A YEAR IN THE LIFE OF JACK MEADOWS

A YEAR IN
THE LIFE OF
JACK MEADOWS

R. L. WATERMAN

Cover artwork by Jessica Shepherd.

Author website: www.rlwaterman.com

For the parents who made me,
and their encouragement which made this.

- PART ONE -

ENCOUNTER

CHAPTER ONE

Jack Meadows was born on a Christmas Day. His mother held the speck of a child close to her face, promising with a whisper to care for this special son with her every breath. Jack's father stood proudly by, removing the dust from his eye.

The parents exchanged a glance over the crown of their newborn son. It was a glance that expressed the joy threatening to burst from their hearts at the sight of their squealing baby boy, determined to wake every neighbour with his high-pitched cries. It was also a glance that expressed something of their sorrow. Jack's parents would never see their boy reach manhood.

Jack's father and mother, having met uncommonly late in life at eight months, ten days, and seven months, thirty days respectively, were past nine months of age on that happy Christmas day.

They would not be around to see Jack reach the established milestone of adulthood at two months and ten days.

They would never see their son fall in love and father grandchildren for them to hold proudly in their arms.

They would only guess at the life Jack would lead, yet

even in guessing, Jack's mother knew by some parental sixth sense that her son was destined to be different.

Their thoughts passed in the flicker of a glance. Meanwhile, I was more than a mile away, treating myself to a final glass of red wine beside the Christmas tree, unaware of anything besides myself and the disappointing day that never quite lived up to its hype.

The night was dark and sounded wet and windy beyond the protective barrier of double glazing that kept my slippered toes toasty. My own parents had long since retreated to the comfort of their bed. I sat, brooding over my future and thoughts of what I could, and should, accomplish. Looking back on that night with the wonderful gift of hindsight, I can see that my musings were rather more selfish than those of Jack's parents, though perhaps they can be excused by circumstance. It was, after all, now half a year since I had finished my prestigious university degree and still I remained jobless and penniless, forced to return to the small Cornish cottage of my parents to scrounge off their generosity and try to forget the immense heap of debt my studies had dropped me in. The path of my life, so meticulously planned, was closer akin to a tangle of spaghetti than the straightforward route I had dreamed into being.

Boxing Day dawned with angry red clouds but I couldn't stomach the thought of another morning trapped in that house. The rooms were shrinking with every passing day. I kissed my mother farewell on the cheek and left the comfortable cottage to take a walk along the Cornish coastline, a rucksack of supplies slung casually over my shoulder and a raincoat tucked through one of the straps. I trudged down the lane to find the familiar coastal path of my youth, leaping over puddles that stretched across the road. A combination of the poor weather and the festive season had left this tourist haven devoid of souls, and so I was left to my contemplation in solitude. The sandy beaches of Cornwall may draw the attention of the masses, but it was always the rugged cliff tops of the county that caught my eye and heart as a child. Jagged shelves of slate rock pointing to the sky at peculiar angles, mirrored in the rough and raging grey of the ocean on an overcast day; who could fail to love the spectacle?

The cove to which I made my plodding way had been a paradise in my youth. The long trek down many a step to the shoreline was well worth the effort to find caves surely still filled with the treasures of smugglers and pirates. We, my sister Andrea and I, became British heroes and explorers, the first to place our feet on the mysterious landscape before us and discover the wonders of beach and cave and ocean. When tiredness tore at our limbs we'd find a flat rock to flop atop of and watch the relentless waves warring against the impenetrable stone, chewing on sandwiches made soggy from our adventures. The future was nothing but the smudge of a rain cloud on the horizon.

Those memories tugged at the corners of my lips, though my mind continued to mull over the problems I faced. Perhaps it was the distraction of one too many thoughts that caused me to miss the rock pool in its stony depression until foot, ankle and leg were drenched with the salty gift of the sea.

Cornwall is a mild place to spend the winter, with cold breezes negated by the warm ocean air, but a shoe full of sea water and jeans soaked through to the skin are not the most comfortable accompaniments to a pleasant afternoon of ocean watching. It was my tipping point. I cried aloud in rage and frustration, scattering a flock of seagulls into the air. I thrashed and kicked my leg in an attempt to free it of the chill fingers that were creeping higher up my calf and causing me to shiver in a gust of wind. My outcry continued in a peculiar one-legged dance as I vented my frustration at life toward the rock pool and its solitary resident, a small crab.

Had I known anyone was watching I would have curbed my flailing, but as far as I was concerned the crab and the squawking seagulls were my only companions.

With a glacier for a leg and a mind clouded with anger I picked up the first loose stone I could see to throw at the ocean with every mite of my strength (it fell short of the mocking waves by some distance). Finally, my energy spent, I sat down hard upon a rock beside the cursed pool and threw a dirty look at the crab whose beady eyes were full of laughter, I'm sure.

I wonder if it was the bout of rage that cleared my mind of clutter, or the lack of any further destination which left me open to my surroundings. Perhaps it was the seagull circling lower that brought my attention to its prey on the ground, or a passing cloud that left a shadow for my eye to follow to see a small man standing, looking in astonishment at the open sky. Whatever the cause, in that time-frozen moment, I found myself staring at a human in miniature, the height of a small sausage. I blinked. The man remained. I followed his gaze to the sky and back to his miniature face. He remained. Finally he turned to look at me, and despite the distance between us and the difficulty in seeing his tiny frame, I was sure he shook his head.

As I surveyed the scene, my mouth hanging open in disbelief, I realised I had disturbed a building work. From where I had torn the stone in my anger a hollow remained, bearing the beginnings of careful carvings, barely visible to the naked eye. I leant closer slowly, for fear of startling the creature, and was astonished beyond belief to notice infinitesimal digging tools resting on a carved shelf and abiding in the hand of my tiny companion. The two of us remained for a time that stretched to eternity, though I'm sure it could be counted in seconds on one hand. He peered up at my face. I peered down at his minute body and wondered if I had slipped and knocked my head in my earlier activity. It would be an amusing dream to tell my parents, if I wasn't so sure that in the telling I would see a worried glance pass between the two. Those looks had been increasing of late. Better the memory of a dream to keep to myself then, one that would surely fade as soon as I woke up.

But there was no hint of waking. The rocky surface beneath me was becoming less comfortable with each passing moment, as was the cold water creeping gradually up the jeans stuck to my leg with icy cold glue.

Why not enjoy the dream? I thought to myself and reached my hand ever so gently towards the small figure. He must have misinterpreted my extended hand of friendship as a threat and before I could say a word he had vanished. I crouched over the exposed building work but there was no sign of life. If I wasn't so convinced that the whole episode was a delusion concocted by a concussed mind, I would have sworn that a tiny rectangular crack at the bottom of a flat piece of stone was the outline of a door.

Subject to the remonstrations of a concerned mother tutting at the state of my clothes upon retreating to the warmth of the cottage, I soon started to think of other things and dismissed my experience as an overactive imagination working within a mind on edge.

CHAPTER TWO

"Tell me about this 'little person,' Tom."

"You won't believe me, I know you won't, but he looked just like us, only tiny. He could only have been a few inches tall, and he was working on a building project. His house maybe. I think I broke it."

"Let me get this straight, Tom. What you're telling me is that a few miles from your home dwells a race of miniature humans?"

"That's what I assume, Doctor, though I only saw the one little person. I'm sure there must be more of them. They're on the beach, I can show you where and then you can see for yourself."

"Thank you Tom, but I don't think that will be necessary. If you really consider what you're saying I'm sure you'll recognise the lunacy of it all. I think it's better for everyone if we take you now."

"Take me? Take me where?"

"Somewhere safe Tom, don't worry."

Fingers like vices clamped down upon my shoulders. Two men in white coats stood behind me. They put their hands on my elbows and raised me to my feet.

"No, Doctor! You don't understand. It is real, I

promise you. I can take you there. I can show you."

"That's enough now Tom, don't make this any harder than it needs to be."

The men were pulling on my arms now, twisting me around and leading me down a dark tunnel toward a van with thick metal bars across the windows.

"You've got it all wrong, I'm not lying," I shouted over my shoulder, fighting against the guards who seemed to grow larger with each passing second until I was no bigger than the miniscule man who had caused this debacle. I could see him in my mind's eye, still shaking his little head at me.

"Tom."

"No, no, I haven't done anything wrong," I mumbled through a mouth full of pillow.

"TOM, will you get out of bed!"

I awoke with a start. A cold sweat had soaked through my bedclothes and I looked around in a panic, searching for bars on my bedroom windows or any hint of white-coated men, come to wrestle me from the comfortable nest of my bed.

"Come on Tom, you promised to help your mother."

Slowly the jumbled pieces started to fit together. I was at home. My father was standing at the bottom of the stairs, calling up to me to fulfil a promise I had made to help with a stock take at the family bakery, Crumbs. I groaned in response to his incessant cries and wearily pulled myself to my feet, rubbing at eyes made bleary with sleep.

Had it all been a dream?

Of course it had. I consider myself to be a sensible man and a vision of tiny humans running around the countryside was not a sensible thought. But there was no amount of cupcake cases or packets of unopened flour and sugar that could keep my mind from wandering back to the cove. It didn't matter how often I berated myself for thinking thoughts sure to land me in an institute specialising in the daydreams of the crazed and unemployed ex-student.

My mother heaved a great sigh as she leaned over my shoulder to correct another error in my counting.

"Get out of here Tom, you're no use to anyone today," she said in the exasperated tone she reserved for those moments in which I half-heartedly attempted to earn my keep. As a child I'd always loved the lingering smell of a perfectly springy Victoria Sponge, the crunch of a fresh loaf of bread and the cloud of flour that dusted my hair and clothes in hours spent eagerly assisting my parents. But early hours at the bakery had lost their lustre for a man in his twenties who had spent his recent years dreaming of business success.

"Are you sure, Mum?" I asked, rucksack already in hand. She sent me on my way with another sigh and a nod and bent her back to the work that should have been mine. I hardly noticed.

I decided a walk was in order to clear my head, and found my feet unwittingly leading me toward the cove of yesterday's adventure.

I'll just go and prove there's nothing there, I thought, quieting the logical part of my brain with a promise of evidence, as the fantasist in me quickened my stride. Retracing my steps was simple, the rock pool was easy enough to find though its resident, the smug crab, was absent on this crisp December day.

I lowered myself cautiously to the ground and sat upon a chilly damp rock to stop and look and listen. The ocean was closer than yesterday and the ground wetter so I assumed the tide had reached this spot. It seemed to be on its way out now so I didn't worry about a fresh soaking. Was I imagining a tiny tapping sound reaching my ear over the rhythmic crash of the sea? I decided to watch the area from the opposite side of the small pool, hoping the distance would be great enough to tempt the creature from its crevice, assuming it existed at all of course. For some minutes I sat, tensed, silent and alert, unsure whether I wished anything, or anyone, to appear to prove or disprove my sanity. It wasn't long before my mind started to wander as mirrored clouds drifted gently across the surface of the still water.

The gloom of the world snapped me back to my senses. Somehow, on that cold and uncomfortable stone, I had fallen asleep. My neck was stiff and my face sore from resting on a balled fist. The winter night was drawing close, stars were twinkling into being and I knew it was time for me to find my way home.

As I rose to my feet something caught my eye. It was the tiniest flash of light. I blinked to clear the focus of my eyes but the light remained; it was a minute flame. I dropped to my knees so quickly I had to stifle a cry as a pebble found its home in my flesh, and I turned my gaze to the microscopic fire. It was so hard to see, the shadows cast by the swiftly setting sun were lengthening and I couldn't be sure my eyesight wasn't playing tricks on me. Despite it all I felt convinced I was seeing the same little person, holding some sort of lantern or branch with a flame to guide his path. He threaded his way carefully across tiny cracks in the stone, more like vast fissures to a man of his size, and made his way toward the rock pool, leaning over the water's edge as if to check on something there.

I stayed entirely still, hardly daring to breathe as I watched the scene unfold before me. Once again I cite the darkening night sky as excuse for my uncertainty, but I am quietly confident that this small person was pulling in some sort of fishing net and checking it for the night's catch. Picking up one or two items too small for me to see in daylight, let alone in the gloom of the streetlight-less beach, the man threw his net back into the pool and retreated towards the space left vacant by my vandalism.

Before I could say a word or make a move he had vanished. I waited until the stars had painted a tapestry of light in the sky above me, until the frosty night had thoroughly gripped me in its frigid grasp. There was no sign. The man did not return. Needless to say, my mind was occupied with the observations of those few minutes as I stumbled over rocks in the darkness towards the path that would lead me home.

How would you have responded I wonder? Would you have done everything in your power to forget what you had witnessed? Or would curiosity have overwhelmed sense and drawn you back with an insatiable desire to know more? I attempted to dismiss what I had seen throughout what remained of the evening, but by the time I was pulling pyjamas over my head I had already formulated a plan to keep watch on the cove and discover its secrets. The age old excuse of needing some time and space to clear my head would earn me a few days free from parental intrusion. It would buy me the time to make my way to the cove bright and early in the morning, armed with a camera, binoculars borrowed from beside my mother's bird watching book (I was sure she wouldn't miss them) and a packed lunch to sustain me through the day. A warm waterproof jacket lay sprawled across the back of my desk chair, ready to protect me from the elements.

During the following two days I staked out the cove as diligently as any private investigator, moving only when the high tide drove me away, and I was not disappointed. Each morning I saw the little man exit through what seemed to be a door carved into a rock. He made his way glumly through the extension I had unwittingly destroyed to go about various tasks outdoors. I watched him collect tiny pieces of seaweed and sticks lying around the place, perhaps fuel for the fire or materials to manufacture clothing or furniture. He checked his fishing net diligently each morning and night. I saw him sit for a few moments on the second day with his feet up on a tiny pebble, watching the pool in quiet contemplation, and I thought I heard a distant shrill voice borne on the breeze that called him back to his home. It was enough to convince me this little fellow wasn't alone in the world. I learnt that only the highest tides washed completely over the man's house, but he always vanished well before the waves drew closer and so I assumed his residence was somehow watertight and a safe haven against the furore of the water.

The man must have been aware of me, sitting like a mountain beside his home, albeit on the other side of the pond that would seem a great lake to a man his size. At first I feared my presence would be a deterrent to his daily activities, but truth be told he simply ignored me and went about his tasks as though I were a new piece of rock dominating the skyline. If I was surprised at his attitude to a person so many times his own size I let it be; I had the perfect opportunity to study this little man and I scribbled notes until my fingers ached. As I watched and waited and wrote and photographed, a vision began to shape in my mind.

"Let's give a warm welcome to Tom Mitchell, discoverer of the Little People. This unprecedented sighting has staggered the scientific community and brought you to the world's attention as the foremost authority on the lifestyle and history of this strange breed of mini-human. Why don't you tell our viewers how you first made this monumental discovery and let us know about your upcoming television show, *The Little People and Me*?"

I was so caught up in my daydream that I almost missed the man's daily weed picking excursion at the edge of the pool. In my hurry to resume note taking I snatched my notebook from the floor, flinging the pen that lay on top of it into the depths of the water. For a moment I froze and so did the little man. He looked directly at me, gave a small shake of the head and continued his work. Work that would remain undocumented. If you ever find yourself recording the finer details of an unknown species, be sure to bring a spare pen.

It only took two days of patient watching, and many a blurry and indistinct photograph with no indication of the scale of the people I had found, for me to grow bored of my life as an observer. I decided to try a new approach. For my third day of interaction with the little man I packed my bag with a multitude of potential treats that I thought appropriate. I reasoned that food is the way to any heart, regardless of its size. That morning I approached the pool with an unsettled stomach playing host to the warring parties of nervousness and excitement. Before taking up residence in my usual vantage point I left the first offering beside the door of the man's home. It was a piece of popcorn the size of his head.

I peered through the telescopic lens of my camera with unsteady hands and eagerly awaited his reaction. The man's tiny features turned to astonishment as he tentatively prodded this giant object with a finger. He walked around it. He bent down to smell it. He finally broke the tiniest fragment from it and placed it in his mouth, nibbling cautiously. After a couple of minutes and no obvious ill effects the man turned his attention towards his house.

"Julie? Get out here Julie," his tiny but surprisingly gruff voice shouted.

To my delight a beautiful and miniscule little woman opened the stone door and moved toward the man. She was wearing a delicate green dress that wouldn't look out of place on a child's doll, though I had no idea what it was made from. My grin grew broader as I refocused my camera and realised the bundle in her arms was a young child, around a year old by the best guess of my untrained eye.

The small family crowded around my humble offering and seemed to spend some time discussing what it might be, too quietly for me to hear.

"It's popcorn," I said. The man and woman's faces

lifted slowly to survey my giant form, as if I'd suddenly appeared out of thin air. The man inclined his head to the house in a signal for the woman to retreat and carry their child away from possible danger. She hastily back-stepped away from me, heavily burdened with the popcorn that I noted she was swift to secure.

It looked as though the man was trying to say something, but at this distance I was unable to make him out. Slowly, cautiously, I crawled on my hands and knees toward him, desperate to avoid any sudden movement that might cause him to follow his family. He watched curiously as I crept closer but made no move. Turning my ear toward him I found that I could just make out his words.

"Who are you, young man?" he asked in the same deep voice.

The thought of being addressed in such a way, by such a small being, made me laugh out loud. Seeing a look of disapproval creep over his features I quickly corrected my manner. "My name is Tom, sir, Tom Mitchell."

"What do you mean by this?" He angled his head toward the house and I assumed him to mean my offering of food.

"Well I've been watching you. That is to say I've seen you gathering, and I thought you might like something different to eat. It's a food we call popcorn. I've more if you'd like, or other things to try," I knew I was babbling but this was a situation beyond even my wildest daydreams. I hastily arranged a few items of food on my outstretched palm, a grape, a peanut, a sugary sweet and a small chunk of bread, spread with butter.

The man studied my face for several long seconds with an expression I can only describe as bemusement. Finally he turned his attention to the items in my hand. He moved closer to assess my offerings, showing no fear of a person who could crush his tiny body in one easy movement. He prodded and sniffed each item in turn before settling on the grape which he struggled to lift in his tiny, well-muscled arms.

"Thank you Tom, we appreciate the gift," he said with a nod and turned to leave, taking his grape with him.

"Wait, please," I cried to his retreating back, "can't you tell me your name?"

The man paused and looked again at my face.

"John. John Meadows."

And with that he was gone.

CHAPTER THREE

I should perhaps take a moment at this point to explain that I was not perfectly calm and collected regarding all that I had seen. A large part of me was still convinced I was dreaming or hallucinating. I was confident that my knowledge of the world was not insignificant and I certainly didn't believe myself to be unintelligent, or deranged. How is it then that I could fail to know of the existence of this race of little people? Surely I should have heard of them. I'd heard stories of pixies and leprechauns and fairies and other fanciful beings of course, but no tales of perfect replicas of humankind in miniature. Not outside of pure works of fiction anyway. There must surely have been studies to find out more about the little people's nature and existence. It was beyond my comprehension that I could be the only person to have encountered the species. I felt I should contact someone about it, but who? I wondered if there was a government department for such things, but who would believe me if I started making enquiries? I'm sure that you yourself will need more convincing regarding the little people, even reading this first-hand account as you are. I pondered contacting some of my old university friends, Ryan and Jerry and Pete, my old flatmates, or even Rosa, for whom the flame of my unrequited love had burned, very secretly, throughout my final year of study. I thought their minds might be more open to the unusual than some, but it was months now since I'd heard from any of them and I laughed to myself at how that conversation would sound. Besides, my dream of being the one to introduce the world to the little people was still burning brightly in my mind, and I knew if I told the wrong person it could be snatched from me. If this was real and not an illusion then I needed to find out more, to stake my claim on my discovery.

The more times I saw the Meadows clan the less I started to question my sanity, and the more convinced I grew that I wasn't simply seeing things and hearing voices, but that introduced new challenges. In those first few weeks there were moments when I could have screamed to the heavens in bewilderment and at the sense of feeling so completely overwhelmed by a discovery that rocked me to my core. These little people were throwing everything I thought I knew into disarray. What else didn't I know about the world? What else had I been told was impossible that could one day appear in front of my startled eyes? How was I to make sense of my own life when I couldn't begin to make sense of the world at large?

Put yourself into my shoes. Imagine if you will, that today you returned home from a long day at the office to discover your pet dog having an intimate discussion with the cat next door. A discussion formed not from barks and meows, but rather a conversation of human words spoken calmly from their animal throats. Is it any less believable than my own discovery? Perhaps you too would feel that everything you thought you knew and understood about the world was crumbling around you. It is impossible to make a discovery of the unusual kind without it affecting the rest of your life. I could cut this knowledge out of my mind no more easily than cutting off my right arm and attempting to continue my normal tasks so disadvantaged.

Knowledge, however peculiar, is a powerful thing.

I don't doubt that my life would have run a very different course if I had made the decision to leave the little people well alone, but by this point I was completely hooked. It seemed I had no choice but to pursue this mystery to see where it would lead.

Strange as it sounds, I was also determined to make amends to John Meadows for the casual damage I had inflicted on his property. I concluded that my strength would be enough to help restore the half-completed extension to its former glory.

And so it was that the moment I heard my parents' voices muffled by the closing of the front door the following morning I leapt from my bed, pulled on my clothes and packed a bag with a light lunch, additional snacks to offer to my new acquaintances and a few tools borrowed (without permission) from my father's collection. I was on my way, muttering a grateful thank you to the weather for staying dry throughout the course of my adventures, before my parents had turned the corner at the end of the street.

The sun had but recently come to visit the day, illuminating the sky with tints of pink that suggested rain to dispel the cold dry days which had dominated the start of this winter. Despite the early hour John was already abroad and engaged in activities around the pool. I took to my surveillance point at the furthest spot from the Meadows' home around the circumference of the water, albeit only two of my strides away, to watch his morning activities. It seemed they were predominantly related to the gathering of food and water. Along with the aforementioned fishing net, my eyes picked out a contraption that looked as though it might collect rainwater positioned beside the shelter of a rock. A tiny piece of discarded crisp wrapper was pulled taut atop a carved and angled container which would allow rainwater to drip steadily into it. John was also expecting rain then, to be checking on the construction. I wondered if filling the pot with a few drops from my water bottle would harbour good feeling with the little people and filed the idea away for an opportune moment.

Someone more patient than I would undoubtedly have sat still for the majority of the day, surveying and recording all of John's activities, but I have never counted myself as particularly patient.

"Good morning, John," I said.

He muttered a reply without looking up from his work; he was tugging tiny fragments of seaweed toward him from the surface of the rock pool with a stick significantly taller than his own height. I wished I was better at lip reading, not that his tiny lips would have been easy to read even if it was a skill I had mastered. I edged closer.

"I said good morning, John."

John looked up impatiently and, speaking clearly and loudly as if I were from a foreign land unable to understand his tongue without the excessive clarity, said, "Good morning, Tom."

I smiled and nodded, a desperate attempt to convey my understanding of his words, though I fear I may have looked more of a simpleton than ever with my head bobbing up and down so violently. John continued his work as if no interruption had marred his gathering.

"Can I help?"

A tiny sigh was borne on the wind as John stepped back to look into my face, clearly frustrated at the distraction my presence provided. I bent to my knees beside the pool and scooped a handful of seaweed to dump unceremoniously beside the little man, dousing him with a shower of saltwater droplets. The resulting tangle of weed was easily as tall as him and I couldn't tell if he was pleased or exasperated at my efforts.

"What am I to do with that, Tom?" He said and poked the monumental pile with his stick. I wasn't sure if the seaweed was for use as food, clothing, bedding or some other purpose but I surmised that my offering would have met any need for a year, and perhaps taken as long to sort through. Thinking quickly I retreated to my pack and pulled free a Stanley knife to strip the weed into more manageable pieces. John watched with his hands on his hips. He showed no fear at what could be a weapon, his expression betrayed only curiosity, coloured with exasperation. As I cut tiny pieces of seaweed from the pile I attempted to engage him in conversation.

"Are your family well? Julie? And the baby?" I asked.

"What is it you want from us, Tom?"

I ceased my work at the abruptness of his question and lay my knife carefully beside the pool. What *did* I want from them?

"I don't mean you any harm. I thought I could help, with this and maybe with fixing your house. I think I might have done some damage."

"That you did," John said.

I resumed my work under John's careful observation, trying to marshal my thoughts. This was a conversation I couldn't have dreamed up in my wildest imaginings.

"It's what you're good at," he said finally, "breaking things that don't belong to you." He must have noticed my frown. "Not you personally, lad, other than my house o'course. You big people, you don't care for our homes and livelihoods what with your giant steps that'll crash through the solidest roof."

"I'm sorry John, I didn't know that you exis… I mean, I didn't know that anyone lived here. I want to make it right."

"It's more bother than it's worth, mingling with the big folk. Our fathers may have tried it some but it's not for us, lad. Better you leave well alone."

I wondered how many little people had found their homes destroyed by our carelessness and my heart sank. It seemed this relationship was to be over before it began. I couldn't bring myself to meet John's eyes and so I continued my work, creating a smaller pile of tidily shaped pieces of seaweed beside him. The silence lingered and John seemed content to ignore my presence again, his point made. He rested his stick against my seaweed mountain and went to inspect his fishing net. It must have been some minutes before he spoke again.

"You can help with the house. But only that, you hear? When it's done you'll leave us in peace."

It was more than I had hoped for. "Yes, absolutely, okay. How can I help? What do you need? I can find a new roof, I'm sure." My eyes greedily surveyed every stone lying around our location, seeking one convenient for our purposes.

John grunted. I took the sound to be a laugh for a faint smile lifted his typically dour expression. "Easy lad," he said, "we start tomorrow."

Before I had a chance to turn around John had vanished into his home and I was left alone, feeling the winter's cruel chill seep beneath my clothes and into fingers moistened by seaweed. I gathered the fruits of my labour and placed them before what I'm sure was the door to their home, hoisting the remains of the seaweed back into the pool.

Despite the temptation of a warm drink at home I spent another hour at the cove, combing the area for stones of a suitable size and shape to replace the one I'd so carelessly tossed to the ocean. I laid out a semi-circle of offerings close to the pool, hopeful that on the morrow one would suffice for our purpose.

It turned out that none of my stones would be suitable however, because John had spent the night drawing up plans for a new extension with his wife, Julie. Despite their obvious pride and initial wish to avoid what help I could offer, it seemed they realised my desire to make amends could lead to a somewhat more elaborate build than the modest room they had made a start on. John seemed almost excited to show me the drawing of his design, featuring a spacious room for his son and a new living area for the family to enjoy together. The loose plan was to take a sheet of slate to create a slightly slanted roof, wedging it carefully between existing stones so as to make it secure and ensure it couldn't fall into the living space or be washed away by an incoming wave. Beneath this roof the separate rooms would be formed, with dividers made of pebbles placed together in a sort of dry stone wall. Those walls would provide extra support to the slate roof, as well as effectively partitioning the space. The external walls would be formed from the more solid rocks around, already bordering the house, and a tiny note scrawled on the edge of the paper said 'pitch,' something for making the new rooms watertight, I assumed. An overhang of slate would create a porch area for sitting on sunny or rainy days, and the angle to it would cause rainwater to run free, rather than pooling above the home.

I was able to get the gist of the idea by swapping to a macro lens on my camera and zooming closely on the design, drawn carefully onto the back of a paper sweet wrapper. It seemed ambitious but achievable. I am not an engineer by any stretch of the imagination, but I trusted that John knew what he was doing and sought to be the muscle to his ingenuity.

The extension we built would seem tiny to you and yet it took us a solid week of hard labour to complete. Hours of traipsing around in the cold and wet to find suitable building materials, coupled with hours of lying on my side and working with fiddly materials in an attempt to put walls together left the skin on my hands dry and cracked and my back aching, but it was worth it. There were moments when I seemed to impress John during the build. He was particularly fond of the umbrella I brought to the cove on that first rainy day; opened and laid on its side it shielded the work area, even if my legs bore the brunt of the rain's fury sticking out from underneath it. His trust for me seemed to grow on the second day when he allowed me to carry him carefully in my hand as we searched for a suitable piece of slate to create the main roof of the structure.

I'm sure I could write for days and still not accurately describe the sensation of laying my hand flat on the floor to allow a miniature man to climb into it. His footfalls were incredibly light and he weighed next to nothing. I endeavoured to walk with my hand completely flat and my thumb raised vertically to give him a handhold. Initially he hugged onto that thumb with his tightest grip but by the end of our journey he simply placed a hand on it to steady himself as I clambered over rocks with the handicap of a missing hand. On more than one occasion I tripped and barely avoided dropping him, surely to an untimely death, as my hands instinctively made to break my fall. Each time I remembered my load just in time and managed to keep John safe, even if my knees told the story of painful jolts on rocky landings.

John didn't seem worried about heights at all. Imagine standing in the hand of a man so many times your own size and not feeling intimidated at the prospect of falling, or terrified at the spectacle of being raised to skyscraper level with no solid floor beneath you. Even the thought sends me to shuddering, but John didn't hesitate for an instant. He recognised that it was required after my first few offerings were not suitable for his purpose. I began to realise there wasn't much the little people were scared of. Perhaps John would have been more cautious if he was alone, but when a seagull flew threateningly close to his head he simply looked at me in expectation until my flapping and shouting drove the bird away. If he saw me as a tool and a bodyguard for the completion of his grand design, then I saw the process as a wonderful opportunity to learn more about the Meadows family and the wider community of little people.

I learnt quickly that John, Julie and their son were not

alone in the world. There was, in fact, a complex network of homes carved into the rocks all about the cove. Several hundred little people dwelt here. The Meadows family lived on the outskirts of the village which explains why I didn't see any other little people wandering past, though in all honesty I'm not sure I would have noticed them even if they had walked beneath my nose. On one of our forays to find suitable stones for the internal walls John called out and waved to a rock as I stumbled along. It was only with a second and closer look that I spotted another little man waving back. He didn't seem surprised to see John riding upon my hand. The news that the Meadows family had enlisted the help of a big person to complete their build had seemingly become widespread already. I was hard to miss after all.

The ingenuity of the little people astounded me when John took me with him to the town kiln. It was situated on a rise that was quite a trek for the little people, burdened as they would often be with pieces of drift wood, but the site needed to be above the high tide line. Wood was stacked within what looked like nothing but an inconspicuous mound of earth and then set alight, and after some few days of careful burning the wood was transformed into charcoal, and a sticky tar-like by-product was produced and filtered into tiny little pots. At least that's how I assume it worked, I'm no expert when it comes to anything outdoorsy; if I needed tar or charcoal I'd visit a DIY shop and ask the staff to deliver it to my door. John took several pots of pitch into the house during construction and disappeared to plug any holes while I continued my efforts on the exterior. We had to work carefully with the ebb and flow of the ocean to ensure John had the longest dry time possible for these delicate operations.

It was with pride and satisfaction that John and I surveyed our work as the sun started to set on the seventh day of our labour. Earlier that afternoon I had carefully laid the slate roof and, after ensuring it was stable, even dared to step on it to ensure it wouldn't fall foul of some other big person casually exploring the cove. The structure took my weight without creak or crack. Knowing the work was likely to be finished that day I brought along a little feast for us; sandwiches in large and small form, crisps crunched into microscopic bites and crumbs of cake. John called to his family to share in our celebration and I knew in that moment I had earned his trust. It was the first time he allowed his wife, and particularly his son, to come into contact with me at such close range.

Julie emerged first, bearing a tray of four tiny cups, one for me I noted with a smile. She looked up at me with a heartfelt grin plastered upon her porcelain face as she reached up above her to pass me the smallest mug I've ever seen.

"Jack," she called over her shoulder, "it's time to eat."

I saw a tiny face peek out of the new stone doorway that John had somehow set to hinge. An energetic toddler ran confidently to his mother and jumped into her arms.

"Where's your other son? The baby?" I asked.

John looked up at me in confusion. "This is our son," he said.

"But there was a baby just the other day. Was it someone else's?"

"No other child here, lad, just Jack."

"Just Jack." I was temporarily stumped. "And how old is Jack?"

John shrugged and looked to Julie. I leant my ear closer to pick up her quiet voice, "Thirteen days."

CHAPTER FOUR

Thirteen days. Thirteen days. Thirteen days.

The words beat a time to my steps. How could a boy who must surely be three years of age, if not more, be only thirteen days old? Perhaps she meant months? But that wouldn't make sense either. It could only be ten days since I had first seen the young Jack Meadows and guessed his age at one. At that point he would have been just three days old.

Was I imagining that John's head of hair was highlighted with more grey than when I'd first seen him two weeks ago? That Julie's step was slower than the day of her quick retreat with a weighty piece of popcorn?

Mental arithmetic was never my strong suit, but even I could calculate that if four to five days were the rough equivalent of a year for this race then these little people couldn't hope to live for much longer than one of my own years. Assuming their lifespan was proportionally similar to our own that is.

I hardly slept that night. My mind ran over the implications of this discovery. There's nothing like the thought of mortality to keep you awake in the early hours of the morning.

I had become accustomed enough to the little people at this point to have accepted their existence as normal, if still a bit perplexing. Perhaps that's why this new revelation was as much, if not more of a shock than my first sighting of John Meadows those couple of weeks ago. As the clock ticked towards 3AM I became painfully aware that in the last six months I had sat, mused, moped and not achieved a single thing; that would be half of the life the new-born Jack Meadows would ever have to call his own.

I put the distance I kept between myself and the Meadows family over the next week down to the promise I had made to John, that the building work would be the end of our relationship. Looking back on that time now I'm sure the reason was different. Saying goodbye had never been a strong suit for me and I was reluctant to get close to something I knew I would lose in a matter of months. Burying one of the little people would surely be more heart-rending than my early experiences of death. I still remembered with a pang the old shoe box, long since decayed, buried in a hole in the back garden and containing my once faithful hamster, Mr Pickles. I expect there was also a sense of shame in the thought that I had thrown away more days willing the clock to move faster than these tiny men and women would ever see.

So it was that in the next week I returned to the cove often, but never once interacted with the little people. I think John saw me and waved as I passed the rock pool beside his enlarged house, but I had already turned away before I could be sure and I certainly offered no gesture in return. He didn't want anything to do with me in the first place; that was my mantra in a week in which I became more and more sulky and aloof.

"What on earth is wrong with you, Tom?" asked my father as I chased peas around my plate with a fork.

"Nothing," I grunted, slouching to the kitchen to drown the pesky vegetables in soapy water.

"He's not a boy anymore, Peter," the whispered voice

of my mother, "you must leave him be. He'll find his way."

"He'd best find it soon. I won't have him scrounging for the rest of his life. He's meant to have left this backwater village and made something of himself by now. That was the plan, Mary. That was the plan."

"Plans have a habit of changing, love." I slammed the kitchen door on their whispered conversation, making sure they heard my angry stomping up the stairs before collapsing on the bed of my youth. Plans have a habit of changing. The plan I had so meticulously crafted for my life lay in tatters around my feet, so maybe it was time for something new, time to take a risk. I vowed to return to the cove tomorrow to continue learning about the little people. The world would surely be even more interested in them, knowing they only had a year to live.

"Thought we were shot of you, son," John said, leaning on the miniscule wooden broom he had been using to sweep sand and seaweed from his new porch. He spoke in an offhand tone, but a glint in his bright eyes suggested he was pleased to see me.

"I didn't want to come back empty handed," I muttered as I started to empty the contents of my rucksack onto the floor beside the tiny home. In a semicircle I placed item after item of furniture pilfered from my sister's childhood doll's house. There was a bed clothed with delicate floral sheets, a wardrobe with real opening doors and miniature coat hangers inside, and even an intricately detailed dining table with four matching matchstick chairs. There were tiny bedside cabinets and little comfortable couches, a metal coat-stand and several garishly coloured rugs, really just tiny pieces of fabric. I brought enough to furnish a miniature mansion, thinking the Meadows family could pick out their favourite pieces, but I could hardly say no as the ecstatic John and Julie carried each of the items between them, one by one, into their modest home.

There wasn't much I could do to help. With the new

roof well secured I couldn't act a crane to lower in any furniture. Instead I took a seat outside and imagined with a grin how cluttered the rooms would become with each disappearing item.

"The other kids say you're a giant," the small and squeaky voice made me jump, despite its quietness.

"Jack? Jack Meadows?" Could this strapping young child be the same baby of just a couple of weeks ago?

The boy thrust out his chest proudly and nodded.

"And what do you tell the other kids?" I asked.

"Well," Jack said with a thoughtful expression, "I said I don't know about that. Maybe you're some kind of weird giant, or maybe we're weird and small. Or we could both be normal, just the way we are." He shrugged and clambered over pebbles as big as himself to sit on a small stone opposite me.

"Shouldn't you be in school, Jack?"

The little boy stared at me blankly. "What's a skool?"

"What's a school? Well, it's a place where you learn all about science and maths and history and how to read and write. Things like that."

"Mum teaches me some stuff like my letters. What's a maff and sce… sci…?"

"Science? It's a subject we learn in our schools, like reading and writing, it lets us know how things work. And maths is all about numbers, adding and subtracting and, and algebra, trigonometry, things like that." Jack's eyes had glazed over; clearly algebra wasn't something the little people worried about.

"After you learn that stuff what do you do with it?" he asked.

It was my turn to stare quietly at Jack.

"Yesterday Dad taught me to check the net for food and the trap for water so we can eat and drink. He says we learn what we need for going on living."

"I uh, well I don't use it all myself, I suppose. But other people do, they use it to invent new things and build us computers and technology like that," I stuttered my reply, silently trying to recall all the hours of my learning and its usefulness in my journey to this point. Jack shrugged and turned his attention to a minute piece of slate resting on top of his rock, with which he started to scrawl what looked like his name. I had to put my eye almost on top of it to make it out.

"Your letters look good." I said and Jack's face glowed with the compliment as he continued to scrawl on the stone, a tiny point of tongue visible at one side of his mouth in a face screwed up in concentration. I watched him work and wondered. Could the little people be born with the ability to speak and with knowledge of the language? Or were they just incredibly adept at learning? Could it be that something which takes a human child years to master could be picked up by the child of a little person in days? I started to think about what they could achieve with this incredible mental prowess if they had but a little more time. The feats of science or enlightenment or even the arts that could be manifest upon the world overwhelmed my mind, and I speculated as to whether I could be the person to bring some sort of higher learning to this race, to help them to see that they could expand beyond day to day fending for themselves, and teaching the next generation to do the same. Granted, they wouldn't be able to spend years in study, but there would surely be some means of recording and passing on the knowledge their days had garnered for the next generations to build upon. I imagined the prestige that would come with introducing the world to the wonders the little people produced. This really could be my ticket to fame and fortune. I was so lost in thought that I didn't realise Jack had finished practising his lettering.

"How old are you?" he asked me, startling me from my reverie.

"Me? I'm twenty-two."

"No you're not!" He laughed. "That's how many days I

have. Well, twenty-one and a half, but nearly twenty-two."

"Oh sorry, twenty-two years," I corrected myself, my head still distracted with thoughts of a syllabus that would change the lifestyle and productivity of these little people.

"What's a year?"

"A year? It's twelve months, or 365 days," I said, glad to have started my instruction so soon.

"You mean a lifespan, right? That's what Mum says is 365 days."

"Well yes, I suppose I do. We call a 'lifespan' a year." I couldn't understand why he continued to stare at me with his head tilted in an expression of puzzlement. Surely I'd explained myself quite clearly, and yet I could have been mimicking old Dr. Patel's lectures on Greek mythology for all the impression it had made on the young Jack Meadows.

"I should go now. Bye Mr Tom," Jack called as he slid from his rock and, with surprising speed, threaded his way through the boulder-sized pebbles that barred his path back home.

"Goodbye Jack," I called, "and say goodbye to your parents for me." He waved over his shoulder and I was alone, once again, beside the invisible home of a species that seemed far-removed from my own.

I didn't have much contact with John or Julie Meadows for some time after that. They were undoubtedly thrilled with my donation to their humble home and said nothing to discourage me from visiting their neighbourhood, but they didn't actively pursue a relationship with me either. I tried not to be offended. I was only supposed to help with the house and then vanish from their lives after all. Besides, I had more than enough contact from the young Jack Meadows to keep me satisfied and my dreams for the improvement of this people alive.

My days settled into something of a routine. In the mornings I would serve on the till at Crumbs or half-heartedly help with baking the day's bread. This coincided with the time Jack spent in lessons from his parents and a wise old uncle (over 340 days Jack told me with wide eyes). At the end of my shift I would grab a fresh crusty roll from the basket, cast an impish grin toward my mother and make the walk down the narrow country lanes to the cove. Jack would be waiting for me, a fraction further from his front door each day. John hadn't explicitly told Jack we weren't to be friends, but we usually made our way a little down the beach to be out of sight, and therefore out of mind. Months later Jack confessed to me that he once told his parents he was seeing other little friends in our afternoon sessions. He was never quite sure if they would approve of his close association with one of the big people, though they must have seen us leave together on many occasions. What parents say and what parents know are two very different things. Whether they approved of our clandestine meetings or not, our time spent together had something of a forbidden air to it which undoubtedly added to its excitement.

I spent our afternoons testing my theories by gently introducing Jack to more complicated lessons that the internet assured me were suitable for his age, or what I assumed his age to correlate to in terms of a more recognisable number. He spent his time ignoring most of my efforts and introducing me to some of the games he loved to play, such as 'Spot the Seagull,' a lesson in self-preservation as much as a game I felt, 'Rock Toss,' whereby your stone had to land as close to the centre circle in a pattern of concentric rings as possible, and, of course, 'Tag.' Jack would giggle with delight as I tried to catch him without trampling the property, or limbs, of any little people as he'd dart between my legs.

In quieter moments he would tell me how the community of little people functioned and proudly inform me of his own accomplishments, such as the time his hand-crafted fishing net first caught a tasty morsel for the family supper. I was so fascinated to hear how their civilisation thrived when its residents had so little time on earth that I almost forgot the frustration of my lessons falling on deaf ears.

Jack's development astounded me. Every day he seemed older, wiser, a more developed young man. In all that time he was unable to grasp the concept of my own age however, though I knew he could count high enough to master the sum. He'd simply stare at me in puzzlement when I explained my kind could live for many lifespans, and once or twice he asked me why I never seemed to age. The concept of a life longer than one year completely eluded him.

After a couple of weeks I hit a turning point in Jack's educational journey when I tried introducing geography into the mix. Jack always responded best when I brought along some pictures to show him, and so I hastily slung an old AA Road Atlas into my bag before leaving one morning. It took some time for me to convince Jack that his cove was the merest speck along the north coastline of Cornwall, and that that particular coastline was itself only a tiny portion of the entire coastline of the United Kingdom. We spent days poring over the old map. Jack loved nothing better than turning the enormous pages by grabbing the corner of a leaf and running as fast as his tiny legs could carry him in the other direction. I'd circumspectly give the page a little help with the prod of a finger, just to get it moving of course. Then he would climb on top of the atlas, and walk along the highways and byways with his little feet, imagining the hills and the valleys through which those roads weaved.

Together we dreamed of exploring it all, from the largest motorways to the smallest tracks of the country, in afternoons spent huddled beneath my umbrella, or in afternoons basking in the cool winter sun. The days seemed perfect, until that one February morning when Jack forgot the rules of Spot the Seagull.

CHAPTER FIVE

Spot the Seagull was a simple enough game. As soon as you saw those white and grey feathers circling above or heard the raucous call of a bird in passing you had to cry, "Incoming" with all your might, and dive for the nearest rocky outcropping. The first person to reach shelter was the winner. It was a game Jack always won when we played together. I couldn't fit under the majority of the cove's rocks.

I've carried a deep sense of loathing for those squawking avians ever since I was a young lad, and first experienced the indignity of a seagull snatching a double-topped ice cream cone straight out of my hand. This day brought my dislike closer to hatred.

It was a typical winter's day, the sky grey and dreary with the threat of rain on the air. It was mild for February, and as I trudged toward the cove I remember thinking I had worn too many layers. It's funny, the things you remember. I sweated beneath my thick winter jumper and waterproof coat, but the discomfort was worth it, because I was looking forward to exploring Yorkshire with Jack that day. We had been making our way steadily northwards through the atlas and we had extra time today with it being my Saturday free from work. I don't recall any sense of alarm until I stepped close to the Meadows' rock pool, faintly surprised to see no sign of Jack rushing toward me. Instead there was John, all but leaping up and down in an attempt to capture my attention.

I knelt down to be closer to the agitated little man.

"Whatever's the matter, John?" I asked.

"Jack!" he exclaimed. "It's Jack!" He was out of breath, panting and pointing desperately past the pool toward the coastline. I surmised that Jack must have made his way to our regular reading spot without me. This wouldn't have caused me any worry, were it not for the rather louder than normal screams of several Herring Gulls swooping low at some target beyond our sight.

"Help him, Tom. Save him!" John's imploring words reached me in my moment of hesitation, and without a second thought or backwards glance I was sprinting the short distance.

Time is a mysterious entity. Some days it slips through your fingers like fine sand. Try as you might to cling on, time rushes forward with the intensity of a waterfall. In other moments time slows to a crawl, and will it on as much as you may, the seconds drag to minutes and minutes to hours and a day feels like an eternity. As I rushed to Jack's aid I knew I would be too late. Time was moving too quickly. As close as my destination was there was no way I could reach it before the worst would happen. Precious seconds were lost as I tripped and stumbled on my way forward.

And then I was there, and time froze.

Our reading spot was a beautiful place. Tall rocky outcroppings shielded it from the harsh coastal winds on three sides, and the one side left open offered a beautiful view to the ocean. It was close to the Meadows house, and yet completely out of sight from it. All in a moment I thought about how long it must have taken Jack to walk there, most of the morning I had spent sleeping away no doubt. I thought that John looked much older and more careworn than I had ever seen him, with a crown now completely covered in wispy grey hair. I thought that my heart would stop beating as I saw a gull swoop at the small figure of Jack, already crumpled on the floor with his legs tucked beneath him, valiantly brandishing a tiny stick in an attempt to dissuade his attackers.

"No!" I cried, and in one enormous leap was by Jack's side, lashing out at the bird and his colleagues with hand and foot, and attempting to shield Jack's frail form with my body. The seagull clearly hadn't expected such a ferocious assault. It took one snip at my hand with its surprisingly sharp beak and departed to a nearby rock, sending an angry shriek in my direction. Its beady eye continued to watch me as I sunk to the floor beside Jack, fearing the worst.

"Jack?" I said quietly. He was lying flat on his back now, his trousers torn, revealing a nasty gash on one leg.

"Tom?" His reply was so faint I almost missed it. Tears stung my eyes as I lifted him. He was as light as a feather in my hand. "I'm going to get you home. Don't worry."

I couldn't bring myself to leave the cove.

I had delivered Jack gently to his grief-stricken parents some hours before and they had carried him inside. I sat and waited for news, occasionally standing and pacing up and down to warm my chilled and sodden body. The promised rain had arrived as a curtain of drizzle that deposited sparkling droplets onto my jacket and coated the entire world with its fine wetness. Sometime during my wait Julie stepped outside and handed me the tiniest little mug of a warm drink. It was only a drop or two. The sentiment warmed me all the same.

"How is he?" I asked.

Julie shook her head, tiredness and concern etched into her aging face.

The sun cast a finger of red light toward me as it stole

beneath the clouds on the horizon. I didn't notice John make his way out to stand beside where I was sitting until he spoke.

"He lives," John said with a cracking voice.

I nodded, afraid any words would betray the guilt that burned in the pit of my stomach. Jack wouldn't have been so far from home were it not for me. Whatever happened to the young boy was entirely my fault.

"There isn't much more we can do till morning. Best you head home, lad, and get some rest." With that he walked back to his house and closed the door to the growing darkness outside. I followed his advice and made my way home, but rest did not come easy. The one time I did drift into a fitful sleep I dreamed of laughing seagulls soaring on the breeze, just out of reach of my fingertips. They taunted me with their cries.

CHAPTER SIX

There was no movement at the Meadows' house when I arrived with the dawn. I made my way to our hideout instead. Despite the rain which had washed most evidence from the scene I could still see hints of the battle waged between little person and bird. Tiny red splatters decorated the grey of the stone and I felt a lump forming in my throat. A solitary white and grey feather attested to Jack's attempted defence. I picked it up and twirled it between my thumb and forefinger for some time to the soundtrack of the relentless crashing of the ocean. I couldn't bring myself to sling the backpack from my shoulder, the weight of it cutting into my skin felt like a physical outworking of the guilt within. I was the one who had brought Jack so far from the safety of his home. Why hadn't he waited for me? Was it the impetuousness of youth? Had the lure of Yorkshire drawn him from his daily tasks early? The iron sky and stormy ocean held no answers to my questions.

Drips of cold rain caught me by surprise. It felt fitting somehow, to stand in the rain, as if the sky itself was saddened at what had happened to my little friend. Less than two months had passed since I first saw the tiny John Meadows, and yet the budding friendship between me and his son could have spanned years. It was only in this moment of near loss that I realised how much I had grown to value the young man. I'd had dear friends before of course, but I hadn't bonded this quickly with anyone, not even Jerry, my best friend and flatmate from my days of study in the city of Birmingham. I thought myself Jack's mentor and him my mentee, a younger brother figure perhaps, and yet in those moments, as the cold rain seeped into my clothes, I realised I had learnt far more from him than him from me. John Meadows was a man of few words and conversations with him were always brief; if he could use an expression to convey meaning instead of speech then it would suffice. Jack was chalk to his father's cheese in this respect, and he had introduced me to this new world of the little people. He had taught me what it meant to live and exist in such a small community, as such a small force in the world. I had repaid him by risking his precious few days of life, pushing him to learn things he never needed to know, for the sake of my own vanity and success. It was all I could do not to run away and never return, but I needed to know if he had survived the night. I couldn't live with the thought of never finding out if he would live to see the coming of age ceremony he was so looking forward to.

I tucked the feather safely into my backpack and made my way to the rock pool and the home of the Meadows family. John was standing on the porch of his house, looking as lost in thought as I must have seemed mere moments ago. I resolved to apologise to him for my part in Jack's being so very far from home, but John spoke before I was able to utter a syllable.

"I never thanked you, lad. You brought my boy home. You saved him," John muttered.

"I, well I, I'm just sorry that I..."

"Don't mention it, lad," John said with a wave of his hand. "It wasn't your fault. No one's fault other than my own. Jack had some fool idea in his head about running off and 'seeing the world,' as he put it. Nonsense. I told him such and off he ran, said he wasn't ever coming home if that's what I thought." He paused. "It was my fault."

So that was it. Jack had run away. I remembered a similar escapade from my own childhood when my father insisted it was only right to give back the toy I'd stolen from my sister, Andrea. I forget what the toy was, but I remember the feeling of childish injustice that insisted she had more than me. I was only trying to even the score. The outrage had been enough to send my eleven-year-old self storming out of the door with nothing but the clothes on my back. My parents hadn't followed. My mother confessed many years later that she desperately wanted to, but my father hadn't allowed it. It was a safer world in those days, and he insisted, quite rightly, that I would come to my senses in a matter of moments. And so I did, as soon as I realised there was no food to be found hidden beneath the slide in the local park, and that the world could be cold without the warm coat I'd left hanging in the cupboard under the stairs.

John must have tried a similar strategy. Had it not been for the seagull I'm sure it would have worked in time, and all our lives from that point on would have followed a different path. My mind started to race. Jack had decided our geography lessons could be more than merely exploring a map, but travelling to see those places in reality. The thought of introducing a little person to the wide world filled me with excitement. I'm amazed how quickly my guilt was assuaged and my mind set at ease. For a moment I almost forgot that poor Jack was injured and fighting at death's door. There would be no travelling together if he didn't survive his wounds.

"Is Jack, is he okay?" I asked tentatively.

"Aye, he lives. Gave us some scares through the night mind, and poor Julie hasn't rested her head for a moment."

"Thank goodness," I exclaimed.

"He lives. How he'll live though I truly don't know, lad. There's no life in one of his legs. He'll be a great time recovering, what with losing so much blood." John hung his aged head as he spoke, and continued in a whisper that I had to strain with all my might to hear. "And I won't be here to help him."

One year.

That's all the little people have, and John was drawing rapidly to the end of his. Jack had told me the specific date his father would die, and it was less than two weeks away. John might be able to help his son adjust to this change in circumstance, but soon Jack would be on his own. Julie was only ten days younger than her husband.

"I'll be here," I said.

John looked up at me, piercing me with a look of pure intensity from his stony eyes. "Well I, I appreciate that," he said with a catch in his throat. "I'd best be back, give Julie a break." With a final nod he was gone once again and I was left alone to wonder what I had signed up to.

I spent the rest of the day ransacking the internet to find doll-sized crutches. It's not a big market. A few helpful guides did suggest how such a thing could be made with a combination of toothpicks, rolled up pieces of paper and plenty of glue. After a few attempts I thought I'd made good progress, though I had no idea if they would be a suitable size for the tiny Jack Meadows, or if they would even support his weight. I'd have to make more as he continued to grow even if they were suitable; he was only 51 days old by my reckoning, and still had some lengthening to do. Still, I was keen to try them, and though I was sure Jack would be in bed for a few weeks I was eager to show my invention to John, and perhaps to prove my worthiness in the great task of watching over his son. I was taking a shine to the thought of being a guardian. It would only be for another ten months after all.

"Won't be at the bakery today, Mum," I called as I ran

out of the door in the morning. The shop didn't open on a Sunday but I was supposed to help with an overdue deep clean of the ovens and worktops.

"But Tom! Thomas!" I ignored her calls as I ran for the lane leading me back to the ocean. If I felt a niggle of guilt at letting my parents down, yet again, I placated it with thoughts of the good I was doing for the Meadows family. I was sure my folks would understand if they knew the details.

"John," I cried as I drew close to the Meadows house but the next words died in my throat. Sat outside on a small stone in the sunshine, smiling up at me with a cheeky grin, was Jack.

"Jack! What are you doing out? You should be in bed."

"You sound like Mum," he said and beckoned me to sit beside him. "I've been in bed for a whole day already!"

By my rough calculation and estimates, one day for a little person would be something like the equivalent of eighty days to us. I suppose eighty days would feel like a long time to spend in bed convalescing and yet I was astounded. Not only did the little people have the means to learn incredibly quickly, it seemed they also benefited from speedy, near miraculous recuperation after serious injury. I couldn't help but notice that Jack's matchstick of a right leg was stuck out very straight and heavily wrapped in what looked like strips of seaweed.

Jack noticed my observation. "Mum says it might get better." He shrugged, unconcerned. Many times since that day I've wished I could view my problems with such childish abandon. We launched into a game of 'I Spy' which consumed much of the morning. It wasn't until Julie came out carrying some lunch for her son that I remembered the crutches I had slaved over the previous day. Julie was thrilled at my ingenuity, having never seen the like of 'bonus legs,' as she called them. So great was her pleasure that she insisted John abandon his gathering to come and inspect my work. Between them they lifted

Jack to his feet, his right leg hanging limp and useless, and slid the devices beneath his armpits, on my instruction. The size wasn't bad; I'm no doctor but the crutches reached the floor comfortably without forcing him to hunch or stand over straight and I deemed that a success. Structural integrity was more of a problem. After a few moments of hobbling, the young Jack Meadows, looking akin to a newborn foal, was saved a fall only by the close proximity of his parents when one of the sticks split neatly in two.

"Never mind my lad," Julie said in her quiet, calm voice and smiled up at me, "it was a good idea."

"I'll fix it," I said with certainty.

And so I did, though it took many goes to get it right. I experimented with different materials, cocktail sticks, cardboard, the tubes of biro pens, even sawn up pieces of my mother's favourite knitting needles. She never did find out what happened to them. At the same time Julie worked hard to make the crutches more comfortable with cushioning made from some combination of seaweed and scraps of material for the pad. John maintained a distance but watched the project's progression curiously. He continued to supply his family with food, the pace of his work slowing day by day.

Within the week Jack was able to move around with almost the same speed as his two legs could have carried him. He took to his rediscovered mobility like a duck to water, and in all the time I knew him never once complained about his lot in life, even on those days when pain and frustration were written on his face. The right leg never did work again and I learnt to spot the pain it caused him in the set of his jaw. Cold days were always the worst. I can only assume the seagull's beak or talons had done irreparable damage to the nerves. From time to time I pondered trying to get a medical professional involved, but the implications of what it would mean to the little people went far beyond improving the life of Jack. He wouldn't hear of it on the occasions I broached the conversation with him, insisting that his bonus legs were more than enough to see him through his days.

Our lives returned to some semblance of normality. John even permitted Jack and I to go and explore, supposing that any risk from the wicked gulls was all but neutralised by my presence. We went for a walk one grey and stony day, and without thinking I detoured to our old spot. Jack's laughter was cut short and his grip on my supporting thumb tightened. Even the bravest soul can be tarnished by a brush with death.

We never returned to that place, and I kept the solitary feather a secret for many moons.

CHAPTER SEVEN

We were co-conspirators now, Jack and I.

Once an idea is born it is very difficult to extinguish. This particular idea had gained the momentum of a runaway snowball tumbling down a mountain. As we discussed the possibility of leaving this little cove to explore the world the idea grew and grew until it took on a life of its own. I'm convinced our scheming was the primary factor that took Jack's mind off the pain that jarred him as he stumbled over rocks during the process of adjusting to a life with crutches. I'm sure the thought of seeing something greater than he knew, of exploring something bigger than his tiny cove, stopped him focussing on how vastly his life had changed. I was happy to provide the distraction. More than that though, I was starting to get excited at the prospect of an adventure. My time at university seemed a million miles away, and I missed the freedom and independence of a life away from my parents. I wasn't sure of the details, but as I started to show Jack pictures of various points around England and Wales and Scotland I found myself longing to see forests carpeted in golden leaves, countryside rolling in gentle rises and slopes as far as the eye can see, and bustling cities packed with people and fascinating buildings. My notebook filled day by day with destinations and thoughts on transportation and costs. We even crafted a crude map of the United Kingdom, and drew our route atop it with arrows marking our way. I tore the page free from its binding for Jack to study more closely. He traced the route with his little feet, adventure lighting a candle behind his grey eyes. In his small and neat letters Jack proudly titled the page, 'Tom and Jack's Great Journey.'

We lost all track of time creating our map so I was in a hurry to return Jack to his parents. In my haste I hadn't fastened my bag, and as I stooped to let Jack clamber off my hand my notebook fell free with a clatter. I shoved it back in and made my way home without giving it a thought, but the next day Jack was nowhere to be seen. Instead the aged John stood outside his home, a scowl on his weathered face. His foot rested on the loose leaf bearing our map.

"Tom and Jack's Great Journey," he read aloud. The silence lengthened as I tried to think of something to say, some argument to support our detailed plans.

"You're not to take him, you hear," he spat at me. He had never looked so angry. "It's too dangerous. He'd be killed, being broken as he is."

"Broken?" A tiny voice from the entrance of the house showed that Jack was aware of our conversation. I couldn't be sure, he was too far away and too small for me to see clearly, but I thought he might have wiped an angry tear from his cheek. "I'm not broken," Jack said, his voice cracking with teenage, sixty-one-day old emotion.

"I didn't mean it that way, son," John said. "But you aren't to go off gallivanting around like some big person. It's not our way. There's nothing you need but what you have right here." He nodded, as if that settled things.

"You don't understand anything," Jack was shouting now. "All you care about is your stupid house and this stupid lake. You never cared about me! You don't care about what happened; you just think I'm broken." Jack pushed past the horrified Julie as best he could and hobbled his way back inside the house, slamming whatever door he had to call his own with a bang that travelled to my ears.

"Jack? Jack love?" Julie's voice grew quieter as she retreated into the house after her son.

John continued to cast a look of dark hatred my way. "You big people. You ruin everything," he said. "You promise me this instant you won't take my son away."

I plucked up my courage, "Surely it's up to Jack where he goes. He'll be of age soon."

"You'll take him nowhere, do you understand me!" John shouted up at me. His whole being trembled with rage. It was the first time I realised that the size of a person's frame has little bearing on the power contained within it. "Promise me."

I've never taken part in a staring contest quite like it, it was a battle of wills between John and I, and it would surely have looked comical to any bystanders. There I was, kneeling on the ground to better meet John's eye but still looming over him. There he was, his tiny hands on his hips, his voice radiating authority as he bound me with words to leave his son alone.

John had a small blade in hand, one I'd seen him use to shred seaweed. He hacked mercilessly at our map with it, walking up and down the page and tearing ribbons from it with careless abandon. A section of North Wales came to rest in front of my knees and I felt the hot sting of a tear come to my eye. All of our plans were in tatters now. I felt keen disappointment, but more than that I pictured the devastated look on the young Jack's face.

"Leave this place, you hear. I don't ever want to see you here again. We don't need you. Nor your kind."

When I made no move he turned and fixed me with a look so dark I'm sure it pierced my very soul. I stood slowly to my feet and turned to leave, fragments of fluttering paper escorting me as they swirled on the cold breeze.

People say things they don't mean in the heat of the moment I reasoned, as I snuck quietly back the next day. Surely John hadn't meant what he said. Trying to hide my 6'1 self as I approached the cove was a challenge. An unnecessary one. I had forgotten what day it was.

I'm not sure if our imaginations colour scenes from years ago with extra detail and depth, or if our subconscious picks up on things we aren't aware of until there is time for reflection. Either way, looking back on that day I can say with confidence that there was an eerie stillness over the cove, as if the weather and the wildlife and even the ocean itself was holding its breath. I expected to see John wielding his little knife to chase me away from his home, or perhaps to see Jack all packed, ready to leave for our adventure. What I didn't expect to see was Julie, sat alone on her porch with her head in her hands.

"Julie? Mrs Meadows? Has something happened?" I asked.

"I wonder if I could ask a favour of you, my lad," she said in a quiet voice, strained with contained emotion. "Jack's gone a'wandering. He isn't likely to return until after John's gone. I know my John's a hard man sometimes, but he can't stand the thought of not saying farewell to his only son. Even if he won't say so himself."

The penny dropped. John's lifespan had reached its end. Today would be his last day on this earth.

No matter how many lives of the little people I see, I still can't wrap my head around the idea of knowing the very day you will die. They even have an approximate idea of the time. Perhaps it's living with this knowledge that makes the prospect of death less terrifying for them than we tend to find it. Jack told me the end of a lifespan was typically a merry affair. Any remaining family would gather together to reminisce with the dying little person and to let them know how appreciated they were. As many of the families of the little people were linked by marriage or blood, the days could easily become rather large affairs. A natural death for a little person was a painless process; they would slip into an endless sleep, comfortable and surrounded by all the people they love.

Then would come the lifespan end celebration. Attendees would toast to the memory of the departed, ensuring that a widow or child was not left alone to suffer in silence. This close-knit community ensured the support of all its members. That's why it seemed so strange that the area around the Meadows home was silent. I'd imagined a scene of many little people crossing rocks to reach the house, each bearing some item of food or drink or a gift for the closest family members. I had pictured the sound of the musical instruments Jack told me were played during the celebration, pipes made from tiny reeds, and small drums carefully crafted from shells and skins made of dried and stretched seaweed. It was music of the sort many humans have mistaken for the wind whistling through the rocks. Today there was none of it.

"Where's everyone else?" I asked Julie.

"They're around or inside, lad, but with Jack not around no one feels much like celebrating. Never in all our days have we seen the like, a son not there for the end." She shook her tiny head.

"I'll fetch him," I said and set out to find my friend. Hindered by his crutches and all alone I was sure he couldn't have gone far and soon enough I found him sat on a rock, flicking tiny stones away from him angrily.

"Jack, you've got to get back. Your mum says it won't be long now."

"I'm not going," he said.

"Don't be daft Jack," I said matter-of-factly, "you've got to go back."

"Why?" he asked, "Why should I? He doesn't care about me anymore, not since this." He tapped his unresponsive right leg with one of his crutches. "I'm broken to him, now I can't look after myself or Mum or anyone." Angry tears left streaks on his red cheeks.

"I'm sure that's not true," I said and hesitated, unsure how to proceed. I've never been one to talk openly about my feelings. "I know parents can be annoying, but there's no second chance on this. You'll regret it if you don't go, you know that."

We sat in silence for some minutes before Jack sighed exaggeratedly and nodded. Together we returned to the deserted porch and I dropped Jack off to run inside as quickly as his good leg and crutches could take him. When I heard the first notes of music piped through the air I knew we were too late.

CHAPTER EIGHT

The family and friends inside had one another for comfort, but I sat alone until the sky darkened. At one point I saw a party of chattering little people exiting the house, carrying the still frame of John Meadows on a bier. I assumed they were removing him to a burial site, but I didn't want to intrude and so I remained where I was. I stayed in my solitary vigil as little person after little person left the Meadows home, calling their goodbyes and best wishes. I hardly noticed that my cheeks were wet.

Sometime in the future, I forget when or where, I asked Jack if he believed in an afterlife.

"Of course I do," he replied without hesitation. "I think there's just too much to us to end after just one lifespan. Don't you agree?"

I didn't reply.

John Meadows was the first little person I had the pleasure to know, and though we didn't always see eye to eye I still counted him as a friend. As I sat hugging my knees for warmth I remembered his gruff appreciation of my gifts of food and furniture and the other little trinkets I'd offered to his family. I remembered the upward twitch of his lips when Julie or Jack walked by. I remembered how determinedly he worked, right up until the end of his life when his back was bent and his voice cracked with the use of age.

Regret is something difficult to live with. I am sure we all find some form of it darkening the doorsteps of our minds, those memories that haunt us late at night or at the crack of dawn, thoughts of projects unfinished, relationships un-mended, days wasted. For the rest of my days I regretted that my last conversation with John was filled with angry words; he died angry at me, thinking I would take his precious son away from the relative safety of his home.

If I felt regret it was nothing compared to the heartache that burned inside Jack. John had breathed his last just as Jack had run through the door. There was to be no goodbye for Father and Son.

As the days went by Jack came to realise, with some subtle prompting from his gently spoken mother, that his father wasn't disgusted at him and his disability as his young mind had first believed. He realised it was care and love that prompted John to prevent Jack travelling into a dangerous world. With that understanding came a flood of guilt for his attitude, and try as I might to make him understand we all make mistakes he was inconsolable for some time.

I didn't wholly stick to my promise to John. I felt my presence might help Jack get through this time and, perhaps selfishly, I didn't want to sever ties with the little people altogether. We didn't talk of travelling anymore though, our conversations were more mundane and our time was limited as Jack was determined to provide food and comfort for his mother in her final few days. I brought food enough to feed a small army of little people each day, and while Jack and Julie gratefully accepted my offerings, Jack was still single-minded in his purpose to supplement them with the work of his own hands. I think it was something he thought his dad would be proud of.

In the mornings I returned to assisting my own parents at Crumbs, more careful to show them my appreciation and affection, and I even found enjoyment in the crafting of delicious treats for the townspeople. I'm sure my mother and father were still alarmed at my frequent absences and lack of any definable plan for the future, but they put up with me lovingly, as only parents can.

I forget exactly when it was that Julie tugged at my sleeve to attract my attention, perhaps a week after the passing of John Meadows. Jack was away from home, working at his gathering so the two of us were alone.

"Tom lad," she said, "I want you to take my Jack away from here."

"But Mrs Meadows, I can't. I promised John I'd keep him here." I had watched enough movies in my day to know you don't break a deathbed promise.

"You promised my dear old John you wouldn't come back here too, don't see you keeping that one up," she asserted shrewdly.

"I know, but I don't want to be the one to put Jack at risk. He's suffered so much already."

"Don't be silly. Our Jack was made for something greater than fishing, I've always known it. He's not the same since he stopped dreaming with you." As she spoke Julie gently pressed a piece of paper into my hand. It had been folded so many times I feared the page would tear as I opened it, but carefully, fold by fold, I unearthed a small section of our hand-drawn map. Julie must have found it after John's rampage and tucked it safely out of sight.

"I've only the two days left lad, then our Jack will come of age and you're to take him to see the world. You promise me that."

I continued to hesitate, unwilling to put hope in a dream so recently dashed.

"Look here, Tom. I loved my John, that I did, but he was a silly soul to not realise all the good you've brought us here, and the dreams you gifted to our dear Jack. You saved him, he's safer nowhere than with you, of that I'm sure. I've never seen him more alive than in his dreamings of seeing that world. He'd whisper them to me you know, when John was nowhere to be found. And I'd dream with him my lad, that I would. It's too late for me now but not for Jack. I won't have him living with any more regrets. Take him with you, go and see all those beautiful things you told him of." The frail old Julie patted my hand and wandered away as my heart fluttered to life.

Tom and Jack's Great Journey was back on.

The elderly Mrs Meadows spent the evening convincing her son of the merits of leaving home to travel, and the next day his face was suffused with a modicum of its old childish excitement.

"When do we leave?" he asked as I walked up.

"Hold your horses," I said, laughing. "We'll have to think about how to afford it and where to start. And I'll need to let my parents know I won't be around for a while. We should wait for your coming of age, maybe a day or two after that we could get away."

"That's ages," Jack huffed, impatience failing to tear the smile from his merry face.

Jack deemed he'd done enough gathering, with the supplies I had continued to provide, to see his mother to her lifespan's end and so we sat beside the pond redrawing our route map. From time to time Julie would join us and the glint in her eye would remind me forcibly of Jack. I could see where his adventurous spirit had come from. By mid-afternoon we had a good idea of where we wanted to go, and I put some of those old maths lessons to good use to put a budget in place that would see us through a few months of travel.

The only problem? I didn't have the money the budget called for.

I didn't want to burden Jack or Julie with that concern, so I left them excitedly talking about the journey ahead as I turned for home, racking my brain to think of any untapped source of wealth. It was too late to buy a lottery ticket for the night's draw. Only one option remained: the bank of Mum and Dad.

"You want us to give you how much?" my father exclaimed.

"Just enough to go travelling for a few months. I won't be staying in five-star hotels or anything, I'll only need fuel and food and money for some cheap hostels. It's not that much."

"Not that much he says. We supported you when you had to go off to your university for that degree, and now we're supporting you when that turned out to be not worth the paper it's written on. And now we're supposed to support you again while you go gallivanting off around the country? It's not happening. Make your own money, then you can spend it how you like." My father's tirade reminded me of John's reaction to the thought of Jack leaving. I tried to react with a modicum more dignity than I felt Jack had mustered, but I couldn't believe our fantastic journey was to be halted again, by something as trivial as financing it. I turned to my only remaining hope.

"Come on Mum, it'd be such an amazing experience. I'll come back and get a proper job after, I promise."

My mother shook her head no, "You heard your father."

"Fine!" I shouted, "I'll go and sleep on the streets if that's what you want."

I should reiterate that I was a young man of twenty-two at this point, still given to outbursts of frustration when things didn't go my way. Perhaps I'd spent too much time with the 'teenage' Jack. That's my only justification for storming out like a child and kicking over a plant pot in the back garden.

"Tom," my mother said behind me, "there are some things you don't understand. Our tenants just handed in their notice on the other house and that's another source of income gone. We think we'll have to sell it just to keep us afloat. What with Bradley's bakery opening up shop just down the road and the supermarket being so cheap... Well things have been tough, Tom. Your dad's under a lot of pressure."

"I know all that, Mum," I said, turning away to hide the surprise I was sure she would be able to read on my face. I was so caught up in the world of the little people that I didn't realise the problems my parents were facing. "I mean, I didn't know it was that bad I guess."

My mother took my hand, "We'll be okay, Tom, don't you worry." As she withdrew her fingers an envelope remained.

"What's this?" I said, tearing it open to see a thick wad of crisp £20 notes. "Mum! What is this?"

"I want you to have it. I always put a bit back from the register at the end of the day. It was meant to be there to help you out when you started a job or wanted a house of your own, but if this is really what you want to do," her voice trailed out.

"Don't you need this now? For Crumbs?" I half-heartedly offered the envelope back to her but she pushed my hand away.

"It's not enough to bridge that river, love," she said. "You take it and have an amazing trip. Just, don't tell your father, okay?"

"I promise," I said and pulled her into my arms for a hug.

My evening was filled with coaxing talk to the old Volkswagen Golf that lay covered with a sheet in the family garage, left there from my days haring around country lanes as a youth. It was a project my father and I had worked on together when I hit my seventeenth birthday, so I was familiar enough with the old girl's inner workings. I tore through boxes on the shelves of the garage to find any spare parts, and felt a great sense of satisfaction after fitting new spark plugs and changing the oil. My blackened hands were itching to get behind the wheel again, but the engine sputtered and died after a valiant attempt at turning over. Our journey would have to wait until I could get my hands on a new battery. Still, everything else seemed in good enough condition so I was confident we'd soon be on our way.

As the night drew closer I clattered around in the loft, throwing down an old tent, sleeping bag, cooking equipment for camping and anything else I thought might be useful. I added those items to the stack of clothes already pulled from my wardrobe and chest of drawers. It was becoming a significant mountain of goods, but I reasoned Jack wouldn't have a lot of belongings to fill the car up with. I could take as much space as I needed with my own things.

That night I fell into bed exhausted but unable to sleep. Excitement warred with fatigue, but I sensed another emotion looming ominously beneath the surface. Tomorrow was Julie's lifespan end. There would be another celebration, another death. I'd spoken to Julie less than John, but that didn't undo the knot in my stomach at knowing I'd never see her tidy dresses or experience her thoughtful gestures again. Her last act had set the wheels in motion for this trip of ours; how could I thank her for that?

CHAPTER NINE

The morning of the sixth of March was beautiful. The ocean was calm, not a breeze stirred the naked branches of trees, their small buds a hint at the bountiful spring to come, and the world basked in the yellow glow of sunshine that was warmer than typical at this time of the year. If nature itself had seemed still and apprehensive on the morning of John's death, today it chose to be gleeful and bright.

Jack greeted me with a beaming grin, and introduced me to some of the trail of little people making their way to the Meadows residence. With many a how do you do I greeted an array of cousins and second cousins and third cousins once removed. Most families of the little people were larger than the Meadows clan; John and Julie had been too late to join the ranks of parenthood for a large brood. No one seemed particularly surprised to see me; I suppose I was a regular feature by this point. Many tiny heads nodded at me politely, though I noticed few were incautious enough to actually offer a spoken word of acknowledgement. They were happy enough for the Meadows clan to be involved with a big person, but that wasn't enough for them to want to befriend me themselves. One or two youngsters were carried past with mouths gaping wide and eyes bulging at the sight of me. I stifled a chuckle, unsure if it would be appropriate, though I needn't have worried. The atmosphere was jovial. It was the very opposite of what I'd come to expect as the norm for funerals, based on my own limited experience of saying farewell to one distant grandparent, and what I'd seen on television of course. I thought the occasions were sombre affairs, with attendees wrapped in black from head to toe. The little people saved their brightest clothes for lifespan end days. Their procession was a carnival of colour.

I resigned myself to several hours of waiting patiently with a book for company. My nose was deep into the pages of my novel when I heard the clearing of a tiny throat. There before me stood the exceedingly frail Julie, supported by her son and surrounded by members of her family. Jack informed me in a quiet moment during the day that leaving her home was highly unorthodox, but she had insisted I be included in the celebrations. I couldn't fit more than a finger into her house and so she came out to me. I felt a lump in my throat at the honour of this inclusion and lay down on the hard stone, my head propped up with a hand, to better hear the stories the little people had to tell of this surprisingly unconventional little woman.

I smiled with the crowd at stories of the rebellious child Julie, recounted by her younger sister, now an old woman herself. I laughed aloud as Geraldine Puddle, a great niece, explained how the two had taken an afternoon off to play games on a day when Julie should have been passing on her knowledge of weaving. Geraldine's words painted a vivid picture, and I could all but see Julie the sea-monster rising from the pool after she'd slipped and fallen in during the excitement of play, all covered in weed. I swallowed against the tightness in my throat as Jack stood to take his turn, and told of a mother who loved him from his first breath and who never failed to look out for him, even when he was causing chaos. Julie's shrunken and spotted hand reached for Jack's. She whispered something to him that he later confided in me, "Make me proud, my beautiful boy."

They were her last words.

The breeze freshened and cooled the sun-baked cove. Distant gulls exchanged pleasantries on the breeze and the waves continued to crash against the rocks. The sounds were too normal for this alien experience. Some part of me expected everything to stop, to still for just a moment as Julie closed her heavy eyelids. Time continued to rush by; it stops for no one.

The tiny Julie had a smile on her face. She seemed even smaller in death. The concerns of the world had fallen from her, and her peaceful visage was beyond the rest of sleep. Without words several of the younger male relations unfolded a sheet, smaller than a napkin, and gently lowered her resting body onto it. Each picked up a corner of material and together they stood to carry Julie's body over a rise. The family followed with footsteps timed to a jolly tune piped by an old gentleman, Julie's brother in law, I recognised him from his bright red trousers. I stayed where I was and listened to the music grow quieter, unsure if it would be proper for me to follow. The pipes released a happy melody under the skilful fingers of Julie's kinsman but it still sounded somehow mournful to my ear. I should have taken more time to get to know her. Julie had quelled her own adventurous impulses to settle down with the traditional and prudent John; that much was clear from the stories shared of her youth. And yet I knew that in the relative silence of the beach at night when John was abroad or already abed, that there were evenings when she would talk to a young Jack about all he could accomplish, should he wish to follow a different dream to the norm. Those seeds, sown by a mother who believed her son capable of anything, had started our journey.

"Aren't you coming Tom?" Jack asked. He must have

hung back as I mused, waiting for me to join him in the funeral procession.

"I think I'd better head home, still a few things to organise for the trip." It was a good excuse. I wasn't sure how much more of the funeral I could bear to witness. Some part of me thought I should be documenting the event in my role as witness to the lives of the little people, but if I'm honest I think I had already laid down that dream by this point. I hadn't documented anything in days, save a few brief notes here and there if they were related to our upcoming adventure.

"Oh." If Jack sounded disappointed he quickly shrugged it off with his familiar grin. "Well I'll see you tomorrow then."

"Tomorrow? I thought that was a private thing?"

"Didn't Mum tell you?" Jack asked.

"Tell me what?"

"Before her end, she said you were to be my Guide for the ceremony. It was witnessed and everything."

Jack had previously told me about the coming of age ceremony. It was a challenge that every young man and woman had to overcome to be known as fully grown, a challenge typically overcome with the help of a parent. Jack had been reticent with the details; I always put that down to it being a sacred little person ritual, steeped in mystery to big person kind. All of a sudden I was being asked to participate, with no idea what to expect and no time to prepare.

"I thought your Uncle was doing it? Bob wasn't it?"

"Billy. Mum thought you'd be better for it. Besides, I doubt Uncle Billy could make the climb anymore, he's not far off his own end."

"But Jack, I don't know what I'm supposed to do," I said, panic shunting grief out of the way in the pit of my stomach.

"Don't worry, Tom! I'm the one who has to do the challenge. You only have to be there. I'll see you tomorrow morning," he called over his shoulder, already following his family to say their final farewells to Julie Meadows.

Once again, and not for the last time, I wondered what on earth I'd gotten myself into.

"You have to do *what*?" I asked?

Jack looked at me in exasperation and explained the challenge again. Slowly. "I have to climb down to the shore, collect a seashell and bring it back up to the Elders. Simple."

"But that'll take hours! Aren't there any special considerations for you with, you know, your condition?" Jack's face became a thundercloud in an instant.

"There's nothing I can't do. I'll do it without you if you won't be my Guide."

"I didn't mean it like that, Jack. I'll help in any way I can, of course I will. What do I need to do?"

"Nothing really. We walk down together and at the shore I'll go forward to find my shell while you watch from behind. The Guide is there to help if it's needed, but mainly to offer advice. Most times the Guide suggests the spot where they found their own shell." Jack hesitated and recent grief drew his features into a frown as he fended away tears. Had things been different, had his parents been younger, had the chasm between himself and his father during his last days not been so great, then this would have been a memorable day for them to share together. As it was he would spend it with me.

"How close do you need to get to the ocean?"

Jack shrugged, "As close as needs be I suppose. Wherever there are shells. Mum told me to watch out for the waves, what with not being able to get away too quick. She said even if the waves seem to be pulling back one can splash you all of a sudden and pull you into the ocean without any hope of swimming free. She almost had that happen on her coming of age day, but her Guide warned her in time to sprint out the way. That's what Guides are for, they can't interfere or anything, but they can advise and support and stuff. It'll be fine. I've got my new bonus legs."

I'd created a couple of new sets of crutches for Jack in the last few days to suit his increased height. He was growing tall, for a little person.

"So what are we waiting for?" I asked.

"The Elders, they'll set me off on my journey."

"Right," I said. We sat together for some minutes before a small delegation of little people arrived. I'd heard Jack mention the Elders before. They were the group that technically governed the community of little people, but they didn't have much of a hand in managing day to day living. They were more involved in events such as coming of age ceremonies and companionship celebrations, similar to our own marriages. The little people didn't pay tax or a salary to the Elders, instead they looked after their own little tracts of land, and helped their neighbours as they were able. Schooling was done at home, common areas didn't require much upkeep, being not much more than rocky outcroppings as they were, and there were no hospitals to manage. The little people didn't fall ill often, and the rare injuries they suffered were managed at home. The eldership was more of a ceremonial title than anything else, that and a living embodiment of the history of the little people, passed from Elder to Elder through oral tradition.

The group of men wore tiny red shirts, embroidered with a pattern showing a wave crashing over a rock. I assumed it was the uniform of the post.

"Jack lad," one of the men said, "You don't have to go through with this if you don't want to now."

"Aye Jack, it might be too hard on you, with just the one leg and no parent to hand neither," another chipped in.

Jack's back straightened and I felt full of pride for a

boy on the brink of manhood.

"And then what? I remain a child? No. I come of age today," Jack said in a bold voice that rang clear above the distant crash of the waves.

"Very well then," said the first Elder. "Jack Meadows, today you'll come of age, should you complete your challenge and bring us back a shell of your own choosing from beside the ocean. This sacred ceremony has been conducted amongst the people for countless generations, and in so doing you promise to pass the practice on to your own sons and daughters. Do you agree?"

"I agree," Jack said.

The Elder nodded. "Well then best of luck to you Jack. And you, Guide, will you assist Jack Meadows in his coming of age, promising not to interfere, only to offer such guidance and wisdom as pertains to the task and that you yourself have to offer?" I hoped I was imagining the sceptical tone in the small man's speech when he talked of my wisdom.

"I will."

"No interfering means no carrying now, you hear," another Elder said, "he's to do it alone or not at all. We won't have no big folk messing with our ancient rites."

"I understand," I said, though I cast a dirty look at the speaker.

"Then be on your way, Jack Meadows, and return before sundown or start again with another sunrise."

Jack set off on his crutches with steely determination and without a backwards glance. My own exit wasn't quite as dramatic. It's hard to storm away from a situation when the person you're walking with needs a hundred paces to match one of your own. Walking with a little person is always a challenge, particularly if you are conscious of needing to be somewhere and feeling the pressure of time. I had the choice of standing still to let Jack progress a little way ahead and then taking one step to catch up, or shuffling my feet in absolutely minute footsteps to try and keep pace with him. Conversation was impossible because of the height difference and so the long walk felt lonely. He was too far below for me to hear much more than a shout. Jack continued for a good hour before we paused for a break. I offered him the lid of my water bottle, filled with a few drops of refreshing liquid. He could just about lift it to his lips to slake his thirst. I slurped straight from the bottle.

"They're out of sight now, why don't I run ahead and grab a shell?" I asked.

Jack was rubbing the muscles in his good leg. The pain from his lifeless limb was no longer constant, but it still dragged on the floor as he hobbled along with his crutches and put a strain on his good leg and his arms, particularly if it caught against the uneven ground as was quite common. It was hard enough for him to walk on level ground, this picking his way across stones and clambering steadily downhill toward the ocean must have wearied him beyond description. I dreaded the thought of seeing him struggle back up the hill bearing a heavy shell.

"I have to do this," he said. "Wasn't there anything you had to do to become a man?"

"We become adults at eighteen, well full adults anyway, there are some things we can do at sixteen. And then again there are some things we can't do until we're twenty-one, especially in other countries. I guess there isn't exactly a marker to say that today you've become a man."

"Sounds confusing," Jack said. "Do you feel like a man?"

Jack's question stumped me. I was a twenty-two year old living at home with my parents, existing entirely off their generosity. In many ways I felt a teenager again. What is it that makes a man? Is it fending for yourself? Providing for your family? The ability to drive? To change a tyre on a car? The first day of work? I still have no answer, and even today there are moments when I'm not sure I've really grown up. I envy the little people their assurance of adulthood.

"Sometimes I do," I said eventually.

"In our eyes this climb is what turns a boy or a girl into a man or a woman," Jack said, "I expect it sounds silly to you, but if we can do this one big thing it means there's nothing we can't do. It means we're strong enough to support our existing families, or to look after a wife or husband and children and start a new family. If I don't do this myself then I'll never truly be a man. I don't want to quit. I can't quit."

"Time to carry on then," I said, and offered an outstretched finger to help Jack to his feet.

We walked on, stopping occasionally for brief rests. Jack's face grew sterner the longer we walked and I knew he was fighting an internal battle to keep going, despite the pain. I felt utterly useless, and strove to drive Jack forward in the only way I could, with encouraging words.

"You've got this, Jack."

"You can do it."

"Don't give up, just a bit further now."

I don't know if it helped, but sometimes my words preceded an extra burst of speed so I like to think I assisted in some positive way. Perhaps having someone there beside you for the walk through a nightmare can be help enough.

The sun had reached its zenith before we reached the ocean. We took another break on the coarse sand. Jack was fascinated by the feel of it; the grains of sand were pebbles to him. We shared the sandwich I'd packed for my adventures that day and talked about nothing of consequence until we were refreshed. Then the hunt was on.

Finding a shell on a beach sounds like the easiest task in the world, but today of all days I couldn't see a single one from high tide line to ocean's edge. *This is all I'm here for, my sole purpose,* I told myself, *to bring Jack to a spot where he can find a shell, and there are none to be found anywhere.* The little people who had undertaken this mission in previous months and years knew exactly where to look, but I was at a loss. The shifting shadows marked the passage of time and still Jack hunted. Finally I persuaded him to keep searching in his spot while I explored further afield to find some token he could return to the Elders. The words which launched Jack's challenge rang in my ears, "Return before sundown or start again with another sunrise." I couldn't stand the thought of Jack having to go through this again. I wasn't sure he could physically manage it.

"Jack!" I cried. I'd almost missed it but there, riding the froth of an incoming wave, was a patch of white bearing the delicate ridges of a common cockle shell. Jack was running as fast as he could manage on his crutches. I think I felt his pain as acutely as he did when he tripped and fell hard on the compacted sand. Before I could take a step to help him up he was on his way again, as fast as if his stride had never been broken.

"The tide must be coming in by now, we need to act quickly," I said.

Jack nodded, wasting no energy on words, and set to work scrabbling at the sand around where the shell had come to rest with his bare hands. A wave splashed in around his worksite, and I instinctively formed my hands into a fence between his fragile body and the ocean to prevent him being pulled back by the current. He hung on to the shell as the water rolled away from him with incredible force. As the water retreated he continued his excavation, and I continued to provide what shelter I could from the waves until we were both wet through and exhausted.

Finally, with an almighty tug that sent him rolling head over heels, Jack freed his shell. It was a beautiful specimen, predominantly white but with a hint of orange between its ridges. A worthy prize indeed. We were elated as we walked together away from the ocean. We were so proud of ourselves that I didn't even notice the large wave crash in behind us and roll forward to dampen my feet.

Jack and his shell had vanished before I could say a word.

CHAPTER TEN

"Jack!" I bellowed.

This was a nightmare. It had to be a nightmare. Sand, water, foam, seaweed, stones, sand, water... there was no sign of a little person anywhere. I ran up and down the small cove, screaming for Jack until my voice grew hoarse. Sand, water, whiteness, the shell! It tumbled out from under a crashing wave and I stooped down, picked it up and pocketed it without conscious thought.

"Come on Jack, where are you," I said as I waded through the breakers and ran my hand across the sand beneath the water, feeling for anything out of the ordinary. My fingers brushed against fabric and I pinched quickly between index finger and thumb to secure what I desperately hoped was Jack.

It wasn't.

It was his tiny leather jacket. I'd found it a few days ago adorning a Ken doll in my sister's old toy chest and offered it to him. I thought it would come in handy if we found our way far enough north for the temperature to drop. The day to day dress of the little people was better suited to the mild Cornish climate, but Jack had loved the jacket so much he'd wanted to wear it immediately. I held the sodden garment between my fingers and peered around the area, but there was still no sign of Jack.

Find me a man who can keep track of time in a crisis and I will be amazed. I trudged through the sand for what felt like hours with no reward for my labour. In reality only minutes had passed, but each second stretched to infinity, each minute was an eternity. Time is a trickster in any desperate situation.

"Tom."

Seawater and sand formed a plaster on my clothes and exposed skin and I sat shivering, my forehead resting on my knees and my arms hugging my cold legs. Now, to make matters worse, I was hearing voices.

"Tom!"

I lifted my gaze as the cry became insistent and rubbed my eyes in disbelief as I saw Jack crawling towards me. In a couple of steps I was beside him.

"Where were you?" I asked angrily, lashing out in anger as relief flooded my senses.

"The wave caught me. I couldn't breathe. It was holding me down and the current drew me to the side, away from you. I managed to snatch a breath but then it pulled me back under. I thought I was a goner Tom, I really did. Just when I thought my lungs were ready to explode I felt a rock beneath me and I clung on to it for dear life. Then I could pull myself up with my arms each time the water rushed away. I lost my bonus legs somewhere so I couldn't get back to you. I could see you running around but you couldn't hear me. I tried walking but I'm all out of balance. All I could do was crawl."

I looked at this brave little soul more closely. The legs of his trousers were torn, and his knees were scratched and bleeding, as were his hands. This mission was costing everything he had to give.

"None of it matters," he said disconsolately, "I lost the shell. We'll never find another in time to make it back up the hill."

"Wait a moment," I said, and pulled the preserved shell from my pocket. The weariness dropped from Jack's face and hope danced in his eyes.

"Can we make it?" he asked, checking the position of the sun.

"We'll have to hurry. I've no spare crutches either; I left the other pair at home." There was no way Jack was going to let me carry him back up the hill, but without his walking aids I wasn't sure how we'd scale it, he couldn't crawl the entire way. "Wait there," I said and left him with another bottle lid full of water to replenish his reserves.

A walking stick wouldn't be anything like as good as my carefully crafted crutches, but it would help. I scavenged the beach for a few likely pieces of wood amidst the tangle of seaweed at the high tide line, and returned to Jack to give them a go. He selected the least sodden and rotten offering and we started the long journey back.

An afternoon has never passed so slowly, nor have I ever felt so utterly useless. Jack scrambled up slippery rocks, one hand clinging desperately to his shell, the other to the stick that offered him some balance on the side of his crippled leg. He was grunting with pain as we cleared the last rise, putting us close to his home. With the very last rays of a blood red sun we stumbled into the midst of the Elders.

"Here," Jack cried, collapsing to the floor as he thrust his hard-won shell towards one of the men.

The Elders crowded around it and spoke together in hushed tones.

"And you did this all by yourself did you lad?" one of the Elders asked.

"Yes, he did!" I replied, affronted. "He carried that shell all the way up from the beach and never once asked for help. If you doubt my word then I, I'll challenge you!" I think it's safe to say I was exhausted as well as Jack. I'm not entirely sure what I was expecting, miniature pistols at dawn perhaps? Fortunately for me the Elders broke into laughter.

"We believe you, lad." The man turned to face Jack, "You have passed the test and today you are a man of the Meadows family. May your footsteps be true and your strength unfailing as you journey to your end."

The Elder took the pretty shell from his comrade and laid it upon the floor. With a united cry from the assembled he drove his ceremonial stick down, shattering the shell into pieces. I watched in confusion as Jack hobbled over, looked at the carnage and picked up one piece to hand back to the Elder who nodded and walked away.

When I returned the following morning Jack was wearing that piece of shell around his neck, the symbol of his adulthood. Some little people, like his father John, tucked their shell necklaces away safe in their houses. Jack wore his proudly until the day his end drew close.

Despite the ordeal at the beach, Jack still wanted to leave immediately. I had to insist he took a day to put his feet up and rest, or at least to put his house in order ready for an extended leave of absence.

"You won't want any rotting food around when we get back, Jack. Give it a tidy up, I've still got to sort the car out anyway," I said to him.

I turned to leave and walked some few paces before I heard his mumble. "I won't be back," he said, or at least I thought those were the words the wind carried to my ears. I didn't think much of it. I might have misheard or even imagined it. Even if Jack had spoken, what of it? This was a place of painful memories for my friend. I'd be happy for him to live out the rest of his days wherever I wound up. Our plan was to travel for several months, and that would be most of Jack's lifespan. After seeing his dogged determination the day before, I resolved to make the trip the best I could. Why would he want to return home to this simple existence after seeing the wonders of the world I could show him?

It was that thought that kept me going as I spent a day of hard labour replacing the car battery with one I'd sourced from a local garage, and then attempting to repair the multitude of faults that showed up once power ran through to the other systems. I even roped my father in to help when he returned from the bakery to find me covered in grease and kicking the tyres in frustration. He disapproved of my plan to travel, but I think he was happy enough to put that to one side to enjoy tinkering on a motor with me again.

By the time we trudged inside for our homemade steak and kidney pie with mashed potato we were both filthy, but happy that we'd restored the car to working order.

The great adventure would begin the very next day.

- PART TWO -

JOURNEY

CHAPTER ELEVEN

"I'll call, I promise," I uttered reassurances into my mother's hair as she hugged me goodbye.

I disentangled myself to say farewell to my father. "Dad, thank you again for helping me with the car. I'll be back before you know it." My father stuck his chin out and folded his arms across his chest, a pose I'd often seen him strike after being defeated in an argument with my mother when he was still convinced he was correct. Still, he took my proffered hand and shook it and then pulled me into a hug, patting me hard on the back.

"Take care of yourself Tom," he said. "Stay safe."

"I will. Love you both," I called as an afterthought and climbed into the Volkswagen to drive as close as possible to the cove to pick up my travelling companion.

Jack greeted me with weary enthusiasm, and I judged it best to start our travels at a leisurely pace. He wasn't fully recovered from the toll the coming of age ceremony had played on his body. His small grimaces told me more clearly than words that his bad leg pained him. I didn't mind a slow day to kick-start the adventure; it would give me an opportunity to perfect my idea regarding Jack's safety in the car. A seatbelt would more likely crush him than save him in the event of an accident, and the last thing I wanted to see was Jack flying forward from the front seat and careening into the dashboard. The little people might be solidly built, but I doubted their tough tiny bodies would withstand that kind of impact. It was also essential to think about what a passing motorist might notice when glancing through the passenger window of my car. I didn't really want Jack on display for the whole world to see. These are the sort of conundrums you need to consider when travelling with a little person.

My plan was to enlist the help of an old shoebox to solve both problems with one fell swoop. The box was cut open on my side so that Jack could converse with me and I could see him at a glance; I trusted the bulk of my body to provide adequate screening from the driver's side of the car. Anyone looking through the passenger window would see a cardboard box locked into place with a seatbelt. That might be unusual, but less so than having Jack on display to the world. At the front and on the top of the box I left the cardboard mostly intact, but cut out thin horizontal strips through which Jack could peer to get a glimpse of the world around him. I carpeted the bottom with soft furnishings, and attempted to create something of a seatbelt within the box itself to offer double protection to Jack. He didn't like the feeling of being restrained by elastic bands and so he didn't wear it much, trusting instead that if we did stop suddenly the cardboard would prevent his body from taking too much damage. He deemed my solution comfortable enough after a bit of adjusting and tweaking, though I think he'd have preferred to sit on the dashboard for the view it would have offered.

The back seat and boot of the Golf were packed full of my belongings. I added Jack's small travelling bag to the collection. He offered much of the furniture in his house to friends and neighbours who were all too happy to relieve him of the high-quality goods I'd donated to the Meadows family, so his possessions for the journey were predominantly clothes and a few miniatures plates and cups to eat and drink from. Other than his fragment of shell he didn't bring any mementos from home. On my insistence Jack made sure there was nothing in the house that would spoil in case he wished to return one day, and shut the doors tight against the threat of the ocean. He shrugged nonchalantly at the prospect of coming back home, but did as I suggested all the same.

By mid-morning we were all but ready. I carried Jack back to the cove for one last look around before departing. I couldn't tell what he was feeling, his small face was expressionless but I could see him fingering the shell fragment at the end of its chain. If I had to hazard a guess I would say he was whispering a farewell to all he had known, and perhaps a final goodbye to his parents. A group of little people of a similar age to Jack gathered near the empty Meadows house to wave him off. He'd not spent much time with them of late, having been content with my company, but they were his childhood friends all the same. I wondered if any would feel envious at the thought of his adventure or beg to be brought along as well, but most of the small crowd wore bemused expressions, as if leaving the cove was pure lunacy and they couldn't quite get to grips with the thought of someone actually doing it. I hung back; I remembered all too well a young Jack telling me his friends thought me a 'weird giant.' After some banter and a few last hugs Jack tugged ineffectively on the leg of my jeans, ready to be carried back to the car.

Our journey had begun.

I wish I could catalogue every detail of my travels with Jack Meadows but alas, many memories have faded with the passing of time. The details of my initial interactions with the little people were carefully recorded, lest I need them in presenting my research to the world, but as that idea evaporated like the morning mist it grew harder to motivate myself to keep a diary of my interactions with Jack and our day to day activities. With a young man's arrogance I convinced myself I would remember each minute intricacy of our journey for the rest of my life, but even the brightest lights dull with age, and the greatest memories become indistinct as the years roll by. One blessing of the short lives of the little people is that they don't live long enough to forget their fond recollections.

You'll forgive me I trust, if any of the following recorded events are out of sequence, or if conversations recalled from one day find their way into the record of another. The original map of our route, today framed and in pride of place in my study, has been of great assistance in piecing together my fragmented memories, for we did stick mostly to our plan. Aside from those instances where circumstances forced us to abandon the activities we'd decided on of course. In those moments we made it up as we went along, a requirement from time to time to protect Jack's anonymity, and even his life.

If I sound forgetful to the point of senility I hope you'll see that isn't the case. I still remember many details from our journey, but I expect you'd soon be bored by a detailed account of each and every day of the months we travelled together. Perhaps it is a blessing in disguise that it is the more interesting days I remember with greater clarity. That first day, for example. We travelled the length and breadth of Britain in my banged up old Volkswagen, clocking up thousands of miles on the odometer, but I'll never forget Jack's first moment in a moving vehicle.

"Are we ready? Can we go?" Jack asked.

"We're ready. Let's go!" I responded, and slipped the car into first gear. I was still readjusting to the old girl's sensibilities and lurched forward into a dramatic stall. Jack let out a strangled scream as his whole box shifted forward and he was thrown into the cardboard barrier. We made a few more adjustments before trying again, this time with a somewhat smoother start. In honour of the sunny March weather I cracked the windows to circulate the warm air within the car. Jack let out a great whoop of excitement as he saw the world pass by in a blur through his peepholes and felt the rush of the wind circling through his box. He discarded his safety harness to jump around (as best a person can jump around with one leg hanging limply in tow). We dissolved into laughter and I had to forcibly remind myself to keep my eyes on the road and not the hysterical antics of the newly grown-up Jack Meadows.

It was the ninth of March when we drove away from the cove in Cornwall; that much I do remember. For almost six months we journeyed, stretching our budget to breaking point to see many wonderful sights. The car was our home for much of the time. Many nights we slept in it, or found cheap campsites or likely looking spots of countryside upon which to pitch the old tent I'd raided from my parents' loft. From time to time we'd stop in a cheap bed and breakfast or hotel room, more for a warm shower for me and a warm bath in the sink for Jack than anything else. Jack found those occasions fascinating, he loved nothing more than stomping on a remote control to see images appear on the television screen. I was forced to highlight our budgetary restrictions on several occasions, when his desperation to keep up to date with the latest episodes of his favourite soap opera, Neighbours, arose.

Food wasn't too much of a problem. Jack ate miniscule amounts, and I was happy to rough it with tins of baked beans cooked over our camping stove. We braved a meal in a bustling pub early in the journey, but it was such a stressful experience trying to keep Jack hidden while circumspectly feeding him morsels from my plate that we didn't repeat it. Takeaways were a welcome enough break from cooking on occasion, and also a great diversion. I vividly remember Jack doing battle with a long noodle from my pot of chicken chow mein. He made it his mission to finish that noodle, though it was longer by some margin than himself.

Once upon a time I might have questioned if there was really enough to see within the United Kingdom to spend six months exploring it, but after travelling with Jack for that time I wonder if I've even scratched the surface. I was always determined to move on to the next destination on our list, but Jack loved nothing more than probing the secrets of every nook and cranny of a place. If the choice had rested solely with him we might never have left Cornwall. Every tiny road held potential mysteries and marvels, and there were many times when I had to apologise to farmers for accidentally driving down their private roads because Jack wanted to traverse every dusty trail.

"What's down there?" he would cry, pointing to a narrow lane unsuitable for heavy vehicles, and off we'd go again, following winding tributaries of main roads through woodlands or fields or to impassable fords. If, in time, Jack learned that it was okay to move on without turning over every rock in every county through the course of our travelling, I learned that it was okay to take my time and enjoy the journey without always thinking where we should be next. It was through those moments of stopping to take in a scene that the real beauty of the country seeped into our souls.

Suffice to say it was an incredible six months. There were hard times of course, and moments where we disagreed. No true friendship is without its occasional arguments. But on the whole I know I will find it difficult to paint a picture with these ineffective words that could aptly describe our trip. From mountain to valley, beach to inland moor, deserted forest to crowded city, I endeavoured to show Jack everything this fair country has to offer.

I was always conscious of time ticking swiftly by. I had the rest of my life to live after this adventure, but this adventure would be Jack's life. I begrudged every long journey to our next destination as wasted time and grumbled and growled through traffic jams. Jack thought nothing of the sort. To him every long journey contained more excitement and more opportunities to take in great vistas in the space of moments. Every traffic jam meant an opportunity to talk about the wonder of the world or to admire the intricate detail he could spot in the most mundane views. He found enjoyment in every single day, in every single moment, even when there wasn't much there to enjoy.

CHAPTER TWELVE

It was a day not long after our journey had begun when the first sneeze rocked my body and caused my eyes to stream. We decided to start our exploration within the county of Cornwall itself, to show Jack that not all beaches were similar to the rocky cove in which he'd spent his seventy-something days. The completely unbroken sandy span of The Towans seemed a likely spot. It was a large enough space for us to sit unnoticed to watch the sunlight dance on the golden sand and the bright blue ocean, and to admire those surfers brave enough to take on the cold water for the thrill of riding a wave. We shared an enormous ice cream cone from the one van brave enough to proffer his trade so early in the year. It was a chilly day for such a treat, but a visit to the seaside isn't complete without that delicious chocolaty flake buried deep into the swirl of a soft, creamy mountain of ice cream, contained within the crunchy nest of its cone. I had to break a morsel of wafer from the cone and scoop some ice cream into it for Jack to enjoy. His hands were a sticky mess by the time he'd finished, but his face was aglow with the light of someone who has experienced that delectable delicacy for the very first time.

The noon sun baked the sheltered spot we'd chosen, so we retreated into the sand dunes for a walk. I carried Jack in my open palm as we wended our way through the tall grasses and trudged through shifting sand. We stopped from time to time at Jack's request, to admire a view or wait for a small bird to erupt from a tangle of foliage. Jack had a sixth sense for the best places in which to look to spot wildlife, a trait bred into the little people over many generations for their protection, I assume. He often tutted at the noise my 'big people' feet would make crashing through the undergrowth, startling away birds and insects and other species he wanted to see. I learnt to tread more quietly as time went by.

Carrying a little person was itself a problem that needed addressing. I didn't mind wandering along with my palm outstretched, but it led to the dull ache of overused muscles in time and it wasn't exactly subtle. If someone stumbled upon our path all I could do was quickly pull my hand behind my back and hope they hadn't noticed a miniature man pointing at some item of interest with an arm wrapped around my thumb for stability. I could make a fist of my hand to cover him, or form a closed shell of both of my hands, but I worried my zeal for concealment would cause him pain or injury. After much trial and error and many a near miss we found a way to use the breast pocket of my polo shirts. I folded small sections of cardboard to make the pocket stand out from the shirt, giving Jack enough space to stand within comfortably without feeling that his circulation was being cut off. I padded the bottom of the pocket as well, so that he didn't need to stand on tiptoes to see out but could rest more comfortably. There was also enough room that if someone did happen upon us he could duck down or sit to avoid detection. I was proud of my ingenuity.

We spent a day admiring the endless stretch of golden sand and a day in the quaint seaside town of St. Ives, eating chips under the watchful eye of a colony of seagulls.

I shielded Jack from sight with a coat slung casually over the backpack beside me and my leg as we ate. That left Jack's view to the front open to see the sea, while he was well hidden in the shadows. After returning to our tent that evening Jack questioned why I was so cautious.

"Does it really matter if I'm seen? What are they going to do?"

"I don't know, Jack, but I don't really want to find out. Scientists would probably want to experiment on you and find out where all your relatives live to study their way of life. I don't know think it'd be good for the little people." In reality I wasn't worried about the rest of the little people but I thought this might be a way to make Jack more cautious; he was certainly an unusual little person, but some part of him still held to the guiding principle that seemed to govern all of their lives, that one should do anything for the good of the people. The truth is I didn't want anything to get in the way of our adventure, and gawping crowds would be sure to do that. Besides, the little people were my secret now, not something for the rest of the world.

ACHOO!

I managed to keep the car in a straight line as my eyes closed against the force of my sneeze.

Jack looked at me as though an alien had overtaken my body and was attempting to evacuate through my nose.

"What?" I asked and wiped my nose on my sleeve, "You've never heard a sneeze before?" He shook his head and I marvelled at the thought of a life without the common cold.

Our plan was to drive down the coast to Lands End on that day but it was a nasty bug I'd picked up, one that led me from peak performance to death's door in the space of hours. This was man flu at its worst. A local shop provided much needed cold medicine, tissues, a microwavable pot of chicken soup and directions to a local bed & breakfast that would likely have a room going free.

"We've a room. Just for yourself is it?" The landlady asked.

"Yes, just for me," I tried to hold on to the sneeze I could feel brewing in my sinuses. The kind woman must have sensed my suffering.

"You'll be straight to bed sounding like that I'm sure. Let me take that," she said, snatching the chicken soup from my hand, "I'll heat it and bring it up. Room three." She handed me the key and we soon found ourselves in a cosy little bedroom. I melted into the soft bed, and tried to admire the chintzy pictures and ornaments that crowded every free space of wallpapered wall. It wasn't exactly to my taste but there was a warm blanket to wrap myself in and an ancient television to watch. True to her word the hostess brought me a bowl of steaming chicken soup, along with a large hunk of bread she'd generously added herself.

"Don't you worry about a thing now. You eat up and pop the dishes outside the room when you're done. A good night's sleep, that'll set you right."

I was more than happy to oblige and hungrily devoured my feast, setting aside a portion for Jack before I started of course.

Jack arranged his travel bed, more a pile of scraps of material than an actual mattress, with frustrating good humour. I explained the fundamentals of the television remote control to my friend and curled up in a ball to sleep the day away.

When I awoke several hours later I noticed two cold capsules resting beside the glass of water by my bed. My befuddled brain praised itself for thinking to secure the next dose of medicine before sleep, particularly as I was quite sure I'd left the box on the other side of the room. They helped to ease my congestion and I dozed again to the sound of Jack discovering the delights of Australian soap operas.

I felt weak the following morning, but much better for a day of rest. I looked around the room and with a puzzled frown noted that the box of tablets was, in fact, on the vanity table across the room.

"Jack, did the lady come in yesterday to bring my medicine over?" I asked.

"No. I did that," Jack said.

I chuckled. "No really, how did you avoid being seen by her?"

"No really," he said with his proud little hands pressed firmly on his hips, "I fetched them."

I looked from the bedside cabinet where Jack was standing to the vanity table. The room certainly wasn't enormous but to a little person it was a vast distance to cover over the thick pile of the carpet which would surely be a menace to a man walking on crutches. Then there was the climb up and down the furniture, burdened with the extra weight of carrying two tablets as long as your arm.

"How? Why" I asked, dumbfounded.

Jack stood to stomp on the On/Off button of the remote control. He wanted no distractions as he told the tale of his heroic feat. He was a born orator.

"As to why, you told the man you got them from they were lifesavers and then said you'd need more later so I knew I had to get them to you, if they were to save your life, especially as you were dense enough to leave them all the way over there," he said, waving an arm in the direction of the table where I could see the box as clear as day. "What would happen to me if you were to reach your end day right here?

"And as to how, well I had my backpack here with a few bits to help, like my knife and that bit of rope I have in my bag for emergencies. Dad always said you should be prepared for anything." He dragged the 'rope' out for my inspection. It was a spool of grey thread of the kind you might sew a button back onto a shirt with. "I had to fasten the end of the rope up here, see," he said and showed me a loop of thread still anchored around the bedside lamp, "then I threw the rest down to let it unravel, and used that to climb down. It wasn't easy mind, I knew I'd need my bonus legs for the journey and they were tricky to manage with the climbing, but I found a way to tuck them through the straps of my bag well enough and off I went.

"It was pretty scary down there. There were all sorts of shadows under your bed and I could hear things moving around. Once I even saw something. It was a monster the like of which I'd never seen, brown and hairy with eight legs pointing off in different directions and soulless black staring eyes, lots of them. It was scuttling underneath the bed and I was sure it would come after me. Its legs were all tensed to jump and it looked straight toward me, thinking me a tasty lunch I expect. I pulled my knife and swung it at the creature hoping to scare the thing off but it didn't work. It scuttled toward me, warned by my blade I think but brave enough to investigate more. I could feel my hand trembling as it drew even closer but I stayed still and didn't drop my gaze in case that would be a sign of weakness to it. Suddenly I felt sticky all over and my other arm was glued to my side, bonus leg and all. I didn't like that one bit so I used my knife to cut these cords it was trying to wrap around me and lunged at it. I missed the eye I was aiming for, put off balance by the ropes it shot at me, but I nicked it on one of its legs and that did the trick. It backed away from my blade under the bed. I had to stop myself going after it to finish the job, but time was ticking and I had to get that lifesaving medicine to you so I let it be and carried on my way, once I'd freed myself of that horrible sticky string all over me anyway.

The walk was longer than it looked from a distance so I stopped for a bit of a break half way over. I kept my knife in hand in case that monster came back for another go. It'd be no good getting eaten right now, that wouldn't help you and we'd both miss seeing all of those amazing places.

"Finally I found the bottom of that massive table over

there and that's when I hit a bit of a problem. It was taller than the one I'd dropped down from. I thought about throwing the reel of rope up to try and get it to cling to something but it was too heavy for me to throw that far. I nearly clobbered myself on the head trying a couple of times. In the end I cut a length from it, what I guessed to be long enough to reach all the way to the top. I made a loop in the end and tried throwing that up to hook it over something, anything, but try as I might I couldn't get it to stay. I was throwing blind, there was no way to see what was up there.

"I couldn't give up though, not with your life at stake like you said, so finally I thought to tie my knife to the end of the rope. I swung it around my head faster and faster and faster and then launched it! It didn't quite make it but it was nearly there, so I tried again, and again, until eventually the point of it must have caught on something up there and stayed put. I gave it a good solid tug and it didn't come down, so I started the climb."

I was impressed with Jack's upper arm strength. I was never any good at climbing the rope in sports lessons in school. I would occasionally make it a couple of feet above ground and then slide back down, facing rope burn and the humiliation of laughter from my peers. I was always one for intellectual pursuits, not physical.

"It was tough going with my backpack," Jack continued, "I'd left the bonus legs at the bottom as I figured I could hop or crawl for a bit at the top and they'd be tricky to manage on the climb. The bag I needed though, to put those tablets you needed in. I managed it in the end and pulled myself up onto the top, even though my arms were aching fit to fall clear out of their sockets.

"The box was all sealed up and I couldn't pull it open, try as I might, so I cut my way in. Hope you don't mind. Then I dragged out that massive sheet of plastic. I could see the tablets there in it but they were trapped and my knife didn't want to cut through the casing. That was a hard blow after making it all the way over. Fortunately I thought to have a look at the bottom and saw it was made of something different, some kind of shiny paper, and that I could cut through. One by one I loaded them into my bag, I couldn't carry more than two so I hoped that would be enough, and then got ready to slide down the rope to the floor. This time I could tie the rope myself so I was happier it wouldn't come undone and leave me with a big fall to the floor. Those tablets were a lot of extra weight so I slid down a bit quicker than I was happy with. Good thing the floor's so nice and padded.

"The monster stayed out of sight on the way back. I must have scared it well enough to keep it out of my way. That's good because the bag was feeling heavier and heavier as I walked back up to my original bit of rope, and I knew I had that second climb again. I had a bit of a rest before trying it, truth be told. It looked like a long way up. Finally I mustered up all my strength and gave it a go. I was fine until about halfway when I could feel my arms growing more and more tired and I started to slip. Thank goodness there's that little knob part way up. I could reach it with my good leg and it gave me pause for enough time to regain my strength, then I was off again and made it to the top. Just in time I think because you stirred and swallowed the enormous things as I was settling down on my bed for a bit of recovery time."

If I peered hard enough at the vanity table I could see a trail of thread affixed to the top of it and dangling to the floor below. The rope he'd used to climb down and back up the bedside cabinet had been hoisted and neatly coiled next to the cotton spool.

"Jack," I didn't know what to say. This brave little person had risked his life and spent hours of his short existence to bring me medicine that would ease my symptoms but nothing more. I decided not to tell him the pills weren't really a matter of life or death.

"Don't mention it," he said and turned the television

back on, leaving me with my thoughts.

At the time of my cold I calculated Jack's age to be around the equivalent of eighteen of our own years. I very much doubted I had performed any such selfless deeds when I was eighteen years old. Watching Jack lost in the quiet conversations emanating from the television, I made a solemn vow to try harder to offer kindness to people. Little acts can make a big difference, I reasoned. I'm sure I've forgotten that vow more times than I've remembered it over the years, but it still comes to mind from time to time when I see a young mother struggling with her shopping bags or an elderly neighbour toiling to keep the weeds from his front lawn. In those moments I remember Jack's selfless act of kindness in crossing a great chasm to bring me two tablets, and I try to do right by whoever I can.

CHAPTER THIRTEEN

I stayed abed all through the next day to recover my strength. The landlady, whose name I have long since forgotten, continued to wait on me. She brought me hearty meals from her own kitchen and offered more cups of tea than the Queen's garden party. I don't know what she made of the small pile of blankets on the bedside cabinet but she never asked, and Jack stayed out of sight whenever we heard the familiar knock on the door.

I dozed through the afternoon while Jack sat enjoying the view out to the garden. It was a beautifully planted space, with many colourful flowers bursting into life with all the enthusiasm early spring brings to nature. Jack later informed me he was so absorbed in the view that he didn't notice the landlady pottering amidst the buds and blooms until she was looking directly at him. He froze, hoping she might mistake him for a doll or a figment of her imagination, but she continued to peer through the window. After some moments she raised a hand in greeting, and Jack returned the gesture.

The woman never mentioned what she'd seen, but she point blank refused to let me pay a single penny for her hospitality or the room. With her parting, "Happy travels,"

I'm sure she looked more to my pocket than to me, assuming from its slightly raised appearance that Jack must be concealed within.

Could I have discovered someone else who had experience of the little people? Perhaps there were other colonies on different beaches along the Cornish coastline that she'd chanced an encounter with. Then again, it's entirely possible that this humble, helpful and altogether kind-hearted woman was simply more open to the prospect of the fantastic living alongside us in this very big and often strange world.

I insisted we must keep our guard up to keep Jack a secret, but such a positive brush with discovery was undoubtedly a factor in our growing apathy toward concealment as the months went by.

Concerns regarding detection were far from our minds as we continued our journey, thoroughly exploring all that the county of Cornwall had to offer. From the dramatic headland of Lands End to the magical mystery of the castle at St. Michael's Mount. From the endless greenery and rocky vistas of Bodmin Moor to the vivid plant life on display from around the world, housed within the alien domes of the Eden Project. From beach after beach (Jack was always drawn to the ocean, I think salt water ran in his veins) to quaint villages with ancient churches plastered in ivy. At this point in our travels I hadn't yet learnt how best to suggest to Jack that we would need to move on if he wanted to stick to our original travel plan and see more of the country. He wanted to explore every detail of the land and I found it difficult to dissuade him. So it was that we must have spent a good month exploring our home county. In a way I was also happy to linger for a long time in Cornwall because it was an area I knew well. There is comfort in the familiar. Once we crossed into counties unknown I would be unable to guide Jack to exciting places because I wouldn't know where they were concealed. The majority of sites we would see from this point on would be new to both of us.

As we crossed the Tamar Bridge into Devon it suddenly dawned on me that Jack's equivalent age would be around twenty-four. He had only recently reached one hundred days, and yet he was older than me.

I dread to think how badly the car smelt after a month on the road. We were experienced hands at this travelling lark by now, and yet somehow it felt as if we were only now leaving. A new county, the next set of places to explore, we both felt the excitement of starting out all over again. And so it was that we gradually made our way northwards through the rolling green countryside of England. Our planned route determined that we would drive north toward the city of Exeter, and then skirt along the south coast of the country before zigzagging our way back east, stopping in London on the way to Wales. We'd explore that land for a time, and then zigzag back along to the west coast, and so on and so forth until we reached Scotland. It would be impossible to see every town, to stop at every spot that looked interesting, but at least we'd cover most of the bases this way. The countryside and quieter spots held more allure to Jack than big cities, something I was thankful for as I felt he was more likely to be spotted in areas of higher population density. Despite it all, Jack was determined to spend some time in the nation's capital, London, and I tried hard not to worry about how we'd cope with that until we got there.

As a Cornishman born and bred I'm sure I could be burned at the stake for saying it, but Devon was (almost) as beautiful as my home county. We spent significant time along the coast, marvelling at the sight of the red cliffs of Dawlish and the beauty of the English Riviera as the locals named it. In time I convinced Jack that the ocean would wait, and we took to driving around the vast openness of Dartmoor. Our week on the moor would have been more pleasant were it not for the weather, but the spell of dry days we'd enjoyed were at an end and the infamous April Showers had arrived. Jack had known heavy rain in his cove back in Cornwall, but in those moments he'd always huddled against a rock edge or sheltered under the safety of my umbrella. I couldn't recall any instance of his actually being out in the open as the heavens let loose.

We had found an idyllic spot for a picnic lunch beside a lazy little stream and Jack wandered a few steps away, following the path of a twig in the slow moving water. The grey sky had looked threatening all day and an oppressive feel heralded precipitation to come, but as yet no rain had bothered us. I ignored the first couple of splatters from the heavy clouds above and hoped for a passing shower, but it was another matter for Jack.

Well do I remember my mother's admonition, "It's only water," as drizzle turned to monsoon on our family strolls into the countryside. Only water it may be, but big fat drops of rain could cause a serious problem for a little person. Imagine a drop of water the size of your hand landing with full force upon your head. One drop would drench you. Several would knock you from your feet. A torrential downpour would be your undoing.

I laughed aloud as Jack ran toward me as fast as he was able while trying to dodge the water falling quickly from the sky. It looked hysterical, until the moment when a couple of particularly nasty drops knocked him to the floor. My umbrella was buried at the bottom of my bag. Instead I grabbed the more easily accessible raincoat and flung it over him like an enormous collapsed tent. He didn't look impressed when I lifted it off him once the area was safely covered by an umbrella propped up against the floor, but at least he was safe, if not dry.

The weather was a consideration that hadn't entered my mind as I planned to travel with a little person. In their day to day routines the little people are never far from their homes, or at the least from rocks under which they can take shelter. They don't have to worry about rain or hail or snow in their sheltered cove. It was a different story out here in the wilds of Dartmoor, and from that day on I always made sure an umbrella was within easy grasp. I also fashioned Jack a rain hat. It looked something like a mortarboard in shape, only larger and with the square board covered with a section of raincoat cut from my own jacket. It wouldn't save Jack in a downpour, but I reasoned it might help keep him dry by diverting a stray drop or two away from his head. It looked funny on his head, though I never told him that and always endeavoured to keep my smirk concealed. Jack wasn't vain by any stretch of the imagination, but in his younger years he was conscious of his appearance.

We were mired in the depths of Dartmoor when I saw a sign advertising the local zoo. I thought it a fantastic idea and Jack agreed. It was a weekday and still early in the year so I assumed the park would be quiet. A lack of time and money meant I couldn't take Jack around the world to see the weird and wonderful creatures it has to offer, so a zoo seemed a perfect solution. We'd already seen plant life from many a country; now we'd do a world tour of animal life to complete the picture.

When you're not a parent or a student school term dates have little bearing on your life. I had no reason to know exactly when the Easter holiday might have started. I'd seen the endless rows of Easter Eggs in the shops I'd entered for our groceries, but I hadn't paid much attention as they'd been there since the week after Christmas. You might think the busy car park would have given me pause, or the general volume level of happy chatter interspersed with frustrated screaming over denied sweets or other treats. It wasn't until I'd bought my ticket, wondering with some compunction if I should be paying for Jack's entry as well, that I spotted the first couple of children tearing past. Even then I dismissed the occurrence as a small group away from school for the day. As I rounded the corner from the entrance kiosk and saw child after child lined up against the capybara enclosure I knew I'd made a mistake. Jack was as concerned as usual. That is to say not at all. And so, despite the crowds of over-excited children and parents dragged at a half-run to the next exhibit, Jack stood proudly with his arms resting on the rim of my pocket, beckoning me closer to the tapirs we were passing.

"Sweet!" cried a little boy a few feet away, "That's an awesome toy!"

"Come on Jacob, don't bother the nice man," his mother urged, guiding her son away with a shove to his back and a concerned look over her shoulder at a solitary man showing off his latest toy to children at the zoo. Jack giggled at my stunned reaction and my hand hovered ready to shove him back into the pocket when another voice had me spinning around.

"Can I see?" A small pack of children stood blocking my exit. I couldn't see any parents in sight.

"There's nothing to see," I said and silently willed Jack to drop down to the bottom of the pocket. He was having far too much fun.

"Let me see," the girl continued, "or I'll scream."

"Fine. Scream if you want to." I regretted the words as soon as they tumbled from my gaping jaw. The girl's face lit up with a sadistic grin and her mouth opened wider than a train tunnel to release a piercing cry that echoed up and down the nearby paddocks. Bystanders turned to stare at the disturbance, including a site security guard.

CHAPTER FOURTEEN

Fear is a beastly sensation. It claws at you, a living being tearing at your insides and filling your mind with fog until even the most straightforward and natural responses sound strained. This could be the moment Jack would be discovered. A myriad of questions raced through my mind but finding the answers was like trying to grab at smoke. Would I be in trouble with the authorities for not revealing the little people sooner? Did a zoo security guard have the authority to arrest me?

"The man won't show us his toy," said the girl, stamping her foot.

"You're not responsible for this group?" the security guard asked me.

"No, no, definitely not. I'm just here to see the, uh, the," I searched desperately for an exhibit sign, "the chickens!" The pack of jackals that had me cornered burst out laughing.

"The chickens? Right. Well why don't you show them your toy and then you can go and see the chickens."

"It's a limited edition. I, I don't want anyone to break it," I struggled to think of any excuse to get me out of this situation. Beneath my head I was sure I could hear Jack giggle to himself. He found the situation, and my reaction to it, hysterical.

"I'll be super careful, mister," the spokesperson of the mob said, nodding.

The whole world was staring at me. The children, the security guard, passing guests, even the chickens looked in my direction with their beady eyes. I was a deer caught in the headlights, and I meekly handed Jack to the girl. "Be still, Jack, be still, Jack," I thought over and over again, willing him to hear me telepathically.

"It's so lifelike," the girl cried with glee and poked Jack in the stomach which caused him to giggle. "What else does it do?" she asked, holding the grinning Jack by one arm.

"That's it. He's a prototype toy. I'm a toy maker. He's a prototype. That's right, and he laughs if you poke him." I'd like to see you come up with a better line in a stressful situation; it was all I could think of. I couldn't quite smother the grin that crept onto my lips as the children took turns to jab Jack all over with their sticky fingers. "I'd better take him back now, the battery's getting low," I said when I sensed Jack's patience was starting to run thin.

"Awww," they chorused. I slipped Jack back into my pocket but I couldn't shake this flock of little lambs that had decided I was the most interesting thing at the zoo. For the next hour they followed us around, occasionally insisting I let them hold Jack again, carefully of course, to introduce him to a meerkat or a pygmy goat. I don't think Jack minded playing a toy, if anything he seemed to enjoy being passed from person to person and getting close and personal with the animals I was denied access to as an adult. All day long I was bombarded with ideas for new toys and potential improvements for the 'Jack Doll' as we'd taken to calling my friend. More than once I cursed myself for coming up with that fictitious occupation. Still, it wasn't the worst day, especially not for Jack. One of the boys in the group, a whiz-kid with technology despite his young age, managed to take a picture on my phone in which I seemed to stand beside Jack, both of us the same height. He muttered about perspective as he ordered me some distance away and carefully lined up the shot with the Jack Doll propped against a wall much closer to the camera. It's one of my favourite photos of the two of us. Our other pictures feature Jack and my foot, or one of us blurred to indistinction as we tried to replicate this perspective idea on our own. I'm a good enough photographer behind the lens, but lining up a timed photograph and rushing to the correct distance was a talent I never mastered.

"What do you think you're doing?" an angry woman shouted at my shadows, cuffing the eldest boy around the ear. "I told you to look around not to go bothering the first stranger you found." The smiles fell from the faces of the children like autumnal leaves as they were marched in a line to a rundown car, waving mournfully over their shoulders and calling their goodbyes to Jack.

"They looked so sad," Jack said to me later.

"I think they were one big family. I bet they don't have many nice toys like the Jack Doll at home."

Jack gazed thoughtfully into the distance. "They have each other. I'd have loved some brothers and sisters growing up."

I thought back to the moments when my sister and I would drive each other up the wall. "Family is important, sure, but you need money and stuff as well, otherwise how are you ever going to get out of living in the same place and in the same life? It's nice to have nice things; I expect they were just sad at missing out on the Jack Doll going home."

"I don't think that's true," Jack said slowly, mulling over each word as he spoke, "when one of the girls tried to put me on that goat she said something to her sister about Daddy going missing again and Mummy crying all the time because of it. I didn't understand what she meant or where he might have gone, but they seemed to miss him. I was happy to be able to make them smile. It just makes me wish I'd had chance to tell Dad how much I appreciated his being there."

Jack was always able to make me think, and to make me squirm about some of my more selfish thoughts.

Nothing of note happened for some time after our adventure at the zoo. I'm sure there were plenty of near escapes as we encountered other people and there were certainly many beautiful scenes to behold as we took to the south coast of the United Kingdom. We watched stunning sunsets where every blade of grass was painted with gold before the day faded softly to night, and we observed cloudy grey days where the whole world was subdued behind a cloak of the finest drizzle. I would never have taken the time to notice the hundreds of different shades of green to be found in a forest or the song of a stream tinkling over a rocky path were it not for Jack drawing my attention to those things. So many times I had plans for us to visit such and such a place on our map, and we'd end up sitting nowhere near my intended destination listening for bird calls or watching the progress of a long line of ants carrying crumbs from some treasure trove of dropped food to their hill.

In those quiet days I taught Jack how to take a photograph. He had to push down on the shutter release with all his might to take a picture, and to throw all his weight against the body of the camera to move it a couple of millimetres to line up his shot. I'd have helped of course, but he was always determined to do things for himself. He didn't say a word when I presented him with a couple of his photos, printed from a supermarket kiosk, but his bearing was suffused with pride at his accomplishment. Whenever we stayed in a hotel he insisted I drag the photos out to decorate his space.

In exchange he taught me how to weave, a skill he'd

learnt from his mother Julie. The process began by stripping a leaf to its fibres, which he could then weave into a multitude of different items, from rugs to items of clothing to bedsheets. I found some bigger leaves to work with and scaled up the model. If Jack was proud of his photographs, I was equally satisfied with my first creation. I deemed the square of weaved material to be the perfect size for a placemat. Over the course of our travels I made several more, with the intention of giving them to my parents as a present to decorate their dining table. Not your typical souvenir, but this wasn't a typical trip.

We continued our travels in parallel with our learning, and from time to time caught up on the exploits of the Aussies on those nights Jack convinced me to opt for a night in a hotel. We spent a good while exploring the Jurassic Coast on our way to the more sandy beaches of Bournemouth and Christchurch. From there we detoured away from the coast into the New Forest National Park, where Jack befriended a pony who nearly knocked him from my hand with a snort. We skirted the city of Southampton and other populous areas and continued the journey toward Folkestone and Dover. I explained that you could catch a boat from those places to take you into the rest of Europe and found a world map to show Jack. I think the size of the world at large stumped him. He was around a third of the way through his life and we'd not left the south coast of England. He shrugged off any discontent soon enough when I suggested it might be time to think about how best to tackle the city streets of London.

CHAPTER FIFTEEN

Even today the thought of London makes me nervous. I wonder if it's the country boy in me, though I've not always lived down that remote lane of my parents, far removed from any form of civilisation. For three years I studied Classical Literature and Civilisation at the University of Birmingham. I might have been cut off from the city at large, living on a campus with a multitude of other students as I did, but even so it was a vastly different world to that of my Cornish upbringing. Living in a city was a shock to senses attuned to the quietness of the great outdoors, one that took time and the help of new friends to overcome. I'd been to London itself a couple of times before this planned excursion with Jack. I took a trip as a child to see the museums and later in life I visited with a group of university friends to explore the capital city (and its bars). It's clear I'm not an expert on city life, but I had experienced enough to know that the sheer density of the population would be a problem in hiding Jack, while still allowing him to see the sights which was the whole purpose of the stopover. If children at a zoo and an elderly landlady had managed to spot Jack despite my best efforts, then what were the chances that the millions of residents of this enormous city could miss him?

It was a thought that kept me tossing and turning all night long.

As it turns out, I needn't have worried about Jack's discovery at all. In the city of London I'm not sure that people even see each other.

We left the car on the outskirts and caught a train, and then the underground line into the centre of the city. Jack had his little head poking out of my pocket the whole time and not one person looked twice at us. We exchanged a glance at one point and I shrugged; looking at the floor or a tablet or phone was the done thing apparently. I wondered if anyone would have looked even if I stood on my seat and cried out to the world to see the marvel of a miniature man in my hand. It was great news for us, but I was strangely disappointed. All my dire warnings to Jack about being spotted, all those hours counting a never ending stream of sheep jumping listlessly over a fence, and I hadn't needed to worry in the slightest.

Not about being seen.

A greater danger came from the constant press of people all around us, especially riding on the tube. The pocket padding I'd made for Jack was designed to keep the fabric of my shirt away from him, not the weight of the rather large and sweaty man leaning much too close in the press of people trying to get where they were going. I was still shy of drawing excess attention to Jack so I didn't want to reach into my pocket and pull him out. All I could think to do was lean gradually backwards until I was all but resting my head on the shoulder of the businesswoman behind me in some kind of crazy curved-spine yoga position.

It wasn't in London where we encountered our greatest danger, even if the pigeons of Trafalgar Square looked hungrily at my pocket. Nor was it in the land of Wales where I faced my fear of heights to climb the mountain of Snowdon, all to give Jack a taste of what it feels like to be on top of the world rather than the bottom. Our biggest peril wasn't at a theme park, where I was careless to the point of recklessness on our first rollercoaster ride, completely forgetting that while I was safely strapped in Jack certainly wasn't. It took a quick catch on my part and a tight grip for the rest of the ride to get him back to safety. We were more careful after that and enjoyed a day of hilarity as the wind whipped through our hair in the gravity-defying rides we conquered. Even in Yorkshire, in that moment when we were both awed by the Dales to the point we didn't see the BMW bearing down on us, even that wasn't the biggest risk to life and liberty. The speeding car only clipped the corner of the Volkswagen's bumper, but it was enough to send us into a spin and to knock Jack brutally into the side of his shoebox on the front seat. I was proud that my design had held and kept Jack from being more seriously injured, but he hobbled around more pronouncedly in the next few days due to the bruising that decorated his ribcage. I tried to hurry through the conversation with the profusely apologetic driver to rush back to the front seat to check on Jack, but she insisted on a thorough inspection of the damage. I eventually convinced her I wasn't too worried about my car, held together with rust as it was, and that I was as happy as she was to keep the insurance companies out of it as the damage wasn't severe. Despite my protestation, she wrote me a cheque on the spot to cover any costs and to apologise for the incident (and I expect to thank me for my silence at the great speed her car had reached), and I worried less about the steadily emptying envelope of cash for a time. All of those dangers and close calls were enough, but our most difficult trial was still to come.

Through it all, the wonders and the dangers and the everyday life with a little person, I marvelled to see the changes in Jack. He maintained his youthful spirit throughout our great journey, and despite the increasing gap in our relative ages we remained close. As the days passed he grew wiser and more cautious, less given to unnecessary risk. Once I caught him watching a family in the distance in wistful silence and I wondered if he regretted this journey of ours which had taken him away from the possibility of a family to call his own. He had made the decision to leave home in his youth; was it a decision this middle-aged man he had grown into still agreed with? He smiled the expression away as soon as he caught me looking and left me wondering if my imagination was playing tricks on me.

Jack changed physically as well. His shaggy mane of brown hair became streaked with grey. He wore his hair shorter now than the shoulder length cut of his younger days. It wasn't easy to see fine details on a little person, but if I looked closely I could see wrinkles spreading across his face. Laugh lines perhaps. We laughed a lot.

Spring had long since given way to a baking hot summer characterised by hosepipe bans and gardens of cracked earth and dying yellow grass. Our travels had taken us beneath mighty oak trees offering a roof of greenery above our heads. They had taken us to the peaks of mountains, letting us linger in sunlight unable to penetrate the dense cloud canopy to the ground far below. We had seen fearsome waves crash against stony shores and endless rolling fields of green stretching beyond the eye of imagination. We had seen star dotted skies on clear and chill evenings, and a sunrise so beautiful that even the memory of it brings a lump to my throat.

"Does it ever make you feel small Jack? Seeing the vastness of all of this?" I asked him once.

"Small?" he replied, his tiny face looking to mine with a knowing smile that was all too familiar by now, "I wouldn't say so."

We were still for some time, surveying the beautiful scene before us. I forget exactly where in the country we were, but I remember the night was closing quickly on our campsite, and yet the sun still sent beams of dappled golden light through the branches of the surrounding trees, engulfing us in a moving tapestry of shapes and shadows. The sky gradually turned a deep shade of scarlet which I had never seen before, nor have I seen again, and the stars blinked their way into life.

"Listen, Tom," Jack instructed me. I wondered what my friend had heard and forgot to breathe as I strained my ears for any whisper amidst the trees. "It's quiet," Jack continued eventually, "everything is enjoying the sun's show."

He was right. Even the incessant calls of the birds, so familiar after months of sleeping mostly outdoors, were stilled. We could have been completely alone in the world. For some reason the spectacle caused my heart to sink.

"It makes me feel a bit insignificant," I said, seeing the mist of the Milky Way painted in the sky above us with no natural light to bar its appearance.

The silence was torn by Jack's laugh, a laugh that had grown gruff with use and age; the sound of it reminded me of John Meadows.

"Insignificant? The way I see it, someone painted the lights in the sky tonight and that means they also made us to enjoy the sight of it. We aren't insignificant. We're masterpieces as beautiful as the stars in the heavens."

The little people had a simple faith, one that seemed less complicated and rule-driven than the vaguely remembered Sunday school lessons of my childhood. I rarely heard them mention what they believed in; it wasn't a part of their companionship ceremonies or the commemoration services they held on lifespan end days. And yet it was as if each little person was born with knowledge of a creator, and an assurance of another life after their first short one. From time to time I tried to find out more about the deity they worshipped so simply, but whenever I brought it up Jack would shrug and say he didn't know the details, he just believed.

Say what you will about religion or philosophy; I defy

anyone to have contradicted the contented smile adorning Jack's face that day. We didn't talk about the deep issues of life and the universe very often, even though Jack became more pensive and thoughtful as he reached his middle days, but at that moment he was completely at one with his maker. I hadn't the faith to match his, but as I continued to study the stars above me and mulled over Jack's words, my discontent turned to a feeling of peace the like of which I'd never known.

CHAPTER SIXTEEN

Our journey eventually brought us to Scotland.

We'd seen many beautiful vistas in the last few months, but there was something about the Highlands of Scotland that took my breath away. Jack must have felt the same because he frequently requested we stop and then, pulled in at the side of the road, he would sit in silence as if soaking each view into his sponge of a memory. It was pleasantly cool so far north, a welcome relief in an August which had broken who knows how many hot weather records.

I decided we had enough money to splurge for a few days and hired us a little boat to explore the great lochs with. It was an old motor yacht with an engine that sputtered and struggled its way over the vast stretches of water of Lochs Lochy and Ness. Our home for the majority of the last month was a tent, so the Marigold seemed luxurious, even if the fabrics were faded and the cushions and mattresses lumpy. There was a tiny kitchen with an oven which I used to cook a pre-packaged pizza on our first night aboard. The small shower room tucked below deck was big enough for me if I tucked in my elbows, and the reluctant stream of water it spewed was gentle enough that even Jack could use it to get clean.

We awoke feeling refreshed, rocked to sleep by the gentle motion of the water beneath us. It's amazing what a full stomach, a long hot shower and a good night's sleep can do. I took over the berth in the back of the boat, the stern I should say. Nautical terminology isn't my strongest suit. Jack chose a section of dining table for his bed and made himself comfortable amidst his mound of blankets.

It took me a good couple of days to master the art of managing a boat by myself. Jack was too small to man the helm or lift the ropes that would secure us to our mooring, so his help was limited to shouting sometimes unhelpful advice in a voice I couldn't always hear. I had to learn to drift the boat toward a mooring spot with the flow of the tide, sprint from the wheel, leap off the side, and quickly fasten a rope in a rough cleat hitch. I can recall several moments where I almost misjudged my jump and was mere centimetres from being submerged in the dark and cold waters of those vast lakes. Fortune favoured me as the weather remained clement, and the people manning the canal locks were friendly and helpful in my obvious ineptitude.

Our trip to this point had been an incredible experience, despite the worries that plagued my mind from time to time, but there was something about our boat journey that made it particularly memorable. When I look back on our months of travelling it is to the Marigold and those endless waters cutting through the wild and untamed hills that my mind wanders first. Perhaps it was having somewhere to call home for a few days and nights, or because it would be on this cruise that our party of two would expand.

"That can't be Tom Mitchell?" a voice called behind me. I gave Jack a push down into my pocket with my finger and turned my back on the ruins of Urquhart Castle to see who spoke.

"Jerry? Jerry Collins?" Before I could do much more than register the appearance of my old university friend and flatmate I was pulled into a rib (and Jack) crushing bear hug. I covered the squeak that came from my pocket with a cough.

"What a small world, eh? What are you doing in these parts?" Jerry asked.

"I'm on holiday. I've been travelling around the UK for a bit, couldn't get a job, you know how it is."

"I hear that. I thought most people went backpacking to Thailand in a gap year rather than a tour of the great British Isles though," Jerry said, laughing.

"I expect most people have bigger budgets."

"True that. I haven't seen you since, well, since graduation I suppose. Are you still down in Cornwall with the parents?"

"Unfortunately, yes. Couldn't get wind of a good job, let alone get hired for anything. I didn't have the money to stay around so there wasn't a lot of choice. I was helping in their bakery before leaving for this trip, but that was about it," I explained. "What about you? Still in Birmingham?"

"That's right. I couldn't find a job either mind, had to move in with Chrissie."

"With Chrissie? I thought you were going to break up with her?"

"Well, I was," Jerry muttered, "but it was a place to stay. I don't think I could have done what you did, gone back home I mean. My parents are okay but I'm done living with them. I'm sure Dad's seeing his receptionist on the side, he seems miserable here on holiday with me and Mum."

"Are you working now then?"

"Only bits and pieces here and there. Chrissie said I had to pay rent, the cheek of it, so I picked up a few hours at McDonalds. The dream of every anthropology student," Jerry said, rolling his eyes. "I ought to get back to the folks anyway. I expect I could sneak away for a pint tonight if you fancy it. It'd be good to catch up properly."

"Sounds great. We're moored up here for the night I expect. I think there's a village close by; meet you there?"

"Wait a minute. We? Not hiding a lady friend on that boat of yours are you?" Jerry dug his elbow into my ribs with a wicked grin.

"Uh," I racked my brains for a way to cover my mistake, "I meant me and the boat, Marigold, she's a fine old girl."

Jerry shook his head with a grin, "You always were an odd one Tom. Seven okay?"

"Perfect. See you then."

I was thrilled to reunite with an old acquaintance but Jack was wary. He cautioned me to keep my guard up and conceal our secret, especially after a drink or two.

"Don't worry Jack, he's a great friend, he wouldn't do anything even if I did let something slip. I'm almost tempted to introduce him to you; he'd love to meet you."

Jack glared at me.

"Fine. Fine! I'll keep my lips sealed."

"How do you know him anyway?" Jack asked.

"We met on our first day at university. We'd both of us moved to Birmingham and didn't know anyone, and we ended up living in the same flat in our hall of residence, the place most first-year students live. Everyone thought it was brilliant, Tom and Jerry becoming such fast friends. That might have been what brought us together from the start." I noticed Jack was staring at me blankly.

"Tom and Jerry? You know, Tom and Jerry?"

Jack shook his head.

"They were a cartoon cat and mouse on television, years ago now. Jerry, the mouse, would always end up outsmarting Tom, the cat, when he tried to catch him. We ended up staying together all through our degrees, with another couple of guys from our courses, Ryan and Pete. I studied classics and he was an anthropology student so we didn't see each other in lectures, but outside of study time we spent a lot of time together, us and the gang.

"I owe him a lot actually; he helped me adjust to city life when I was a bit lost. He took me under his wing I guess, which was a massive help trying to find my feet a new place. He's a good friend.

"I wondered what he'd been up to, him and my other friends; it's so long since I heard from any of them. It'll be great to catch up, it's so easy to lose touch when you all go off in different directions and start doing different things."

"Seems like you'd stay in contact better if they were really great friends," Jack muttered under his breath. I ignored him.

"Best you stay here on the boat tonight and then we don't have to worry about anyone seeing you when I meet with Jerry."

"If that's what you think is best," Jack said, "but please be careful." I felt satisfactorily smug at the thought of Jack being jealous of my other friends. In reality I'm sure he was only concerned about his security, and perhaps annoyed at my willingness to ditch him for a night because it was too difficult to take him with me. His months of aging had left him wise enough to not be swayed by something as petty as jealousy, or at least not as much as when he was young. I'm not sure the green-eyed monster is something we can ever truly vanquish. If truth be told I was looking forward to a night off from 'babysitting' the adult Jack Meadows, now the equivalent of fifty-something years old. I thought an evening free from worrying if anyone might see something that could put him in danger sounded wonderful. Meeting Jerry was the perfect excuse.

Darkness settled over the land and still Jerry and I laughed and reminisced and drank our way through the varied selection of whiskies that decorated the walls. With every draught I felt more inclined to divulge the secret I had carried for the last seven months. It's a mystery how a confidence can suddenly seem a great weight when you realise how long you've borne it. I knew Jerry would be fascinated at the thought of the little people and their society, and that he would appreciate my efforts in trying to instruct the young Jack Meadows all those months ago, even if I didn't get anywhere with it. I bit my tongue and kept the conversation centred on other things.

"I've an idea," Jerry said, "I'm sure I could persuade the parents to travel together tomorrow and meet up with them further down the loch. It'd be more fun on your boat than seeing Mum and Dad throw daggers at each other all day long."

"Sure! Sounds great," I said with a hiccup. "You go tell your parents and tomorrow morning we'll track Nessie down!"

As we stumbled towards the mooring by the castle where our boats were tethered to shore, I suddenly remembered Jack and wondered what he would think of the extra company. Company that didn't know he existed.

Despite the protest of my inebriated mind, Jack and I spent much of the night discussing, debating and downright arguing the merits of telling Jerry everything. I insisted on my honour that he could be trusted and would be a wonderful travelling companion for the day. Jack threw back every argument I'd badgered him with regarding keeping him out of sight of anyone, be they friend or foe. We both considered the landlady in Cornwall who had seen Jack with no negative repercussions, but he was still unconvinced. I had done too good a job informing him of the flaws in humanity, including our desire to do anything to make a quick buck, often at the expense of another living creature.

"You were way more fun when you were younger," I threw the comment in his face at one point in our argument. "You wouldn't have hesitated having Jerry along then. You'd have been the one to welcome him."

"People change, Tom, I'm not that young man anymore and there's more to think about here than me. I've got to think of my people. How do I know Jerry wouldn't tell others about them?"

Gone was the child more concerned with his own fate than the lives of his kin, even though he hadn't seen them for half of his one lifespan.

After hours of traversing back and forth over the same conversational ground and crafting the pros and cons lists that lay scattered over the table, we finally agreed to introduce Jack to Jerry. Jack's final stipulation was that we were not to tell him of the cove where the other little people lived.

I was exhausted but I felt happy in my victory. It was decided. The next day we would introduce Jack to another big person for the very first time.

CHAPTER SEVENTEEN

Jerry leapt nimbly on board the Marigold, holding the coil of rope that had bound her to her mooring. Jack and I thought we should cast off and then make the announcement, providing us with plenty of time to discuss the situation before we reached land, and any other humans Jerry could divulge the secret to. I concealed Jack in my berth for the time being. Before long we were trundling along as fast as the Marigold could manage, battling against waves stirred by a strong chill breeze that whipped through the valley and caused water to slap against the boat's sides and spray to douse anyone who dared step outside the cabin.

"Jerry," I began, unsure how best to broach the subject of Jack, "there's something I have to tell you. But I need you to promise you'll never breathe a word of it to another soul."

Jerry laughed; he must have assumed he was the butt of a strange joke until he saw the serious expression on my face. "What's going on? You're not dying are you? That's not the reason for this travelling?" Jerry's face filled with concern.

"No, no, nothing like that!" I reassured him. "You'll

think I'm crazy when I tell you this, but hear me out okay."

Jerry looked bemused but nodded an affirmative and settled himself on the bench opposite the helm station to listen. He was true to his word and didn't interrupt as I recounted my initial meeting with the little people, my shock at discovering the length of their lifespan, Jack's incident with the seagull, his desperate desire to see more of the country and our subsequent travels. Jerry was working hard to keep a straight face as I talked, but he burst into laughter the moment I reached the present day in my tale.

"You expect me to believe that? Somewhere in Cornwall there's a race of intelligent miniature humans? I think last night's drinks went to your head mate."

"Take the wheel a moment," I said and Jerry slumped into the driving seat. His chuckles followed me through the boat as I walked on feet made unsteady by the rolling waves.

It wasn't until I returned, bearing Jack on my outstretched palm, that Jerry's laughter was strangled silent. The song of the wind howling through cracks in the boat's exterior, and the constant buffeting of water soaking the windscreen were the only sounds for moments that stretched into infinity.

"This is Jack," I said, daring to break the uncanny silence.

"Hi," Jack said, lifting a hand in greeting to Jerry.

"How much did I drink last night?" Jerry muttered and shook his head as if to clear his vision, only to find the image of the little person refused to vanish.

"You're Jack?" he asked finally.

"That's me," Jack replied.

"You're the little person that lives for one year?"

"I'm a person who lives for one lifespan, yes," Jack answered.

"And, and you're real?"

"As real as you."

"Right, right," Jerry struggled for words and I looked on in amusement. I wondered if I'd looked so gormless when I first tried to come to terms with the existence of the little people. I noticed him pinch his own arm in a test to check the status of this waking dream. "Everything Tom told me is true?" Jerry asked, staring into the tiny face of my friend. "There are a whole lot of you living down in Cornwall?"

"That's right," Jack said. I noticed he divulged no additional information about his old friends and relatives.

"I think I need a drink," Jerry said.

We let the silence linger, Jack and I, to give Jerry a chance to adjust to this new information. We were asking him to accept in a couple of hours what had taken me weeks to settle in my mind. Jack sat down to read an eBook on my phone; he found this easier than a real book as he could turn a page by hitting the right-hand side of the screen with his outstretched palm. He usually had a sore hand and a crick in his neck after a long reading session, having to look from side to side and top to bottom to read a single page, but at least he didn't have to stand up and drag a heavy paper leaf to uncover more of his story.

Jerry continued to pilot the Marigold so I took a seat on the bench opposite and gazed out of the window at the choppy black water surrounding us. We could have been sailing on ink, for all I could see beneath the surface.

"Tom, if this is real and not a wind up you've got to let me in on it," Jerry said in a whisper he clearly hoped wouldn't carry to the engrossed Jack.

"Let you in on what?"

"What you've got going on here with these little people. Don't you get it? I've wanted to get my PhD since leaving uni but no one'll fund anthropology studies unless there's a possibility of unearthing something unusual. I'd be inundated with offers if I pitched this. Imagine it, the first study of an entirely new race of mini humans! I'd need to borrow Jack for a few weeks, to properly study him. Then I could go down to where the rest of them live and see how they exist in a community. I'd have to bring some research students along too of course, and it'd be interesting to take some of those little people out of their familiar environment to see how they coped with life in the wider world. Seems like your buddy Jack has coped okay with that so I'm sure it wouldn't be too harmful.

"I bet I could write a book at the same time. This could be my ticket out of the rubbish life I'm living, Tom. It could be the answer for both of us. We can split any royalties from the book so you'd be set for life too."

I could feel a knot forming in the pit of my stomach, like an icy hand clenching at my innards that made me want to squirm. I wish I could say it was only concern for Jack that caused me to ball my hands into fists tight enough to feel the bite of my short nails, but I know a part of me returned to those first days of knowing the little people and the lure of the fame and fortune that revealing their presence could bring. From time to time those thoughts still entered my mind, months later, but then I would remember my friendship with Jack and the experiences we'd shared over the course of this year. Not to mention the kindness of Julie who allowed me to share in the most precious moment of her life, her end, and even John who had grudgingly granted me my first opening into the lives of the little people. No. No matter what temptation plagued the deepest corners of my mind, I couldn't risk destroying that content community. I convinced myself that Jerry's rambling talk was him reacting to the shock of this revelation. I knew him to be a good man. A few sidelong glances at Jack told me he'd heard every word of the speech. He gazed at the phone as intently as ever, but he'd not turned a page for some time.

"Jerry," I started.

"Don't give me any excuses Tom, you're onto a good

thing here. It wouldn't hurt you to share it. Imagine how different our lives could be."

I chanced another glance toward Jack who, at that very moment, turned to look at me. I could hardly make out his expression, so far away was he, but in that glance I knew I could never jeopardise everything he was so insistent we protect. His one condition to the trust he placed in my judgement of Jerry was that we protect the other little people. In that shared glance I knew I could never betray that confidence.

"Jerry, I think you've got the wrong end of the stick here. I'm not out to make anything off the little people, they're perfectly happy where they are. Jack wanted to explore and I'm helping him do that, that's all there is to it."

"You can't tell me you've never thought about this mate, you're not an idiot. This is our chance," Jerry said in the persuasive tone I recognised from those moments he'd hoodwinked me into all sorts of nefarious activities as students. A significant part of me wanted to capitulate from habit, but I knew I needed to stand up to him this time.

"No Jerry. I'm sorry, but I've made a promise to protect these little people and I can't keep that if I let people run all over their home."

Jerry lapsed into thoughtful silence again.

"Fine. Fine," he said at last, "but can I at least travel with you? It's not as though I have anything important to get back to. Chrissie'd be glad to see the back of me for longer I'm sure, and my work before this trip was only temporary."

"That sounds like a great idea," I said, relieved. In hindsight I should probably have checked what Jack thought about all of this, but I knew if Jerry got to know Jack he'd see I was right and that it'd be better to leave the little people well enough alone. It's not like I was going to tell him where the cove was, it would be a couple of weeks with some extra company. That was all.

Jerry okayed the decision with his parents on the phone and we moored next to their boat to gather his belongings. Then we were off, threading our way up the winding canal to the city of Inverness.

If I had any lingering concerns about Jerry joining our company they were quickly quashed. He was as quick to make a joke as ever and within a couple of days Jack was completely at ease around him. It was a help having another pair of hands to conceal Jack, and we managed to pick up some pocketed polo shirts for Jerry in the city so that he could carry Jack from time to time. I'm not a short man, but Jerry was even taller and Jack enjoyed the different perspective on our walks away from the boat. An extra person made it possible to explore more freely as there was always someone to be on the lookout for any potential threat. Eating out was an enjoyable experience again, with Jack sat on a chair tucked under the table waiting for the morsels we sneaked him.

The deep-seated doubts Jerry had inspired in me after first meeting Jack were utterly vanquished on the day we turned the Marigold to its owner. The marina was tiny; it consisted of a scant handful of boats moored up alongside four wooden walkways. The vessels belonged to several different companies and were let out to tourists. It was mid-August at this point, the height of the tourist season, and today was a changeover day. The narrow walkways were flooded with a constant flow of running children excitedly clambering over their boats for the week. All our belongings were packed and Jack's things were hidden in my bag in case of seeing an odd person or two, but we hadn't anticipated the clamour we encountered. This carnage was nothing like the day Jack and I had picked up the boat.

Jack was riding in my pocket as we tied off our ropes for the last time and climbed out of our trusty home from home, weighed down with possessions. I had developed sea legs by the end of our week on the Marigold, and now walking on land was a problem. The whole world was swaying gently up and down, up and down, confusing my head and my stomach. That altogether unpleasant sensation, combined with the carrying of a heavy suitcase and the dodging of a hysterical stampede of children who bore no regard for other people using the walkways, left me feeling rather unsteady. I stumbled and before I could right myself I had overbalanced and toppled into the water, narrowly avoiding clobbering my head on a sailing boat moored close by. I came up for air spluttering and humiliated at the laughter of nearby children, my pride the only injury to my person. I swam to the walkway and clung on tight and only then realised my breast pocket was empty.

Jack was nowhere to be seen.

CHAPTER EIGHTEEN

"Jerry," I cried, "he's gone, Jack's gone." My mind was as sodden as the clothes that threatened to drag me to the bottom of the canal, panic was overwhelming my senses and I struggled to think.

In an instant Jerry was on his hands and knees on the walkway, peering into the water in every direction for a hint as to the whereabouts of the little person.

"There!" he said, pointing to a spot a few metres out. Jack must have fallen out of my pocket as I'd toppled inelegantly into the water, and been pushed further from the walkway by the ripples my flailing doggy paddle had caused. Any motion I made caused enormous waves to crash over the top of Jack's head. Even turning in the water to find his position caused a disturbance that threatened to overwhelm the tiny man. Jack was a reasonable swimmer, he learnt in the rock pool beside his home on that faraway cove in Cornwall, but aside from the drama during his coming of age ceremony he'd never had to battle waves like those my body was creating. That and the lack of function in his right leg left him floundering in the inky water.

"Stay still, dammit," Jerry hissed and before I could

respond I saw him dive from the walkway in a perfect arc, still fully clothed. Jerry had been a swimmer at university and I was impressed at his technique; the dive caused minimal splashing and hardly any agitation to the water surrounding Jack. He surfaced almost exactly where Jack was lashing the water with tiny arms in an attempt to keep his head up. Jerry snatched Jack in his hand before anything could swamp him again, and swam back with a one-armed front crawl to where I now stood, dripping all over the floor.

Jerry passed the shivering Jack into my hands. His skin looked slightly blue as he sat on one outstretched palm. In one miniature hand he held tightly to his cockle shell necklace; it must have floated off his head in the water but he'd been quick to snatch it and cling to it like a lifebelt. As the crowd pressed in behind me I clasped my hands shut over Jack's frail form to stop the curious onlookers seeing anything untoward.

"Honestly," Jerry said in a carrying voice, "all our money's in that wallet you idiot, don't lose it again." He gestured dramatically at my cupped hands and stalked off towards the car park. A kindly member of staff pointed us in the direction of a shower block and soon enough we were washed and comfortable once again in dry clothes from our bags. If it weren't for Jerry's quick action I'm sure Jack would have been seen. Or worse, he could very easily have drowned. That was an outcome I tried not to dwell on.

The three of us took a moment to breathe once we reached the safety of the car. Jerry started to laugh in his infectious way.

"It's hardly something to laugh at," I grumbled but couldn't keep the smile from spreading over my lips. In moments the three of us were giggling hysterically, easing our frayed nerves with the release only laughter can bring.

"Where to now?" Jerry asked, once he'd recovered enough to speak.

"North," Jack and I chorused, and the journey continued.

Jack resumed his old trick of asking us to pull over to explore every nook and cranny along the coast, up and down tiny lanes more suited to travel on horseback than by car. Because of his detours it took us several more days to reach the final destination on our planned route, John o'Groats.

The internet reliably informs me that a journey from Lands End in Cornwall to the far north of Scotland could be done in around thirteen and a half hours of non-stop driving.

It had taken us more than five months.

When we first started travelling I was focussed entirely on the destinations we must reach, be it this final haven or any place on our way we wished to visit. It took me five months on the road to realise that the journey itself was the important thing. If I had been responsible for our trip we would have reached this point in under a month, but what would we have missed along the way? It's a lesson I hope to continue to live until my last breath. I never want to stop taking the time to hesitate and see what's around me, instead of hurrying on to the next objective without a moment's pause. There is more to witness in this world than we can imagine, but only if we take the time to look.

Jerry hadn't been with us on the bulk of our journey, but he had captured the spirit of our adventure. The three of us sat together on the edge of the world, watching the perfect blue of an endless ocean.

"Quite something, isn't it," Jerry said and the two of us nodded in reply. We were lost in our thoughts. Despite our long planning sessions, back when Jack was a boy, we never discussed what would happen now. This was the final place on the grubby, well-travelled map of ours. What was next for us? Return home? Continue to explore back down the country? I wasn't sure if Jack wanted to carry on and wasn't entirely sure how to ask. It would be nice to see my parents and enjoy some home cooking, but I wasn't really ready for the adventure to stop yet. I'd enjoyed myself all the way, but with Jerry in our party for the last couple of weeks the days had been filled with fun. I was well aware reality would kick in at some point, the money would run out and we would have to return to responsibility, but did that have to be now?

The sun descended into the horizon's threatening clouds and lined them with silver before we moved from the cliff and found a couple of rooms at a nearby guest house. We gathered for fish and chips wrapped in newspaper to discuss our options.

"Well Jack, we made it," I said eventually, "what next?"

Jack hesitated before speaking as if he weighed each word carefully, "I'm not sure what's left for me back home, but I've thought more and more that I need to get back there. I don't know how, or even why, but I feel like I need to stand ready to protect the people, does that sound crazy? I've had my adventure and lived my life to its fullest, now I want to help them live the lives they want to lead. I don't know if that makes any sense."

"It makes perfect sense," I said, selfishly disappointed at the looming end to our adventure.

"What about you Jerry?" Jack asked. "What will you do now?"

"Oh I suppose I'll go back to Birmingham, see Chrissie. Maybe you lads can drop me off on the way down. You'd be able to see where Tommy boy and I did our studies."

"That sounds great."

Jack and Jerry continued to talk but I drifted out of the conversation. Something about the words Jack had said was ringing in my ears.

"Protect them," I mumbled.

"Excuse me?" Jerry replied.

"We can protect them, I bet we can. Jerry, aren't there tribes in the Amazon rainforest that are completely uncontacted? They're protected aren't they? People aren't allowed to go near to where they live."

"What are you suggesting?" Jerry asked. "Try and get a law put in place to stop people going where the little people live?"

"Exactly! I'm sure there must be a conservation act that could be put in place, something to stop people going there at all."

"Is that possible?" Jack asked, the wildfire of my enthusiasm igniting a light behind his own eyes.

"It'd be a long shot, but it might be possible," Jerry said thoughtfully, "people are definitely more conscious of protecting things like that these days, safeguarding civilisations and cultures and whatnot. It'd be a hard battle, but I remember something in my course about how some untouched tribes were protected. If we could find a library I bet I could dig out some information that'd be a help. It would give us a starting point if nothing else, and an idea as to whether anything like this has been done before so close to home."

"We could get to Glasgow by lunch time tomorrow, if we didn't stop anywhere," I said, casting a pointed glance in Jack's direction. He grinned sheepishly and nodded. His little grey eyes were alight with an infectious passion, and I think I'd have signed on the dotted line there and then to commit my life to the cause of protecting the little people. Jerry seemed excited too, he talked us through what he could remember of various laws protecting certain subsections of humanity until late in the evening.

Jack was unusually quiet as we followed the A9 towards the city of Glasgow. He was true to his word and didn't suggest a single diversion. That, if nothing else, made me realise how very serious he was. Jerry had made an early call to the University of Glasgow to see if there was any chance of borrowing their library. He struggled to reach someone with the summer holiday in full force, but when he finally got in contact with a person rather than a voicemail message they seemed happy enough to let us in. I'm not sure what story he told them, something about preparing a thesis for his PhD and a sudden flash of inspiration requiring additional research right away. He must have told the lie with conviction, because there was a young woman waiting to let us into a building packed from floor to ceiling with books when we arrived.

Jack and I spent the afternoon tracing patterns on the dusty bookshelves while Jerry dug deeply into textbooks we struggled to understand. By the end of the day he'd written reams of notes and declared we would definitely have a case. "We'll need to hire lawyers and garner public support. That'll mean releasing some details about the little people." Jerry explained. "Are you happy to do that, Jack? It's the only way to keep them safe in the long run."

"I think so. They'd be secure in the meantime, right? Before these laws were put together?"

"Of course, we can keep the location of the cove a secret between us and the officials who would need to know it. It'd help me to know how big an area we're talking about now though. This is a small country with a large population so it will definitely be easier to protect a smaller zone."

Jack looked to me and I nodded enthusiastically, it felt great to do something meaningful and I was keen to follow it through. We dug out a map of Cornwall from an atlas on a shelf and Jack pointed out the location of the little people, suggesting which area would need to be shielded from public view.

"That's great, that's not too big an area. This could really be possible," Jerry said eagerly. He copied down details of the cove's location and the area Jack had identified as containing the homes of the little people on a new piece of paper, which he added to the top of his pile of research. "We can do this, I'm sure of it. Tom, we'll need to do some fundraising to help us pay for lawyers and whatnot, maybe you can think about how best to approach that. I don't know about your bank account but I don't have enough in mine to cover all this is likely to cost."

"I'm on it," I said and started to sketch down my own plan featuring social media campaigns, websites and celebrity endorsements. I was exhausted when I fell into my bed in a cheap hotel in the centre of the city. The scratchy sheets and lumpy mattress betrayed the price of the room, but I was tired enough to sleep anywhere after the long drive and the excitement of the day before.

"Tom," Jack's tiny voice floated to my ears, "I wanted to say thank you."

"Thank you for what?" I asked, leaning up on an elbow to see his shadowy form in the dark room.

"I know I didn't trust you about Jerry, but you were right, he is a good man. And now we'll get to keep the people safe forever, and it's all down to you."

I smiled and quickly drifted into dreams of becoming a hero to the little people, one who was able to keep them free from harm for all future generations. I imagined the endless adoration, the thrill of being the only human allowed into their reserve to interact with Jack and the other little people.

Sunshine struck my face, waking me from a deep, contented slumber and I realised I must have overslept. I was surprised Jack didn't wake me up, his piercing shouts were as good as any alarm clock and he was always up earlier than me.

"What time is it Jack?" I murmured sleepily, rolling over to look for my friend on his bed of blankets on the bedside cabinet. I rubbed eyes made blurry with sleep and realised both the pile of blankets and Jack were gone, replaced with a piece of card that read 'I'm sorry.'

I sprang out of the room in my pyjamas and startled the cleaner who was busy stripping the bed in the empty room that was Jerry's.

Jerry was gone, and so were my car keys.

CHAPTER NINETEEN

I was a naive fool. With hindsight I could see the cues I hadn't picked up on at the time. Why hadn't I thought it strange that Jerry was so quick to give up on his idea during that initial boat journey across Loch Ness? Why hadn't I noticed those moments when he looked at Jack with an odd gleam to the eye, as if Jack were a winning lottery ticket and he the ticket holder? I had trusted to friendship to beat the lure of financial gain. I wonder if spending so much time with a little person had caused his ideals to rub off on me, making me blind to the darkness in people.

Jack and I experienced peril from many different quarters during our travels; wild animals and pets and crushes of people and car accidents and rollercoaster calamities and hailstones almost as large as Jack's head. I anticipated dangers like that. I'd foreseen the risk from strangers and circumstances, but I never expected it to come from a friend. I felt the betrayal like a physical kick to my stomach.

I was alone in Glasgow without a car, without the majority of my things and without Jack. Whatever Jerry's plan might be, I was sure it wasn't one that would benefit

Jack or the little people at large. How long would it take him to go public about their existence? He knew the precise location of the cove and the houses of the little people contained within. We had drawn the giant X on the treasure map that would see him set for life.

Guilt and anger warred within me like two opposing armies, launching their assaults across the battleground of my unsettled stomach. If anything happened to the little people, to Jack, it would be entirely my fault for trusting that conniving former friend of mine.

I must have paced a mile or more around that small room until a stubbed toe broke my reverie with a string of curses that would cause my mother to gasp in horror. I sank onto the bed, my head in my hands, and tried to calm down.

"This isn't helping Tom, get a grip," I said aloud and took a few deep breaths to still the runaway train of my mind.

Jerry was nothing if not thorough. Along with the car keys and Jack, not to mention the bulk of my clothes and all of the camping equipment and other accoutrements still in the car, he'd also taken the cash from my wallet. I whispered a silent thank you for the envelope concealing the bulk of the remaining money. I don't think I'd ever mentioned that source of finance to Jerry, and so it remained, tucked into the bottom of my wash bag.

"Okay, think. You have some money, but no car. That's okay. He'll have to go back to Birmingham, that's where he lives and where his contacts at the university are. All I need to do is get to Birmingham, and then I can track him down." Talking to myself seemed to restore my sense of equilibrium and I threw the possessions I did have to hand into my backpack. I nearly missed Jack's shell necklace resting on the bedside cabinet. I had a sneaking suspicion he probably took it off himself during his kidnap, to let me know he hadn't left of his own accord. I knew he would never go anywhere without it. I snatched it up and wrapped it carefully in a sock in my bag.

"I can catch a train. I might even beat them back to Birmingham." With that decision made I was out of the blocks like an Olympic sprinter.

I missed the direct 10am train from Glasgow Central to Birmingham New Street by five minutes, but the harried woman at the ticket office told me there was another at midday. I thrust some cash toward her and took my ticket, fidgeting restlessly during the intolerable two-hour wait.

The journey itself wasn't much better. It seemed that every time I glanced at my watch only a minute or two had passed. Time slowed to the amble of a turtle. The clicking of knitting needles carried across the aisle and grated my frayed nerves, making me all the more aware of every individual, dragging, eternal second.

"You look like the cat that got the sour cream," the grey-haired woman said without pausing in her knitting stride, "it can't be all that bad now can it?"

I was tired, angry and eaten alive by guilt. It was all I could do not to scream at the elderly passenger, "How could you possibly know how bad it all is? I doubt you're on this train because a person you called a friend, a best friend, robbed you, stole something precious and is probably doing it irreparable harm right now."

The relentless tapping of the needles halted for a split second and then continued. "Well now," she said, "he doesn't sound like he was much of a friend."

I felt the anger deflate from me like a popped balloon. It left me exhausted and sad. "We were great friends once. We caused a lot of mischief back in the day."

"And let me guess, he was the one who'd initiate that mischief and you'd follow along. Then one day you stood up and refused to follow along so he took what you wouldn't give him. Is that how it goes?"

I stared at the old woman, bemused by her uncanny ability to see into my situation. "How could you know that?"

"Ah my boy, when you've lived as long as me you'll start to see the same scenarios play out time and time and time again too. There's nothing new under the sun, a wise man once wrote. Friendships like that, well they're all well and good when we're young, but sometimes you need to let go of what's past to look for stronger bonds. Friends shouldn't drag you along kicking and screaming to what they want to do, they should encourage you in what you want to do. Don't you have any friends like that?"

I lapsed into a thoughtful silence. I had always been the Robin to Jerry's Batman, the one to follow in his shadow. Now that I took the time to think about it my friendship with Jack was very different. Jack wasn't forceful in dictating what we should do; instead we both supported the other when there was something we wanted to see. We stopped for him to admire nature and he would share that with me, and at other times we stopped for me to admire architecture, something he wasn't remotely interested in, and I would try to explain my fascination of the Gothic Revival style to him.

I missed Jack all the more at that moment and wondered where he could be. Was he in the car at this very moment? Had they stopped somewhere? Where they already in Birmingham? I felt hopeless at my inability to help my friend.

I had to find him.

When the train where time stood still finally pulled into Birmingham New Street station I had formulated a plan. Not a great plan, it's true, but it was somewhere to start. Despite my years living in the city I wasn't altogether familiar with it, having spent the majority of my days in student hotspots. I could remember the way to the cathedral grounds from the train station however, and reasoned it would be a good place to put stage one of the plan into operation.

I managed to find a quiet corner, despite the perfectly manicured green attracting sunbathers desperate to enjoy the late August warmth. My fingers sped across the phone as I started to dial every number in my possession even remotely connected with my time spent at the University of Birmingham. I hoped I could find one old friend who might know Jerry's current address.

"Jem? It's Tom. Yeah, great to hear from you too. Oh you know, same old, same old, looking for a job and whatever. Hey, look, any chance you know where Jerry lives these days? Jerry Collins. No? Okay, no worries, thanks for your time. Yeah, yeah we must catch up soon. Bye."

By the end of the twentieth identical conversation I could feel desperation threatening to overwhelm me like a flood. There weren't many contacts left in my phone book.

"Steve, long time no speak," I said to one of my last potential sources of information.

"Tom? Tom Mitchell? Wow, haven't heard from you in what? A year? Look man, I'd love to catch up but I'm about to walk into a meeting."

"Please Steve, really quickly, do you know where Jerry Collins might live?"

"Jerry Collins? Nope, sorry."

My heart sank. "Oh, okay, no problem."

"Sorry I can't help."

"Wait, Steve, what about Chrissie? Chrissie Everett I think it was? She was the year above us but she'd sometimes hang around with Jerry and the others."

"Sorry Tom, I've really got to go, I'll text my sister, she might have an idea. Bye for now."

And that was that. My great plan had come to nothing and now I had no idea how to locate Jack. I couldn't exactly knock on every door in Birmingham. Evening was drawing closer and I reasoned I wouldn't be able to do much without some rest, so I wandered the streets until I found a budget hotel and checked myself in for the night. It was after I forced a few bites of food down my throat and evening turned to the blackness of night that my phone startled me by ringing.

"Yes? Hello?"

"Tom? It's Steve, sorry I had to run earlier."

"Oh Steve, no problem at all, hope you had a good meeting."

"Yeah, yeah it went okay. You sounded pretty desperate earlier for Jerry's address, is anything up?"

"I'm back in town for a few days, was trying to catch up with some people still around the area," I said, reluctant to divulge too many details.

"I see. Well Sara knew Chrissie's address so I have it here if you want it."

"Steve, you're a legend, thank you!"

I upturned the contents of the desk to find a pen and scribbled the details on the back of my hand.

"Thank you, that's perfect."

"You're welcome. If you want to catch up I'm free tomorrow night, I'm sure I could get some of the old gang together."

"Yeah," I said distractedly, "whatever you say. Got to run, good talking."

I hung up the phone before he could say goodbye and tracked the address down on a map on my phone. It was too far to walk. I would take a taxi first thing in the morning.

"Chrissie, hi," I said as she opened the door.

"What on earth are you doing here? I thought you were in Scotland with Jerry?"

"He's not here?"

"No. I've not seen him since he left with his family on that trip. Then I get no more than a text to say he'd met up with Tom Mitchell and would be away longer. And not a word since." Chrissie folded arms across her slender form and watched me with a pout on the full lips that had undoubtedly attracted Jerry.

"Do you have any idea where he might be?" I asked.

"Not a clue. If you see him first you can tell him from me he needs to find someplace else to live. I've had enough of that layabout taking me for granted."

"Me too," I muttered and turned away to the slam of the front door behind me.

It was twenty-four hours since Jack had been stolen, and I had no idea where on earth he might be.

I had no idea if he was still alive.

CHAPTER TWENTY

It took more than two hours to walk back to the centre of Birmingham. My feet were raw and blistered by the time I returned to those more familiar streets. I trudged dejectedly the whole way, racking my brains to come up with an idea to find Jerry and, by extension, Jack, but I was drawing a complete blank.

I depleted the dwindling funds in the envelope with a second night at the hotel. There wasn't much I could do wandering the streets with no clue where to go, and I hoped returning to base might give me another idea. I fell into a restless sleep to the low drone of the television and found myself trapped by the tangled sheets on waking. A news report on screen snapped any lingering weariness from my brain.

"And this is the discoverer, Jerry Collins, who I believe will be starting a PhD in September to study what he's calling the 'little people' at the University of Birmingham, is that correct Jerry?"

"Yes Gail, that's right."

"What can you tell us about these little people of yours?"

"Well Gail, they live in rocky coves in Cornwall. I can't

tell you the exact location of course, we can't have it overrun before we've investigated it thoroughly," he said in a conspiratorial tone to the reporter. "They're quite like us in a lot of ways, not as intelligent of course, more like pets really, though it's going to be fascinating learning more about how they've managed to survive with such rudimentary knowledge of anything."

"And you have one of the little people with you now, is that right?"

"Yes I do. I'd like to introduce you to Jack." Jerry held a small glass tube to the camera, within which stood the tiny Jack Meadows. I stared at the television screen and felt a hot flush of anger tighten my chest. It wasn't Jerry insulting the intelligence of the little people, who I knew to be as resourceful as us, that caused my hands to ball into fists. It wasn't even that he was claiming my discovery as his own. The thing I couldn't bear to see was the condition in which he was keeping Jack. There was no sign of his crutches in that glass fronted prison, and yet the space wasn't big enough for him to sit down in. Goodness knows how long he had been forced to stand on his one good leg with his right hanging limply beside him and his tiny hands hard pressed against the glass for extra support. Jack's face was expressionless and I felt incredibly proud of him in that moment. He refused to give Jerry the satisfaction of seeing him in pain or afraid.

"How old is Jack?"

"Well that's the amazing thing Gail. Jack here is less than a year old. I've discovered that his kind only live for one year. This fellow would be the equivalent of a man in his fifties I believe, but in reality he is only around two hundred and fifty days old."

"Well that is incredible. We'll be eagerly awaiting more information about these little people, and of course the book which will document your journey through a year with one of these little fellows. Thank you Jerry, and back to you in the studio Andrew."

I sunk my head into the pillow and, I'm not ashamed to admit, shed more than a tear or two at the plight of my friend. This was getting out of control. Jack was being tortured at the hand of Jerry, who was unquestionably mounting an expedition to the cove at this very minute. He would disrupt the world of the little people. I could see two options before me: continue the hunt for Jack, or get on a train to Cornwall to do my utmost to protect Jack's people. Jack was an adult now, as old as my own father in relative terms. When you see a gradual transition from day to day, the steady scaling of the tendrils of a climbing rose, the slowly slimming figure in the mirror, it's easy to ignore the subtle alterations. I sometimes imagined Jack as a young man still, one keen to throw off his civilisation to explore for his own pleasure. But that wasn't who he was anymore and I knew, without a shadow of doubt, that were he here beside me he would tell me to leave him and protect the little people.

I had all but made my decision to do just that when I leapt out of my skin at the wail of a passing police car on its way to some emergency.

It was so simple I couldn't believe I hadn't thought of it already. I would go and help the little people, but I had to try one more idea to find Jack first.

"Hello, police?" I asked on the phone.

"Yes sir, how can I assist you today?"

"I'd like to report a stolen car."

Early the following morning I received a phone call to explain my car had been found, and that I could come and collect it at my earliest convenience. It seems a diligent member of the public had reported a vehicle that looked abandoned, in the car park of a shabby hotel on the outskirts of the city. The police officer surmised that joyriding kids had probably taken the Volkswagen for a spin and left it in an out of the way spot, but I knew better. There was little obvious motive to the crime, so I was happy to deter the man on the phone from pursuing any further investigation. I didn't want anyone to snoop through the inside of that vehicle, what with spare crutches and clothes for a little person scattered around the place. The officer couldn't see any harm in satisfying my curiosity as to where the car had been found and happily divulged the address. Within minutes I was in a taxi and on my way. I would collect the Golf from the police later, Jack was my priority now.

"Not so clever are you Jerry," I muttered under my breath to a peculiar look from the cabby.

I asked the driver to drop me off a couple of streets away from the hotel so that I could creep up unnoticed. My mind was running at a mile a minute and coursing with concern for Jack, but I couldn't suppress the grin at the feeling of this real-life espionage. I felt like a lanky and severely inexperienced James Bond.

I could see the building from a distance. It looked tired and worn from the outside, its light coloured render long since blackened by passing traffic. Peeled and cracked window trims surrounded the old glasswork. Jerry must have assumed this to be the last sort of place I would look for him. If it hadn't been for the car he would certainly have gone unnoticed.

Finding Jerry's residence seemed like the least of my problems as I faced the once proud lodging. I had no idea which room was Jerry's, or any inkling of how best to go about breaking into said room. I was distractedly musing on potential strategies for scaling the sheer walls as I moved closer to the main entrance of the hotel, and only noticed the door opening at the last moment. I dived out of sight into a tangled mess of brambles that was once a flower bed as Jerry walked past, chatting animatedly on his phone. If he noticed the car was missing he didn't seem concerned. I thought it more likely he had decided not to drive it around in case I happened to spot it, and therefore hadn't thought to check if it was still parked haphazardly where he left it. A BMW estate with blacked out back windows stopped in front of Jerry and he climbed into the backseat. A literary publisher perhaps, come to wine and dine Mr Collins, the future author of the fanciful tale of the little people, a true story stranger than fiction. Enraged as I was at Jerry, I had to admire how quickly he'd manoeuvred a book contract. I wouldn't have known where to start. With a sickening feeling creeping into my stomach I realised there was no way he could have arranged all of this so quickly. He must have been making contacts while he was still travelling with us. All those evenings he'd wandered off to call Chrissie; he must have been using that time to set this up. This was his plan all along, from that first moment he agreed to travel with us. I had to fight the temptation to run from my hiding place and rugby tackle Jerry to the ground.

I couldn't see clearly from my position in the bushes, but Jerry didn't seem to have any possessions on him. I hardly dared to hope that he might have left Jack in his hotel room.

Jerry was long gone when I pulled myself out of the mess of weeds and thorns. I picked foliage from my jeans and scowled at an angry red scratch running the length of my arm. I looked around in a desperate search for inspiration and identified a corner shop across the street. Within I found a few items to help with the farfetched scheme I concocted. My basket contained a box of Ritz crackers, Sellotape, a roll of parcel paper, a notebook and a box of pens. In an alley beside the small supermarket I untidily wrapped my box of crackers and addressed it to one Mr J. Collins at the hotel's address. I tried to write what looked like postal order instructions on the notepad, but my scruffy handwriting would betray anything more than a casual inspection. Sticking a pen behind my ear in what I hoped was the casual and confident demeanour of the delivery person I made my way into the lobby of the hotel.

The exterior of the building was a good reflection of its interior. The few chairs scattered around the lobby bore stained and torn upholstery and the tiled floor looked grubby.

"I've got a delivery," I said to the teenager behind the desk. He scooped a pen from the desk and made ready to sign for the package without ever looking up to see what I was holding. "Sorry," I said, "I was told I have to give it directly to the recipient."

The youth shrugged. "What name?"

"Collins," I said. I couldn't believe this was working.

"J or M?" he asked.

"J, J. Collins."

"212," he said and was back to playing a game on his phone with a level of dedication he failed to show in his work.

I adopted a swagger and strutted confidently to the staircase, stunned at the success of my daring manoeuvre. It was the best idea I could come up with but I hadn't thought for a moment it would actually work. I doubted my ruse was necessary at all; I could probably have walked in and asked for the room number with no preamble, given the lackadaisical nature of the staff member on duty.

206, 208, 210, 212, I read the numbers as I passed each room until I was standing before Jerry's hideout. I'd made it this far, but there was still the problem of the locked door before me. I'm always amazed at how quickly a mind under pressure can work. In scant seconds my mind wandered over all the days of my life, wondering what had brought me to this point. It's true, I'd always been a bit of a rogue, particularly under Jerry's influence, but I had never broken any laws. I was too worried about my own future endeavours to risk stepping too far over the line. Now I was here and contemplating how to gain access to a locked room to steal something, albeit something that was stolen from me. For all those thoughts swirling like a fog through my mind one thing was crystal clear, no matter the consequences I had to save my friend.

What would James Bond do? I thought and struggled to remember any film or television series that had demonstrated the art of breaking and entering. I didn't have a hairpin so I couldn't try to pick the lock that way, nor would I have any idea how to do so. There was an old library card in my wallet that Jerry hadn't deemed it necessary to steal with my bank and credit cards. Hadn't I seen some hero open a lock by jimmying a credit card into the crack between door and wall? It was worth a shot. I'd been lucky so far, maybe the luck would hold for a few more moments.

It didn't of course. With mounting frustration I tried twisting the card this way and that to no avail. The hotel might not have looked like much, but the locks on its rooms were good enough to keep this novice burglar out.

I slipped the battered card back into my wallet and was pondering my next move when the door opened before me. Silhouetted by the glow pouring through the room's window behind him stood a man, a bit younger than me I'd guess. He was shorter than I was, but his shoulders were broad and his frame looked powerfully built.

"Thought I heard some noise out here. What do you want?"

"Uh, um," I struggled to think of an excuse for my presence. "Oh, parcel delivery," I said at last. Whoever this ally of Jerry's was didn't seem to be the sharpest knife in the block, and he merely shrugged as I stuck the notebook in front of him for his scribble of a signature. I suspected he had been placed here for his brawn, not his brain.

"Don't suppose I could use your bathroom, mate?" I asked. "It's been a long shift."

"I'm not supposed to let anyone in," the man said gruffly.

"Come on mate, I'll only be a moment. Who's going to know?"

"Fine, be quick about it though," he said and stepped

back from the door to point me in the direction of the room's ensuite facilities.

I made my way across the room with a slow swagger in an attempt to take in every detail. It was a mess; that seemed about right for Jerry, having experienced his slovenliness as a flatmate for three years. Items of clothing were scattered carelessly over the backs of chairs and the bed, and remnants of hurried takeaway meals lay in a heap on the desk. There was a pervading odour of sweat mingled with old food and dirty laundry. Whether that was a smell familiar to all the rooms in this establishment or the result of two men living in close quarters in the small room I couldn't be sure.

As I swung around for one last survey of the space before closing the bathroom door I saw the man pick something up and start tossing it, end over end. The something looked like a glass tube and within, I'm sure, was Jack.

I shut the bathroom door and perched on the edge of the bathtub to think. Jack was proud and brave but would he survive this torture? He had another hundred and twenty days to live, I was not going to let that time be shortened by some careless buffoon Jerry had hired to watch Jack while he was off wining and dining his way to a lucrative book deal. This had to end. Now.

The man was stronger than me, of that I had no doubt, but I would have the element of surprise. I could lunge at him and try to knock him to the floor. Aside from a scuffle with my sister when I was eight I couldn't remember ever punching another human, the physical was not my forte. I had always found ways to avoid a fight. I regretted that now, with no knowledge of how to defend myself or bring an opponent to the floor. There wasn't much to help me in the bathroom. I could try to beat him with a toilet brush but I doubted that would prove effective, unless he was particularly squeamish. I felt sure Jerry would have briefed this man to defend Jack against any eventuality, why else would he have been there at all? There was nothing for it, I couldn't think my way out of the situation in the limited time I had so I would have to rely on my wits and his lack of them.

"Hey, excuse me," I called from the bathroom with the door still closed, "the door seems to have stuck, any chance you could give it a yank?"

I heard the barrel of a man stomp noisily toward the door and I held on tight to the handle, leaning back so my weight would prevent it from opening.

The man grunted as he tugged on the door but my mass was just enough to prevent it opening. On his second attempt I let go of the handle at the very moment he wrenched at the door with all his might. The solid wood hit him in the nose with an almighty crack. He hopped up and down cursing and trying to stem the drops of blood that streamed from his broken nose. I didn't hesitate but pushed past him, made a grab for Jack and rushed toward the exit with my heart beating in my ears.

He wasn't as dense as I first hoped. Despite the pain that must have been pulsing through his face like an electric shock he chose not to chase me but instead to bar the exit with his bulk.

"That's your game then is it?" he growled. "You put that down right now, it ain't yours." He took a threatening step towards me, looking utterly terrifying with eyes maddened by pain and with blood still dripping from his wonky nose.

"He isn't anyone's," I said and backed slowly away. The man continued to walk towards me, one slow and menacing step at a time. "You shouldn't listen to Jerry, he won't share any profit with you," I didn't know what I was saying but I knew I had to keep the man distracted. With every step he took toward me the gap between his back and the door widened. "If I were you I'd leave now and run away before he gets you into any trouble. He's bad news."

"Bad news is he? Well so am I," he said, and lunged at me. I sprang out of the way by instinct alone, and rolled over the bed in a move I'd gloat about for years. There was the gap, I could make it. The man was rising from the floor where he'd landed when I'd slipped through his grasp and I was running for my life, faster than I can ever remember running. Somehow I even managed to scoop the keys to my car that I noticed casually resting on the desk which lay beside my escape route. As I reached the door I fell hard to the floor, and almost lost my grip of the glass container that housed my friend. Something heavy had struck my ankle. I looked back in horror to see the man holding onto my leg with a vice-like grip.

"Let go," I cried angrily and kicked back hard with my other foot. I had no idea where I was aiming but I must have struck his already wounded nose. He howled like a dying animal and for the briefest of moments loosened his grip on my ankle. It was all I needed to kick free, scramble to my feet and sprint so fast down the stairs it felt more like falling. I could hear him chasing behind me and shouting curses at my retreating back. "Run, run, run," I chanted internally to my every footstep. The other man might have been stronger but with my longer stride and adrenalin fuelled desperation to escape I managed to put some distance between us. I led him on a merry chase, running down street after street in an attempt to lose him. My lungs were burning and the stitch in my side was a dagger tearing my flesh apart. I knew I couldn't run much further, red spots were masking my field of vision. I saw a side street and sprinted down it, almost losing my footing as I took the corner too sharply. It was a small road dotted with rubbish and recycling wheelie bins. I dived behind a line of four bins pressed together and tried to slow the ragged breathing that would surely give my position away. Running footsteps came to a halt close by. The beating of my heart sounded like a hammer bashing an anvil to my ears, and I had to exert all my will to persuade my exhausted limbs to stop their twitching and lie still and quiet.

"Dammit," the man cried and stalked past my hiding spot.

I had escaped.

CHAPTER TWENTY-ONE

I don't know how long I sat in that filthy spot, clutching the glass tube like it was a life preserver and I a man floundering in the ocean. I didn't want to risk Jerry's man catching us unaware if he retraced his steps. My lungs couldn't take another chase.

Once my rapid breathing had slowed and the red spots had faded from my eyes I lifted up the glass tube to see how Jack was faring. His prison contained tiny air holes, at least Jerry had thought of that, but it was still a horrendous place for him. I wondered how long he had been contained within, unable to sit down or even bend his legs. His hair was matted and his clothes were dirty, as was the inside of the tube. I doubted they had even let him out to go to the toilet. I was reluctant to break the glass in case it would hurt Jack or attract unwanted attention to our position, but with a bit of exploring I found such drastic measures unnecessary. A section at the bottom of the container twisted away to release Jack onto my waiting hand. He instantly crumpled to his knees.

"You came," he said.

"Of course I came," I answered quietly.

The afternoon passed by but neither of us suggested

moving. I quietly filled Jack in on my tale, how I'd tracked him down and freed him from his captor. He sounded suitably impressed by my detective skills, but I was more interested in finding out what had happened to him since we left.

"It was dark when Jerry came into the room," Jack said. "I think he must have taken a spare key from the lady downstairs, they knew we were together after all. I thought there must be some emergency when I saw him standing over the bed but I think he was only checking to make sure you were asleep. Next thing I know he'd grabbed me, blankets and all, and was stepping quietly out of the room. I tried shouting but I was too far away for you to hear me. He put me in the travel box in the car and drove off. I kept trying to get away, so he wrapped me in thick springy brown bands that made my arms and legs ache. I was stuck. All I could do was sit quietly and wonder what would happen.

"We drove through the night. I must have fallen asleep because when I woke we were in a big city. He didn't waste any time, even though he'd been awake all night. He checked into that hotel where you found me but then we were on our way again right away. He left the car there and we took a taxi to a big building, he said it was part of the university. He showed me to some people and tried to get me to speak like some kind of performing animal, but I refused to talk. They still seemed impressed by me though and they poked and prodded me a lot. They even stuck a tiny needle in my arm and took some blood out. Someone brought out a 'specimen tube,' I think that's what they called it, and Jerry put me in it. The people he talked to suggested he should keep me quiet for a bit while they did some research but he didn't want to. He muttered about that for a while after meeting with them, he kept saying it couldn't hurt to let people know sooner. He made some calls soon after that, and some people came to do an interview with him on an enormous camera. After that he was meeting even more people and talking about how he could write a book. They bought him nice meals and offered lots of money if he'd go right ahead and get started. I think he was more concerned with that than the research the men and women at the university wanted to do.

"It was a pair of those people who suggested he should have someone around to look after me in case I wasn't there, now that he'd gone public with it all. They seemed to think there was a lot of money to be had where I was concerned, and that someone might want to steal me to get rich. He was happy with that and asked some student called Rob to stay in the room with me for some money. That freed Jerry to come and go without having to worry about me being there all alone, or taking me with him everywhere.

"I hated that tube they put me in, but Jerry would at least lie it down at night so I could sleep a bit. Rob wasn't as nice. He spun the tube around and around until I was sick and then laughed and did it again. Jerry told him off when he saw him do it and I thought that'd be the end of it, but he just waited until Jerry was out of the room and then came up with new ways to make me ill. He was cruel."

That was an understatement if ever I heard one.

"That's about it really," Jack said, "Jerry wanted to keep me under wraps after that first public appearance so I was mostly at the hotel with Rob."

"If I could get my hands on him right now," I started angrily.

"Don't be too mad at Jerry," Jack said.

I stared at him blankly. "What?"

"He's not all bad."

"He could have killed you!"

"Oh I don't think so. Rob maybe, but Jerry definitely wanted to keep me alive. I'm sure mostly for money or whatever, but he did sit beside my tube one evening and say how sorry he was for putting me through this. He might have labelled me a stupid pet to the media, but he knew I was intelligent really and I think he was genuinely sorry about what he was doing to me.

"His life hasn't turned out the way he wanted it to, and he couldn't see a way out or a means to achieve his dreams. Then suddenly along we came and it seemed like the perfect opportunity to put things back on track."

"That's not an excuse to do what he did!"

"Maybe not, but it lets us know why he did it. There's no telling what desperate people will do, even nice ones."

"You can't tell me you forgive him for all of this?"

"I wouldn't trust him again, not as far as I could throw his shoe, but forgive him? Of course I do."

I was speechless.

"I think you'll understand when you're a bit older Tom. Choosing to hold on to all that bitterness and rage, choosing not to forgive him, it can't hurt him at all but it sure hurts me. Sometimes you just have to let things go."

Jack's words made sense, but the living, writhing ball of anger that swirled inside me would take a long time to diminish. Forgiveness never came as easy to me as it did to Jack.

We waited until it was dark to move from our sanctuary. At one point I feared Rob had discovered us, but it was only a mangy cat seeking scraps from around the dustbins. It was too late to think of retrieving the car, so instead I suggested we find a place to stay for the night, somewhere more comfortable than this dirty alleyway. Despite all the hubbub I'd managed to keep hold of my backpack and the depressingly thin envelope. Jack was riding in my pocket again as we snuck out of the alley, peering backwards and forwards in the gloom. There was a small bed and breakfast close to us, so my phone informed me. The couple running the place welcomed me warmly and offered a hot meal for an extra few pounds. I accepted it gratefully and devoured every morsel, aside from the pieces I passed on to Jack of course. In the height of adventure it's easy to forget things like your stomach, but in the safety of the quiet room I realised I was starving.

"What now, Tom?" Jack asked as we rested from our ordeal.

"I think we'd better stay out of sight for a while, lay low somewhere. If I can get the car back tomorrow we could drive south a bit and find a campsite. That'd keep us out of the way until the media furore dies down."

"That's the safest option, but I think we need to go back to Cornwall, to the cove," Jack said.

"I'm not sure that's the best idea right now, Jack. Jerry knows its location. With you gone I bet he'll head straight there, otherwise he'll have no little people to report on and he'll lose everything he's worked for these last couple of weeks."

"All the more reason why we need to get there first. If anything happens to them Tom, well, it'll be our fault."

Part of me still hoped I could convince Jack to extend our travels, maybe even to take a ferry down to France to stay well away from the spotlight. But even if I had been able to convince him I knew in my heart of hearts it wouldn't be the same. Everything had changed. Jack was always a light-hearted soul, but after his capture there were moments when a dark shadow would colour his features, moments when he'd be tormented by nightmares and wake from his sleep with a cry. Memories of his ordeal stayed with him. As humans we live long enough for painful recollections to fade, if not completely vanish. Jack would live his life remembering every detail of his nightmare. He was resolved to protect the little people before Jerry's kidnap, now it was a determination the like of which I'd never seen. We might have continued our travels, but Jack would never be able to rest until he was sure no other little person would suffer a similar fate.

"We can't leave until tomorrow. That'll give him a big

head start, assuming he leaves right away," I said finally.

"He won't leave immediately. I doubt Rob would have confessed to losing me that quickly, he'll try and find us instead I think. I remember Jerry saying he'd be out for the whole day and most of the evening, so he probably doesn't know I'm gone yet. And even if he does, he wouldn't be able to disappear instantly. He'll have to go and talk to the university people and get a team together if he wants to find the little people quickly and do it all reputably. He'll need to talk to his book contacts too to try and save that deal with me gone. I think we can do it Tom. I think we can beat him there. We have to try."

Jerry had already shown the world a little person, and told anyone watching they could be found on the coast of Cornwall. To the best of my knowledge he hadn't released the exact location of the cove, I suppose he wanted to keep that information to himself so that he could be the one to study the little civilisation without being badgered by the public. That gave us the narrowest of windows to drive down and prevent any further damage being done to them. My anger at Jerry and my desire to stop his fiendish plans battled with concern for keeping Jack safe, and I couldn't help but think returning him to Cornwall would be returning him to danger and more pain. In the end, despite all the arguments my brain could concoct, there was no choice. I had started this. It was me who had taken Jack from the cove. I was the one to introduce him to the wider world, and the one who foolishly trusted Jerry enough to reveal the existence of the little people. I had better be the one to set things right.

The race to Cornwall was on.

- PART THREE -

HOMECOMING

CHAPTER TWENTY-TWO

"Mitchell, M-I-T-C-H-E-L-L."

"Make, model, colour and registration number please."

"I went through all this with the police already. Can't I just have my car back please?" I said, biting back frustration. I had spent the better part of the morning waiting around, answering the same questions over and over and over again, and filling in endless forms.

The woman at the desk started at me blankly and repeated the query in a monotonous tone, "Make, model, colour and registration number please."

With a pronounced sigh I repeated the information for the umpteenth time.

"Proof of identification."

I handed over my driving license and waited, again, while it was photocopied, again.

"Do you need us to contact someone about ordering a replacement key?"

"No, as I already told that other guy, I found the spare key so it's fine."

"Do you have a catalogue of the inventory of the vehicle for us to check against its contents now?"

"You mean did I keep a list of everything in there? No,

of course not! There's camping gear and a suitcase of clothes and I don't know what else. I don't care if anything's missing." I could hear Jack's chuckle rise up to my ears and gave the pocket a circumspect nudge. We were both frustrated at the delay when time was of the essence, but Jack had a knack for seeing the funny side of any situation. It was a character trait that not even his recent ordeal could snatch away from him. My lack of patience at the red tape surrounding the release of the car was providing him with great amusement.

"Okay sir, I believe we're ready to release your vehicle now. Please follow me to confirm the condition of the car is as you remember it."

"Finally," I muttered under my breath and followed the woman to a small lot with a few vehicles inside. She even walked slowly. "That's it," I said, pointing at my old Volkswagen.

"Thank you sir, please take a moment to inspect the vehicle and its contents."

I all but ran around the car to give it a cursory inspection, noting nothing but a new scratch along the passenger door that highlighted Jerry's lack of regard for my things. The key worked to unlock the door and it looked like everything was still in place. If Jerry had taken anything it was inconsequential now anyway, we were going home.

"It's fine, it's all there."

"Thank you sir. Please sign this form to confirm you are happy that the car has been released to you and is in an acceptable condition and you will be free to go."

"Thank you!" I signed the form without reading it and placed it firmly back in her hands. "Can I go now?"

"Yes sir, you can go now." The corners of her lips twitched into the briefest smile as she waddled back to her office.

Jack's travel box was still belted into place on the passenger seat; it all looked the same, as though the last few days hadn't happened. I slipped him inside and started the long journey, hours later than planned. We were in a hurry but I still insisted we stop at a service station on the M5. The possessions in the back of the car were jumbled but I was able to find some of Jack's spare clothes. He had washed the stench of captivity from his body at the bed and breakfast in Birmingham, but with nothing else to wear he was forced to change back into the same filthy clothes. Now he cast them away from him in disgust and put on a clean pair of tiny trousers and a shirt and looked instantly happier for the transformation. We threw the old clothes away. They were tarnished with dirt and with memories sooner forgotten.

"Something's missing," I said as I looked at him appraisingly. "One moment." I fished in my backpack for a balled up, slightly smelly sock and unravelled it to find Jack's cockle shell necklace. I carefully placed it around his neck like a medal.

"Wasn't sure I'd see this again," Jack said gruffly and patted the shell. He stood straighter then and lifted his chin proudly to the world, despite the pains it had caused him.

Time passed quickly on our long drive; it sped by far faster than that unbearable train journey from Glasgow. Having company again undoubtedly had something to do with it, or perhaps it was just that the danger seemed more remote than in the case of Jack's kidnap. I found myself enjoying our final trip, and I was not excessively aware of the passage of the minutes. Jack's position could not have been more different. I noticed his frequent glances at the clock on the dashboard. "How long now?" he would ask from time to time. It strikes me as a peculiar phenomenon that two people in the same situation can experience the passage of time in two completely different ways. For me, time was a fast flowing stream, propelling us forward toward the unknown fate that awaited us at the cove. For Jack, time was an insufferably slow trickle, preventing him from being where he desperately wanted to be.

As I drove I wondered how often the little people considered time. Were they conscious of it sweeping forward and swiftly counting their numbered days? I doubted it. It seemed more likely that they rarely thought of it, not wearing the watches that keep us so aware of the passing of every moment of the day. I doubt there were many instances like today, where a little person willed the clock to move faster.

The map on my phone suggested our journey should take little more than four and a half hours, but that didn't take traffic into account. It was a Friday afternoon, drawing toward a Friday evening, and we soon joined the masses making their way down to Cornwall for a final weekend by the seaside before the school term started again. Caravans aplenty filled the roads and left us trapped in long queues, particularly as we left the motorways behind and took to narrower roads. Though it was full evening when we finally arrived and we were both tired and hungry, Jack insisted the cove should be our first stop. I pulled the car into a lay-by not far from Jack's old house, there being no designated car park for such a small patch of coastline. Unfolding my legs out of the car felt beautiful after the long drive. The stroll across the rocks that I had been so adept at before we left on our travels seemed like much harder work than I remembered.

I was about to reach into my pocket to pick Jack up and pop him on the floor near his old home when I heard voices. Pretending to bend over and tie a shoelace instead, I nodded to the passing crowd. In all my days stalking this cove I had never seen another soul, not even a rambling dog walker. Now there was a group staring intently at the ground with every footstep. Not far behind them I could see another group walking up the hill from the ocean.

"Any luck?" one of the young men called to me in passing.

"Luck?" I asked.

"With the little people? We've not seen any sign yet, but they've got to be out there somewhere right?" He grinned and moved on, taking careful steps and watching closely for any sign of movement.

An excited cry brought the group running close to the rock pool I knew so well. "I saw something moving," a female voice said, "I'm sure I did."

"It's a crab you dolt," another voice replied and the group moved away. I breathed again.

"We'll have to come back tomorrow Jack," I said quietly, "first thing in the morning, before anyone is out of bed. We don't want to draw any undue attention to them if they've not been spotted."

Jack reluctantly agreed and we climbed back up the rocky path to the car, my legs protesting each step.

This was something I hadn't anticipated. I expected to arrive and find the area taped off as Jerry and others in white coats carefully turned over every stone, but I hadn't foreseen the attraction the revelation of the little people would have on the general population. The pursuit of Jack's relatives had become a treasure hunt. When I turned on the news later that evening I discovered the one interview Jerry had given showing Jack had gone viral on social media, with the #findthem tag trending for days. All online fads die down eventually but we couldn't afford to wait. Somehow we had to warn and protect the little people from the incursion of more determined minds who would be arriving any moment now, and who knew the exact location of their homes.

We discussed options on and off all the way home, but neither of us could come up with a credible idea regarding what to say to the little people. Our strongest plan was simply to tell them the truth and open the floor to suggestions from the people themselves. Not much of an idea I know. Jack was confident that his people wouldn't want to leave their homes unless the situation became desperate, but I was almost positive moving to a new site would become a necessity.

"Mum? Dad? I'm home," I called as I pushed open the front door.

"Tom? Peter, it's Tom, he's home!" my mother shouted up the stairs. "Tom, we didn't know you were on your way back, you should have called." She enfolded me into a hug, quite a feat considering her head didn't quite reach my shoulder. I checked in with my parents periodically throughout the last few months, sending messages and the odd photo to let them know where in the country I was, but in all the drama of the last few days I had forgotten to get in touch.

"Son, it's good to see you," my father stood at a distance as if inspecting me for any changes, but within a couple of long strides he crossed the kitchen to give me a rough hug.

"You must tell us all about it, Tom, about all the things you've seen. We want to see all the pictures," my mother said.

"Of course. But tomorrow, okay? I've driven for hours today. I'll be out early in the morning though, I promised a friend I'd help with something. Night guys, love you." I left my parents staring at my retreating back in dumbfounded silence and ran up the stairs to my room, Jack concealed in my pocket.

We stayed up for a good while despite our exhaustion, and quietly debated how best to approach the organisation of a meeting of little people without alerting those desperate to find them. Finally, when I couldn't keep my eyes open for a moment longer, I set a pre-dawn alarm, sunk my head into a pillow that smelt of home and fell instantly into a deep sleep.

I think I dreamed of chasing Jerry around Cornwall with a cricket bat, but I can't be sure.

It's certainly what I felt like doing as I dragged my aching and bone-weary body out of bed in the dark. The first rays of sun were painting the world with colour as we began the familiar walk to the cove. As I'd suspected, many people wanted to find a little person to call their own but not so much as to be willing to be up at the crack of dawn. The waking cries of a myriad of gulls and the slow rolling gait of the ocean were the only noises to be heard.

"Where should we start?" I asked Jack. I knew where the Meadows house was of course, but other than a vague knowledge of the direction I had seen the other little people come from I had no idea where they lived.

"Put me down over there." Jack pointed at an unassuming rocky outcropping and I willingly obliged. "I'll go and have a look inside, wait here," he said.

I fumbled with the zip of my coat with fingers made frozen by the chill early September breeze. I waited and waited and waited, wishing I'd brought a book to read. At one point I thought I saw Jack in the distance, vanishing into another rocky formation but I wasn't positive, it could have been another little person or a figment of my imagination at such a distance. Still I waited and saw no sign of Jack as the sun reached higher into the sky. I wondered how the discussion was progressing. I hoped he was presenting the arguments we'd discussed the night before eloquently enough to sway the stubborn population of the cove.

"Tom?" I heard the tiny voice carried on the breeze and turned to find Jack standing not far from where I sat. "Jerry must have beaten us here. The little people are gone."

CHAPTER TWENTY-THREE

I've never felt anger like it. First he took Jack, then he claimed my own discovery as his, and now he'd taken all of the little people away, the people Jack was so desperate to come all this way to save. I was seeing red and definitely not thinking clearly. I could picture Jerry now, jumping into a car, rushing away from Birmingham while I was trapped trying to free my car. I could see him rounding the little people up like cattle to take away and study in some kind of cruel experiment. I was enraged at the thought of hundreds of little people lined up in glass jars, kept on a shelf ready to be poked and prodded, becoming lab rats for all sorts of research. I imagined the little people moved to a zoo, to become a spectacle for human children, just another curiosity from some part of the world.

Gradually the mist of furore dissipated and common sense reared its head.

"Jack, this can't be right. Think about it, Jerry couldn't take them away, he'd need to study them in their natural habitat not take them out if it. If he had beaten us here I think he'd be trying to stop us getting to them, but he wouldn't have removed them without the chance to make a study and take a tonne of photos. Did you check everywhere for them?"

"Every house I know and the meeting hall. There were no people in any of them."

We sat together, alone with our thoughts. My mind concocted all kinds of calamities to explain their absence. Had a contagious disease torn through the population and left them decimated? Had they been discovered by someone else? Had the tide rushed higher than ever before, overflowing the rock pool and flooding their houses? None of the options fit with the evidence before us. It was as if the little people had grown wings and flown away. Perhaps they really were the fairies of folk tales, given to sprouting feathers when threatened. I wondered about asking Jack if that was a possibility but a voice stopped me in my tracks.

"There, over there." I scooped Jack into my pocket and scrambled over the slippery rocks as quickly as I was able as the murmur of many voices closed in on our position. Once there was some distance between us and the homes of the little people I stopped and sheltered behind a large rock where I could hide while keeping an eye on proceedings.

A group of ten people was approaching Jack's former home. They carried large boxes of supplies and tools between them. In their midst stood Jerry.

I balled my hands into fists and fought every urge to charge at him. He would have floored me long before I could throw a punch of course, but the brain doesn't think clearly when it's maddened by rage.

"Start over there," Jerry said and pointed directly at the site of the Meadows' house. We couldn't see clearly, concealed as we were, but we heard the tap-tapping of a hammer or chisel or some other tool designed to gain forceful entrance into the family residence. My anger burned hotter as I remembered all the hours of work John and I put into making that place a wonderful home for Julie and for Jack.

"Nothing there, boss," a woman's voice called.

"What do you mean nothing there?" I saw Jerry stamp toward the group, all of them hunched over and peering at the floor. With sadistic pleasure I noted that Jerry looked tired and worn. Dark rings coloured the skin beneath his eyes and his stiff walk revealed the tension in his muscles. I stood for a better view to see him crouch down and stare into the exposed home. "It's empty." He sounded disappointed. "Try over there," he said and pushed one of his team in the direction of the other houses with a not-too-gentle shove.

We watched the work party closely as time ticked by. Each time the team uncovered a house there were cries of excitement, quickly replaced with groans of disappointment when another residence was found empty.

"Jack," I whispered, "did you check to see if there were any belongings left inside the houses?"

"No, I was only looking for people so I ran in and out quickly. Now that I think about it everything did seem quite barren."

"I think they left before Jerry could get here Jack, why else would their possessions be gone too?"

"But why would they leave?" Jack asked. It was another mystery, but his face brightened at the possibility.

"I don't know. Maybe with all the extra people traipsing around here after Jerry's news report they didn't feel very safe?"

"Could be," Jack mused. "Where would they have gone though?"

I had no answer to that question.

"I'm going over there," I said.

"What? Wait, Tom. Don't." There was a note of panic in Jack's voice that I had never heard before. The bruises he received at the hands of Jerry and his assistant Rob had yellowed, but they still marred his skin.

"Don't worry, you'll be safe," I said, giving the top of his head a gentle push into the relative sanctuary of my pocket.

"Jerry, how nice to see you," I called in my coldest voice.

He spun around to face me, and I noticed that his gaze dropped to my breast pocket before meeting my eye. I was so angry I found it hard to believe he could remain standing under the intensity of my glare.

"How did you do it?" he spat at me. "Where did you put them?"

"Out of reach of you and your cronies, that's for sure," I replied. Realisation dawned on me. Jerry thought I was the reason for the absence of the little people. "You might as well give up."

"Give up?" Jerry moved closer and hissed into my ear, "You stole my chance from me. I was going to be somebody. This is not over. I will not rest until I find them."

"You've already lost Jerry. Drop it while you still can."

"Or what? You and your little pet will take me down?" He snorted, "I'd like to see you try."

"How can you call him that Jerry?" I said in a hushed voice to keep his friends from hearing. "They aren't pets, they're people. You spoke to him, you know him. He's intelligent, as intelligent as us."

"If he was intelligent he'd have spoken when I told him to. It's his own fault that's what people think of him."

I started to laugh, "That's why you told the woman on the news they were pets? Because he wouldn't talk on command? And now you've got the whole of Cornwall and more besides out looking for little people they can take home and keep." I shook my head, amazed at the absurdity of it all.

Jerry glared at me for a moment, but then his face broke into a smile. He looked almost like the carefree man I used to know. I'd have believed it, were it not for the smouldering anger behind his eyes. "Tom, listen to me, this is for their own good."

I gave a bark of laughter. "For their own good? Coming in here to destroy everything they know so you can get rich exploiting them?"

"You think this is about me?" For a moment Jerry looked genuinely stunned. "That's the last thing I'm worried about Tom. I'm like you; I want to protect these people. But you can't just bury your head in the sand and assume no one's ever going to find them. We have to understand more about them so we know how best to look after them. That's all I'm doing here."

"If that's all you're doing here why on earth would you tell the world about them? Why would you stuff Jack in a tube and parade him on national television?" I clenched my fists at the memory.

"Protecting them is a pipe dream if we don't have any money Tom. I was genuinely doing that research in Glasgow mate, we can protect them, but no amount of campaigning is going to raise the money we'd need for this. Publicising it, well it gives us a chance. Don't you see that?"

I stared at my old friend. It seemed as though he genuinely believed the rubbish he was spouting at me.

"I figured you wouldn't understand," he said in response to my silence. "That's why I had to take him. If you weren't going to look out for their best interests then I figured I'd have to."

"Their best interests? You think this is in their best interest? Destroying their homes? You think having your lackey Rob torture Jack was in his best interest? You're an idiot Jerry" I all but shouted at him.

"We'll see who the idiot is at the end of all of this, won't we," Jerry snarled and turned away from me, his mask dropped. "Get back to the cars, we'll make a new plan," he instructed his team and off they marched, leaving the complete destruction of Jack's hometown in their wake.

We stayed for longer. When I was sure Jerry and his

team had left I placed Jack on the floor to pick through what was left of the houses. Now that most of the homes were exposed to the light of day we could both search for any clue as to where the little people had gone. I was amazed at how thoroughly the houses had been stripped. If it was the influx of people searching on Cornish coves that had caused them to move, as I suspected, then I was impressed with the efficiency of the little people. They could only have had a few days to clear out, and yet even items of furniture were gone. The only evidence of little person habitation was the layout of the rooms within their houses, and unless you were looking particularly closely those could have been natural formations. Jack's home was the only one that showed more evidence of a dedicated building work. Jack walked slowly around his ruined childhood home, tracing the walls John and I had built with his hand as if reawakening memories by touch.

"They could have gone anywhere," Jack said.

"We'll find them."

"We'll have to find them quickly. Jerry will be looking too."

I hoped I had bought some time persuading Jerry that the little people were in my keeping, but I didn't doubt he would still scour the coastline around here, just in case. He had ten people to work with compared to our two, and if he saw us searching he would know we didn't have the little people safe and sound after all, and would surely intensify his own hunt. It was a tricky dilemma we faced. Our only boon was having a little person on our team, and I hoped it would be enough to give us the advantage in spotting any subtle signs they might have left during their evacuation.

The race was still on, and more heated than ever.

As darkness rolled over my bedroom that night I knew the thoughts keeping me from sleep should have concerned the fate of the little people, but those weren't the reflections plaguing me. My heart felt oddly constricted by the treacherous thoughts of my mind. The only image I could see was the face of one of Jerry's assistants. It was the most beautiful face I had ever seen. When I met her gaze for the briefest of moments as Jerry turned away, I was sure a soft smile had turned up her lips. It was that smile I pictured as I drifted into a restless doze.

CHAPTER TWENTY-FOUR

I have always hated races.

I well remember the cold sweat soaking into my too long and too skinny frame on the morning of every school sports day. We lined up on the field in our shorts and t-shirts, my fellow students and I, and awaited the countdown to run ourselves ragged in endless laps until one of us was crowned the victor. I never earned that title.

This was an altogether different sort of race but I felt a pressure in my chest that mimicked that of the childhood me wishing for victory against the odds.

We decided to try for a casual approach, an offhand exploration of the coastline without making it obvious we had as much of a clue as to where the little people were located as Jerry. I'm sure my parents were dumbfounded. Their son had finally returned but he was as aloof and mysterious as before he left to drive around aimlessly for six months. I assured them I would soon have things back on track, once I completed the project that so transfixed my attention.

"You do what you need to do, son," my mother said and to my surprise my father nodded. As I left the room I heard them speak in hushed tones.

"I don't know what it is that's got a bee under his bonnet, but have you ever seen him so driven?"

"No Mary, you're right. We'll let it play out for a while but one of these days he'll have to buckle down and get a job. We can't keep on supporting him like this, we just can't afford it."

"I know, love, but for the first time I feel sure he will settle down soon. Something's changed in him in these last few months; you can see it when you look him in the eye. He's grown up."

I didn't feel very grown up. Then again I still don't. I have drawn the conclusion that growing up isn't something we feel, it's something that creeps up on us like a thief in the night until the day we realise it to be the truth.

We started our exploration from the original cove, walking down to the shore and then back up and away from the ocean in a diagonal search pattern. I carried Jack in my hand as we inspected the land in case he could identify details I might miss. From time to time he would ask me to put him down and proceed to search around a rock or pool or clump of seaweed. Nothing heralded any sign.

We saw no trace of the little people for days.

Our nerves were feeling frayed. We judged that the little people couldn't have moved too far, burdened as they were by belongings and the very young and old, but there was no hint of their passing and no suggestion of a location to which they could have retreated. Had they survived to reach their journey's end? We had no way of knowing.

As the days ticked by we saw plenty of other people. The holiday hunters continued to keep their eyes peeled for any trace of tiny footprints. Their enthusiasm started to wane as the week drew on, with no additional news reports and no sightings of any little person to whet their appetites. We saw less and less of them each day. Jerry's team was another matter entirely. They were out every day, usually in pairs, to comb every inch of the local beaches and coves in meticulous detail. We managed to stay out of sight so I had hopes our own search was still hidden from Jerry. I was confident Jerry wouldn't be able to stay here with his group to keep looking indefinitely. Media interest was at a minimum because there was nothing new to report, and I expected the university would call him back soon. They couldn't commit endless resources to a hunt which yielded no results, other than the original little person who had now disappeared. Jerry was growing bolder in his methods. Only yesterday a couple of his researchers had knocked at the door to my parent's house and asked if they could look around the garden. They informed my mother of a great search for some rare species of plant that only grows near here and is threatened with extinction, and could they please look around her garden for any evidence of it. She gushed about the lovely students over dinner, and I knew at once that Jerry had sent them to check if I'd secreted the little people to her garden. He must have been aware of a time limit on the endeavour to grow so daring.

The next day we set out to re-explore a rocky section of cliff-face that had piqued Jack's interest, when I bumped into the mystery girl whose face still floated in the periphery of my mind.

I quite literally bumped into her. She was exploring the same area, and as I stepped over a rise I didn't notice her in my path until we collided. I caught her slight body in my arms instinctively, to keep her from losing her footing on the unstable surface. Fortunately Jack was in my pocket at the time and not in my hand, or I would have had a hard time explaining him away.

"Sorry," we said simultaneously. I realised my arm was still wrapped around her waist and dropped it awkwardly to my side, very aware of the lobster red blush creeping across my cheeks.

"It's Tom isn't it?" she asked.

"Yes, Tom, Tom Mitchell, I live over there," I said all in a rush, pointing in a vague direction over my shoulder that was almost certainly not where my parent's house lay. My mind turned to jelly. I struggled to put aside the thought of the flowery scent of her perfume and the gentle wave of her blonde hair to stitch a normal sentence together.

"You're here with Jerry? Another anthropologist?"

"An accountant."

"Wait, what? An accountant?"

Her face broke into the widest smile I have ever seen. I'd never known a face like hers. Most people smile with their lips, or possibly with their eyes if they are truly happy. Her whole face was involved in the task of smiling, she radiated joy.

"My brother's an anthropology student," she explained, "he said he was coming down to the beach for a project and they needed as many bodies as they could get. It sounded like a good enough excuse to see the sea." She turned to look at the ocean and I saw its endless blue reflected in her sparkling eyes.

"What's your name? If you don't me asking of course, you don't have to answer, I don't mind." I willed myself to stop talking.

The smile was back. "Amy."

Amy. I rolled the name around in my mind, it sounded as beautiful as she looked.

I was smitten.

"Accountancy, that must be interesting," I said, struggling with the niceties of small talk.

"Not the word most people would use to describe it I'm sure," she said with a laugh that reminded me of the tinkling of rain hitting a canopy of leaves in a forest.

"Oh I think it's interesting, very interesting. Have you been accounting long?"

"I only finished my degree this summer. I start work at

a firm in November, so no, I've not been accounting for anything yet," she said with another laugh that brought sunshine to an overcast and gloomy day.

I loved that laugh. It infected my very soul with mirth and brought a smile to my own lips. They hadn't had much to smile about since the night of Jerry's betrayal, and the warmth of it was enough to cast the weight of many cares from my back. It's amazing, the power of a smile.

"You don't seem quite like the picture my brother painted of you," Amy said. "To hear him and Jerry talk I expected to see you with a pitchfork and pointy tail." The laugh again, oh that laugh. In an instant I knew I'd do anything to keep her laughing. It was such an infectious sound that I joined in, despite the concern over my tarnished reputation. Anger seemed such a waste of energy all of a sudden.

"Jerry was my best friend," I said, determined to restore some credibility in her eyes, "but he's changed. He said he wanted to study the little people, to study Jack, but all he wants is to be successful and make a lot of money. I don't know what he told you or what your brother said, but I never did anything to him. I had to save my friend, that's all there is to it. You understand?"

"Honestly? No, I have no idea what you're talking about," she said with a sparkle in her eye. "But are you saying there really are little people? I honestly thought this was a wild goose chase."

"Oh no, they're real, they're definitely real, I've known plenty of them." I could feel a nagging sensation on my chest as Jack tried his best to kick me to silence through the fabric of my shirt, but I felt as though my vocal chords were overtaken by an alien presence desiring nothing more than to impress this Amy. "I wish I knew where they were now of course. I know where Jack is, but none of the others, they're all gone and it's all my fault really and I have to find them before Jerry because who knows what he'll do if he finds them first. It's all such a huge mess and

I've got to try and set it right but it's hard to know how. Sometimes I think it'd be easier to give up and run away from it all and go and travel some more, but Jack would have none of that I'm sure. We'll have to keep on looking and so will Jerry and who knows who'll find them first."

Amy stared at me in stunned silence as I continued to ramble on and on.

"You don't know where they are? Jerry was convinced you had them hidden somewhere," she said when I paused to draw breath.

"I, uh, that is to say, I mean I might know, I think they might be, somewhere," I stumbled out some words; realising too late I had revealed my lack of knowledge regarding the location of the little people to one of Jerry's own team.

"Well I'd better be off, so long Tom," she said and was climbing away over rocks before I could think of anything to say to stop her.

"What on earth is wrong with you?" Jack near shouted when I pulled him out of my pocket.

"I, I don't know, she was pretty," I finished lamely.

"Oh Tom." Jack sighed and shook his head. "There's nothing can be done about it now, we'll have to keep looking and find them first."

And look we did. For long days we searched, over rock and under rock and along tiny streambeds and around rock pools and anywhere we could think to hunt for Jack's relatives. We widened our search, traipsing further and further away from the cove, thinking the little people must have managed to travel a greater distance than we first thought. Our disappointment was dulled only by the knowledge that Jerry seemed to be having as little luck as us.

I was determined of course, but I admit it wasn't only signs of the passage of little people I found myself searching for. As each new morning dawned I hoped upon hope to see a trace of Amy. I wasn't disappointed. She appeared with startling regularity wherever we happened to be hunting. We started to while away the afternoons chatting about this and that, and Jack grew increasingly frustrated trapped in the darkness of my pocket for minutes, or even hours at a time.

"Put me down here Tom, I'll explore myself."

"Come on Jack, you know that's not safe. What if one of Jerry's people sees you? Or Jerry himself?"

"I'll go alone. You do whatever you want." The tiny Jack stalked away from me. I was too love-struck to notice his annoyance.

"I'll meet you here later then, okay?" I called after him. I think it's safe to say I wasn't exactly fighting to keep him with me that day. There were other things on my mind. As the ageing Jack hobbled off on his miniscule crutches, waving one in the air to show his acceptance of my parting comment, I noted how desperate he must be. He was marching out alone in close proximity to two of the greatest dangers he had faced in his short life: the seagull who took his mobility and the man who took his freedom. You might think those thoughts would have urged me to call out an apology, to put aside all selfish thought and help him with his tireless effort to track down his kin, but no, the stab of guilt I felt was not enough to dissuade me from my own search.

The conversations I shared with Amy over the previous few days had been wonderful. I eventually overcame my tongue-tied mouth to find out more about her. She told me about her family, how she was the middle child and always felt compelled to prove herself, even though the greatest combined accomplishment of her sisters was the day one of them became the employee of the month in the supermarket where they worked the checkout. She talked about her dream to run an accountancy firm, a small affair, designed to help business owners manage their finances so they could be free to do what they do best, without the added concern of money. She spoke of her love of fantasy tales, of having read Gulliver's Travels as a child and how that influence factored into her decision to come to Cornwall. She would talk and I would watch her animated face and think it grew more attractive with each passing day. I don't suppose you could call Amy a classical beauty, like the models airbrushed onto the covers of magazines, or the full-pouting face of Chrissie, Jerry's ex (I assume) girlfriend. I think it was the passion and the humour and the beauty of her soul reflected in her face that I fell in love with so quickly.

I felt like an addict denied the supply of my vice as I traipsed up and down the coastline and saw nothing of her. It was a sunny day but it seemed devoid of colour and life without her laugh carrying toward me on the breeze.

"What do you mean you're not doing it anymore?" I heard Jerry's voice, floating over the rocks from Jack's original cove.

"You heard me." Amy, precious Amy, I could hear the musical tones in her voice even from a distance.

"Come on woman, it's a simple enough job. Stop him searching and find out what he knows. That's what I'm paying you for. You've done it well enough up until now, what's the problem?"

I didn't hear her reply.

She wasn't anything to me. She never expressed any interest in me, why should I be surprised she was reporting back to Jerry on our conversations? That her role in this escapade was to keep me occupied? All in that instant I pictured her laughing with Jerry at night about my confiding in her that I felt I was letting my parents down, and would soon have to give up on this mission to become a responsible adult. Jerry had been my best friend for three years but somehow even his betrayal stung less keenly than this. I felt as though someone had shot an arrow through my heart. The blood was pumping so loudly in my ears that I couldn't hear anything and my vision was suffused with red. She used me. I thought we were getting to know one other but she only turned up each day to find out what I was doing and to stop me helping Jack.

Jack. Where was Jack? I had left him alone while I succumbed to the wiles of this siren and now he was alone and in danger.

In my peripheral vision I saw Amy turn to look at me as I stumbled blindly away. I think she might have called after me, but I was too angry and too hurt to hear her words.

CHAPTER TWENTY-FIVE

Was that the stone I left Jack beside? Was it there he slipped into the crack between two rocks? Or was it over there? Was I in the wrong place altogether? Anger still clouded my judgement, but it was soon overtaken by the blind panic spreading from the pit of my stomach and gripping me with its cold fury.

I couldn't remember where I had left Jack for the life of me.

Jack was too small for his cry to carry far. He would struggle to grasp my attention even if I chanced to walk a metre from his location. I doubted he could find his way back to the house. I always carried him and the world must look very different from the floor compared to the view from my pocket. Even if he were able to find the way, it was such a long journey for a little person it would surely take weeks to complete.

Not for the first time and certainly not for the last time in my life I felt a complete fool. I seemed doomed to put my trust in the wrong people.

The sun set in a glorious display that evening. Any tourists still lingering about this part of the county were treated to a light show of reds and oranges and the most vivid blues colouring the heavens. I saw it but hadn't the heart to appreciate the sight. The lengthening shadows were merging into darkness and it dawned on me that I would have to leave Jack alone in the wild to fend for himself for the night, and try to retrace my steps on the morrow. In that moment of despair something caught my eye. Not far from me was a little person, hopping from stone to stone with incredible agility.

"Jack," I cried, "am I ever glad to see you!"

He must still be angry at me, I mused, as he paid no attention to my shout.

It took me longer than I'm proud to admit to realise Jack wouldn't have been able to leap around so freely with his unusable right leg. The crutches were nowhere to be seen. My observational prowess hadn't picked up on the fact that this little person had a tatty backpack thrown across one shoulder and was, in fact, wearing a dress. As she continued her hurried journey long blonde hair, flowing almost to her waist, streamed behind her. All at once it seemed impossible that I could have mistaken this little woman for Jack.

"Wait," I shouted to her, "I don't mean you any harm."

I was close now and she revealed vivid, if tiny, bright blue eyes before vanishing from sight as completely as a drop of water spilt into the ocean.

"Hey, hey wait! Come back!" I pawed around the area where she stood only moments before but could find no evidence to suggest this mysterious little person wasn't a vision cast by the growing gloom and flickering shadows. If I hadn't known other little people I would have dismissed the encounter, but I could see cracks in between the rocks easily big enough for the disappearing act. She had taken sanctuary there and even now must be making her steady way away from me, or hiding in silence until I departed.

"Wait till I tell Jack about this," I muttered to myself and made sure to take a mental photograph of my surroundings to remember this location.

There was still the matter of finding Jack of course.

He was sensible. He was wise to the world. I was sure he would have found a hole to hide out in for the night by now. I could keep looking all night but I wouldn't find him.

I repeated those words to myself all the way home but their reassurance didn't help me sleep. My alarm clock ticked the seconds onwards and I lay staring up at the Artex ceiling, watching every mistake I have ever made play back in my mind's eye like a horror movie. I don't know what it is about the silence and stillness of the night that brings the memories of past blunders to life, but even events long since passed and put to rest can creep back into the periphery of your mind in those quiet moments. Blundered conversations with girls mingled with exam failures and the many times I had seen that disappointed look creep onto the face of my father. I tried to live up to his expectations, I really did. I finished the degree, spent months tracking down leads in the job market that would make a lot of money, but a lucrative career eluded me. Not many months ago I was convinced a good job was all I needed to make me happy. I was confident it would be the key to unlock the door to everything else, the house and the wife and the children and the stuff that would keep me content. On that muggy September night I realised how very wrong I was. I couldn't tell you precisely what I did want now, but I came to realise that people were more important than things, that friendship was more important than money in my pocket and that honesty, trust and loyalty were characteristics significantly more important than wealth. As my lead-lined eyelids drooped and shut out the world, I remember thinking of the crucial importance of giving my mother a big hug in the morning, to thank her for all of the sacrifices she made for me over the years.

"Jack!" I shouted, "Where are you?"

I spent most of the morning struggling to remember the exact route we took together the day before and I knew I must be near to where I left Jack. In hindsight, shouting about the presence of a little person all alone in the world wasn't my wisest decision, especially knowing Jerry and his team were still close by. My mind was focussed on other things, on reuniting Jack with his family and on the revelations I had mulled over until the early hours of the morning. Perhaps it was those very thoughts that heralded a turning of my fortunes, because suddenly there he was, waving his arm to draw my attention to him.

"Jack, I'm so sorry."

"Forgive me, Tom," he said at the same time and we both burst out laughing.

"There's nothing to forgive, Jack. I shouldn't have left you on your own like that to chase after a woman. I'm sorry."

"No, no it's my fault, I should have been more understanding. Who am I to stand in the way of young love?"

It was so easy to forget that this eight and a half month old man would be approaching the equivalent age of sixty. He was less than a year old and yet I was the young one.

"None of that matters now anyway, I found something amazing," I started.

"Me too," Jack said eagerly, "after I couldn't find you all day I settled in a crevice between a couple of boulders over there." He waved his arm in the direction of a tiny crack between two small stones. "Just inside I found a jacket someone must have left and some footprints too. We're getting close, I can feel it."

"Oh footprints, yes, that's a great find, much better than mine. I only saw another little person after all."

"You what?" Jack exploded. "Why did you let me go first?" I couldn't help but laugh out loud at the sight of this old little man, bedraggled from his night of sleeping rough, all but jumping up and down in his excitement.

"Tell me everything," he implored.

I scooped Jack into my hand and told him the whole story as we walked to the place I discovered the little woman.

"Don't be too hard on her, Tom, that Amy of yours," Jack said once my story was complete, "it sounds as though she changed her mind about where her loyalties lay after spending a few days with you. That's a good enough sign isn't it?"

A butterfly of hope fluttered inside my stomach. "Well, maybe, but our first priority is finding this little woman again, not Amy. She was right around here," I said and popped Jack back onto the floor to examine the ground more closely than I was able to.

Our optimism dampened after the passing of another day with no additional sign of the woman, short of a few footprints where I spotted her the previous evening. Still, we were closer than we had been for weeks now so I bolstered Jack with words of encouragement and my certainty we would find them the very next day. I was so distracted by my discourse that I barely reacted in time to shunt Jack into my pocket as the front door to home flung open in my face.

"Tom! There's somebody here to see you," my mother announced with a sparkle in her eye and a grin on her face. In a whisper she added, "You didn't tell me you'd been vanishing off to spend time with a beautiful woman."

"Amy?" I said, pushing past my mother to see her sat at our dining room table, a cup of tea in hand.

"Come on, love," my mother said and nudged her husband toward the lounge. "Let's give these two a bit of space shall we?" I had no doubt the two of them were huddled behind the closed door, jostling for position at the keyhole like children to better eavesdrop on our conversation.

"I saw you yesterday, I know you heard what I was saying to Jerry," Amy said in her singsong voice. I felt a stab of sadness that I was responsible for robbing her face of its beautiful smile.

"It's okay, it's not like we really know each..." She cut me off with a raised hand.

"Let me finish. I was working for Jerry to help look for these little people, and it's true, I did tell him what you told me, that you didn't know where they were either." She looked down at her hands as she spoke, "I'm sorry about that, but he was paying for me to be here, I thought I owed him the truth. That's when he decided I'd be better employed tailing you rather than searching. He told me to try and get you to talk more to find out what you knew, but also to see if I could stop you hunting as he figured that'd give him the better chance."

"I know all that," I said but was silenced by the spark in her eyes.

"For the first day, maybe two, that's what I thought I was doing, stopping you from looking around, but then I started to get to know you and it changed. I wasn't there to do my work; I was really looking forward to our conversations. I wanted to find you, not because I would be paid a bit of extra pocket money, but because I couldn't wait to find out more about you. You heard some of what I was saying to him but I saw you leave before I told him to screw his money and his job. Besides, I don't like the way he treated his team, like he was the king of the castle. Even if I was convinced the little people were real and stumbled into a warren full of them I'm not sure I'd tell him where they were. It's best for animals to remain free and in their natural habitat I think, not be taken away, especially if they possess intelligence, however limited it might be." I heard a faint snort from Jack in my pocket. He took Jerry's comments about the stupidity of the little people personally.

I felt a tingling sensation rush up and down my fingers and realised Amy had placed her hand on top of mine on the dining room table. "I don't expect you to forgive me

Tom, or to trust me, but please don't think too badly of me. I didn't mean any harm."

I think Amy took my silence for resentment. She slowly drew her hand away and made ready to stand. In reality I was so flummoxed by that brief contact my mind had turned to mush and I could think of nothing bar the softness of her skin.

"You don't need to worry now anyway," she said as she stood to her feet, "Jerry and his group are leaving first thing tomorrow morning."

"Wait, what? Why?"

"Didn't you hear? Some kid in Devon claimed he found a little person and posted a load of photos of him online. Everyone went mad again for a day but it turns out he did it all with perspective and the 'little man' was actually one of his school friends. Thing is, the picture looked the same quality as that interview Jerry did that started all this off, so now everyone is convinced his was a hoax too. Even the journalist who interviewed Jerry has said she must have been hoodwinked by a lifelike doll in a glass tube."

"You mean..."

"I mean it's over. The university has said he can't use their name for a wild goose chase and is insisting he bring everyone back. If your Jack truly is real then staying perfectly still that time and saying nothing has saved him. As far as everyone's concerned, Jerry played a prank on the country. It makes sense when you think about it. Who could really believe in a race of miniature humans without ironclad evidence? I'd say you're the only person now who believes it. You and Jerry anyway."

"And you? Are you leaving too?"

"That's right," she said, "I'll be out of your hair. Jerry's refused to take me back up with his group and that baby brother of mine has taken his side of course. He's loyal to a fault my brother, even though his hero was just exposed as a fraud. I'll have to take the train I suppose."

"Maybe I could take you to the station," I offered.

"No, that's okay Tom. I'll find my own way. You've a job to finish and no interruptions to worry about now." She cast a rueful smile over her shoulder as she opened the door, and then she was gone and the familiar kitchen-diner of my childhood home seemed diminished.

"Why didn't you stop her?" A tiny voice floated up from my pocket.

"It's too late. Besides, this is our best chance to find the little people. With Jerry's team gone we won't have to worry about looking over our shoulders the whole time. We know the general area at least one of them is in now, it's only a matter of time until we find them."

I put all the confidence and positivity I could muster into my words, trying to disguise the pain I felt that I would never see Amy's smile again.

CHAPTER TWENTY-SIX

The day was young when we returned to the area where I had sighted the little woman. We looked for clues once again, paying much less attention to our surroundings than had been required over the last couple of weeks. With no Jerry around we didn't worry about staying quiet or keeping Jack out of sight. We both felt optimistic and happy and were determined to find this mystery little person today.

Our positivity was not without justification, for it was around eleven o'clock in the morning when Jack saw her, or more rightly when she saw him. I was exploring on the other side of a small rise, but downwind as I was I could make out their conversation if I lay completely still.

"Who are you?" a small female voice asked.

"I'm Jack, who are you?"

"Jack? Not Jack Meadows?"

"That's right. How do you know that?"

Silence lengthened and I lifted my head very slowly to see if the two little people had moved out of earshot. In that instant several things happened.

First, the little woman pounced at Jack and started to pound him all over his body with her tiny but furious fists.

"Ow, OW," Jack cried and attempted to wrest control of the hands that bruised his skin.

Second, I looked up and saw Amy poised with her hand over her mouth watching the scene unfold before her, her eyes wide with shock at this, her first sight of the little people.

Third, I heard a familiar voice cry, "I've got you now," and saw a blur of motion as Jerry leapt towards the two tiny combatants locked in a skirmish on their stony battlefield.

They say your life flashes in front of your eyes in the moments before you leave this world, that in the mere seconds you have left to breathe and to exist and to continue to live you have the time to relive every important memory. I think that's because the mind goes into overdrive in any stressful situation. In those moments every second becomes an aeon. I was closer to Jack and his aggressor than Jerry, but I was lying on the floor and he had the element of surprise. Could I reach them first? These thoughts and more raced through my mind at the speed of a bullet train. I weighed my options. I could jump to my feet, leap over the rise and attempt to snatch the two little people into my hands. There was risk in that strategy, I could trample them in my enthusiasm or grasp them too firmly in my haste and cause injury. What's more, I would then be encumbered with full hands as an angry bull of a man charged at me. Not the best idea. I thought I could perhaps enlist Amy's help, catch her attention somehow and have her make a grab for the little people while I turned my attention to Jerry. It was a better solution, but it relied on me catching the attention of the startled accountant who was too shocked to stir. Besides, her betrayal was a recent wound to my heart, as far as I knew she might simply hand Jack and his adversary to Jerry. It seemed likely they had come here together anyway, how else would one explain their coincidental arrivals? I swallowed my frustration at the apology I now assumed to be a ruse and turned my mind back to the problem at hand. The way I saw it I had one final option: prevent Jerry from reaching my friend and his compatriot. I could try to distract him, or to trip him. Perhaps I could tackle him to the ground. I judged the latter to be the only viable idea to prevent him doing any damage. I would only have one shot.

I rose to my feet and threw all of my body weight into a lunge as Jerry drew alongside my hiding place. The two of us crashed down in a tangle of limbs on the hard and unforgiving rocks. Time resumed its normal pace and suddenly Jerry was striking out at me, trying to push me off him to reduce the advantage my elevated position offered. He was a more powerfully built man than I, more broad in the shoulder and much more suited to the sports he had played his whole life, not to mention the swimming competitions he had mastered. It must have looked quite the spectacle, me, a rake of a man, trying desperately to keep this muscled monster bound beneath me. In the periphery of my vision I could see that Jack and the woman had stopped their fight to gape at the two of us. Jack grabbed the woman by the hand and tugged her away from me and Jerry, locked as we were in our wrestling bout. Then I saw Amy move, as graceful as a swan she leapt from her lookout post, dropped to a crouch beside the two stunned little people and scooped them into her outstretched hands. My cry was strangled when Jerry took advantage of the distraction to land a knee in my stomach and steal all the wind from my lungs. He grabbed my wrist and managed to lever me off him and onto my back. I lay panting, re-evaluating the way I made decisions as pain flooded my midsection. Jerry didn't bother to restrain me but rose to his feet and stumbled to the spot where the two little people had stood only moments before.

"Where are they?" he growled at Amy who stood with her hands behind her back. "Give them to me, now." I could see her backing away, feeling carefully with her leading foot to make sure she didn't stumble and fall, thereby crushing her delicate and priceless cargo. Could it be? Was Amy on my side?

"They're not yours to take," I shouted at Jerry's retreating back, stirring my courage to take another leap toward him. My arms caught him around his waist and once again we smashed into the hard ground. I felt wetness running down my arm and thought we must have stumbled into a rock pool. Pain stung my forearm as Jerry pushed himself up against it and for a moment the world disappeared behind a fog of darkness. I could hear him clatter on, threatening Amy to hand over the little people, and I did all I could think to do. I stuck my leg out in the direction I guessed Jerry to be walking. A jolt to my leg sent my body reeling with pain but in that instant I heard Jerry fall to the floor and lay still.

Brightness gradually returned to the world as my vision started to clear. I looked at my arm in a detached sort of way and discovered the wetness I felt was blood. It continued to drip from a deep wound on my arm. The sharp stone I fell onto had created a gash as the momentum of two falling men dragged us along the rough surface. I felt queasy.

"Stay still," Amy said. I blinked at her in confusion.

"Where's Jack?" I managed to mutter.

"He's here," she said, pointing at the bag she wore draped over one shoulder, "with his friend."

"Oh." It was all I could manage to say. I felt divorced from my arm as I watched her tear my sleeve free with the help of a sharp piece of slate, and then use it to bind the jagged wound. I closed my eyes against the pain, trying with all my might not to cry out or shed a tear or expose my weakness in some other way.

I heard a groan and saw a groggy Jerry roll into a sitting position and hug his knees.

"Where are they?" he asked in a muted tone.

"They're gone," Amy said, "I let them go. You won't

find them again now."

Jerry moaned, a strangled sound of frustration and pain and anger and sadness all rolled together.

"It's over," I managed to say. We stayed in that tableau for a long time, Jerry and I on the floor, Amy standing over us, one hand on the bag both she and I knew held the prize Jerry was willing to risk so much for.

"I guess you won," Jerry said eventually, glancing in my direction. He looked tired, defeated. "I never meant to hurt anyone," he mumbled quietly, "it was only a matter of time before someone found out about this, you know that's true. I did mean to protect them, I really did. All I wanted was to understand them. It was me or someone else Tom, you know that, right?" Jerry entreated me with his eyes but his justification fell on deaf ears. As I looked across at him though, a bruise already colouring his forehead where it struck a rock during his last topple, I was surprised to feel all the anger and resentment that I held toward him fade away, replaced with pity. He had taken the chance to get to know Jack even as I had, but instead of allowing the magic of the little people to infect him and change him for the better he only saw an opportunity to better his own life, however he rationalised it in his own head. Was I so very different to him? If I had met the little people on a different day or in a different way I might have made the same decisions as him. We weren't all that dissimilar, Jerry and I. I think I finally understood Jack's concept of forgiveness. I chose to forgive Jerry in that moment, and instantly felt released to move on with my life.

Jerry finally stumbled to his feet and made his way back to the road and his long journey home. I never spoke to him again. I felt no satisfaction when I heard from a mutual friend years later that Jerry was completely discredited in his field after the events concerning the little people. As far as I know he never did achieve his doctorate. I hope he found satisfaction in another area of life, in family or in lasting friendships that were not so easily cast away to make a quick profit.

As for the rest of us, we waited for some time after Jerry had left before moving.

"You'll need to go to the hospital," Amy said eventually.

I nodded dumbly. Pain and shock had stolen my capacity for sensible thought or speech.

Slowly Amy reached into her bag and drew out Jack, clasped in a loose fist.

"I can't believe it. I knew you believed it but I couldn't make myself accept they were real, not truly, not even after seeing him in that interview. This is actually happening." Amy held Jack up before her eyes and peered intently at his lined face and grey head of hair.

"Jack?" she asked finally.

He nodded but said nothing.

With wide eyes Amy started to back away from me. "What are you doing?" I asked, finding my voice again.

"This is incredible Tom. We *do* need to share this with the world; Jerry was right about that, even if he was going about it in the wrong way. Everyone would love to hear their story, don't you think?" I recognised the way she looked at Jack now, as if he was her own private goldmine. It was a look I'd seen creep onto Jerry's face. A look I don't doubt my own face had shown when I first met John Meadows.

"No Amy. Please," I pleaded, trying to stumble to my feet to defend my friend once more.

I saw Jack place his entire hand on the tip of Amy's index finger and look up at her. She looked down into his face, a perfectly formed human face. In a clear and carrying voice Jack said, "You're better than him Amy, don't do this."

The madness trickled out of her eyes, leaving the joyful gleam that first attracted me to her.

"You are intelligent," she said.

"Yes. We have less of a tendency to state the obvious than you big people as well," Jack said with a roll of his grey eyes.

"I'm so sorry, Tom, Jack, I don't know what came over me."

"No harm done," Jack said and smiled up at her. With a gentleness that touched my heart I watched Amy place Jack on the floor and do the same with the other little person contained within her bag. I felt my eyes welling with tears of relief, tears I swiftly blamed on the gaping wound on my person.

"If you're Jack," Amy said nodding to him, "then who are you?" she asked to the other little person standing beside Jack and sending a look of pure loathing in his direction.

"I think that's something we'd all like to know," Jack replied as each of us turned to look at the delicate woman with the streaming blonde hair.

CHAPTER TWENTY-SEVEN

"I'm Sophie Lake," the little woman said in a proud and clear voice. Up close I noticed that her blonde locks were streaked with patches of white. She was younger than Jack, certainly, but by no means a child. In my limited experience I thought her to be middle aged, but it's so hard to guess with any great accuracy.

Jack, Amy and I made ourselves as comfortable as possible to hear the story of this, the only other little person we had seen in the endless search for any evidence of their kind. Amy and I sat on the stony floor and Jack and Sophie perched on a rough ledge level with our heads to make conversation as easy as possible. I found myself leaning on Amy and knew it was for more than support for the weakness I felt following the brawl with Jerry.

"I was born after you left," Sophie said, casting a disdainful look at Jack, "but I know all about you. Everyone does. You're the person who went off cavorting with the big people, leaving behind everything you knew. Funny isn't it, only a couple of generations after you leave and there are suddenly big people traipsing all over the place and ruining the life we've lived here for who knows how many lifespans. It's hardly a coincidence is it? No one here thinks so. We all know you're to blame for the mayhem we've had to live with." Sophie spoke in a high pitched and confident tone, casting daggers at Jack with her eyes as she spoke each word.

"We had to leave when the big people started stomping all over our houses, we had no choice. There was a cave-in at the old Cotton place. Their little lad was inside at the time. And that wasn't all, only a day later we found Trevor Clay on the ground with a serious head wound. He went out against all warnings to check his nets because he was hungry and the next thing we know he's being lifted off into the sky and then dropped. We're pretty sure he was taken by a big person who let him go for some reason. Maybe he bit them. When he woke up he didn't remember anything so we can't be sure.

"The Elders came knocking on everyone's doors that night and said to gather in the meeting hall. We snuck out in ones and twos until we were all there. Even the youngsters were brought along, yawning but happy enough to be up after hours. They didn't understand what was going on, even if they did pick up on some of the worry the adults were feeling. The Elders said we needed to move from our homes, that we'd come back to this place soon but it was important we get out of the way for a bit. We discussed it back and forth for hours through the night, but in the end everyone was in agreement. It's happened before, this extra foot traffic of the big folk. The Elders say so. They said it normally lasts a few days and then quietens down again so we'd be back at home before you know it. They said we needed to take everything from the houses, in case some big person stumbled on them and then came looking for the people that lived in them. That very night, tired though we were, we went back to our homes and started moving out our furnishings and possessions in the dark. The Elders said to bring one bag each and to put the bigger bits into hiding. Did you know there was a big cave close-by for that very purpose?" Jack shook his head. "Neither did I, but there is. It's a squeeze to get in with chairs and beds but it's possible. You go through a gap in a crag and down a little passage and there's a wide open place under cover from rocks. That's where most of our things are. We took only a little with us, thinking we wouldn't be out of our homes for long.

"Well that was days, weeks ago now. We weren't equipped for such a long time out and about, but the scouts the Elders sent out said there were still too many big people abroad for us to risk a return. They wouldn't even send anyone out to forage for food, they said it was too risky. We've been hiding in caverns with hardly a bite between us. Some of the young'uns and older folks are looking worse for wear now. I snuck out without the Elders knowing to find some kind of food for those most in need of it. That must have been when you saw me," she said, nodding in my direction, "I was bringing back a few bits I'd found. Enough to keep us alive at least.

"It's not been easy, that's for sure. I'll bring you back with me if you like Jack, but I should warn you there won't be a warm welcome. I'm not the only one that thinks the Meadows' buddying up with a big person brought this on us."

Jack shook his head in wonder. "You shouldn't have been out here on your own, it's far too dangerous." Sophie stuck her chin out and jumped to her feet, planting them into the stone and looking as though she was ready to go another ten rounds with Jack.

"What do you know about danger? You with your great protector. I'd do anything to help our people. Anything." Sophie spat the words at Jack as if they were arrows and I saw a flush creep across Jack's face. His sentiments echoed hers now, but for most of his days he'd been less concerned at the fate of his people. "Besides, if I didn't bring food back we'd only die in those caves anyway. I might as well risk a quick death out here rather than sit and suffer a slow one." She folded her arms across her chest and positively scowled at Jack. As much as I wanted to rush to his defence I wasn't sure it would do much good.

"Is it really as bad as that?" Jack asked quietly. Sophie's proud stance deflated like a balloon and she sank to sit on the floor again.

"Yes. We'll die if we stay there. All of us. But where are we to go? With so many big people around we'll die if we leave as well. Not everyone can hide as well as me." Some of her earlier pride coloured her tone again. "But what about you? Tell me your tale."

Jack spent a great deal of time relaying our adventures. I expected him to skirt over the details when it came to us being the reason for the invasion that had so disrupted the lives of the little people, but he told the story with complete honesty. Jack didn't try to put the blame on Jerry or on myself, but stated the facts and left Sophie to make her mind up. She was less angry after hearing the full explanation and nodded with a contented smile when she heard that Jerry and his researchers were gone.

"That means we can go home," Sophie said.

"We can go home, but there isn't much of a home to go to," Jack replied.

"Show me."

Amy helped me to my feet and wrapped my good arm around her shoulder. I've never felt so happy to feel such pain.

We each carried a little person. Jack rode in my pocket and Sophie in Amy's hand. As we clambered over the final obstacles that separated us from the cove I heard Sophie cry aloud, and was devastated to see tiny tears leaving trails on her face. They seemed out of place on someone so bold and brave. I don't think a single house escaped the ransacking of Jerry's team. The devastation was worse than I'd imagined. Jerry must have ordered his people back to methodically tear through the homes of the little people, in case he missed anything. Roofs were torn clear from structures and solid rocks chipped and hammered into until rooms were exposed to sunlight and rain. It would take an incredible amount of effort to restore this place to a habitable state. It might be impossible to do so without removing the natural look that had shielded the little people from unwanted attention. Jack told me once that the little people had lived here for nigh uncountable years, with families taking existing cave structures and making them into homes for their families. They had expanded of course, over the years, but the heart of this network of homes remained unchanged from the days when the little people pioneers had first found it. This place with its happy homes was all Sophie Lake had ever known. To see it despoiled must have broken her tiny heart.

"I need to tell the Elders of this," she said in a voice made firm by willpower alone.

Jack nodded and the four of us returned to the scene of the fight. On the way back we decided that Amy would take me to the hospital while Sophie would take Jack with her to the temporary shelter of the little people to discuss the situation regarding their former homes.

As to what would come next for the little people, none of us knew.

Amy and I had plenty of time to talk on our long drive to the hospital, and during my long wait to be seen. Amy explained she had intended to find a way to the closest train station first thing in the morning, but decided to take one last stroll by the ocean.

"I've never lived so close to the sea," she explained, "but I love it. I can't think of anything as relaxing as the sound of wave after wave crashing into the rocks."

She also mentioned her hope to catch another glimpse of me. There was enough blood left in me to flood my cheeks with warmth.

I still bear the scar of that day's exploits but I don't mind the mar on my arm's flesh. It reminds me of the day when Jack reconnected with the little people and a day when I was able to really get to know Amy Anderton. She even held my hand as the doctor stitched me back together.

"What will you do now?" I asked her on the journey back to my parent's house.

"If I'm honest I would love to see how this plays out. I don't need to be anywhere until November, but it was Jerry paying for everything and I can't really afford to stay in a hotel until then. I guess I'll have to go home to my parents in Bristol for a while, until the start date at my new firm."

"Why don't you stay here with me? That is to say, I mean, stay here with my parents and me, in our house. We have a spare room, my sister's old room. I'm sure they wouldn't mind."

"I couldn't impose like that Tom, not after everything I've done."

"I insist," I said, and that was that. We settled into a contented silence and I watched her face glowing with the orange of passing streetlights as the miles drifted by. Amy looked nervous as she pulled my old Volkswagen onto the drive, but after my mother welcomed her with an enveloping hug and a well-stacked plate of food she was soon smiling and laughing as if she'd lived in the Mitchell home all her life. I ignored the sly glances my parents passed between them; they seemed to think this a good match. Secretly I agreed, but I could hardly profess my undying affection so soon after making Amy's acquaintance. I was sure there were rules about such things.

We were so late back from the hospital I knew it was useless looking for Jack again that evening. We would have to catch up with him the next day. I hoped the little people hadn't been too hard on him, and that he had found somewhere comfortable to lay his head.

For myself, I had my first uninterrupted night's sleep for weeks. Perhaps it was the pain and exertion of the day that drained me of all energy, or perhaps it was something to do with who lay sleeping in the room next door. Whatever the reason, I slept soundly and contentedly with a feeling that it was all over at last. We had defeated Jerry, returned Jack and he had found his people. Granted, they would need to find somewhere else to live or a way to repair their old town, but I was sure they would be able to handle that. They were a resourceful bunch, the little people. Our adventure had surely reached its happily ever after.

Or so I thought.

CHAPTER TWENTY-EIGHT

"The conditions they're living in are awful, Tom. They're not sustainable, not even for the short term. We need to find them somewhere else to go," Jack told me. He spent over an hour explaining everything he had seen and all that he had found out about the plight of the little people. They were living in cold and damp caves, fine for what they assumed would be a night or two but not for the lingering stay they were forced to make. The little people were hardly ever ill, I had never known Jack to suffer from a cold or a stomach bug; he was the epitome of health. In the conditions his kin were forced to endure now some were actually coming down with diseases, and that worried Jack more than anything else. One elderly woman met her end five days before her allotted time. It hadn't been the gradual and dignified slip into a peaceful and eternal rest, it was a drawn out and painful affair with a racking cough tearing through her fragile frame until her energy gave out.

"The Elders do nothing. They won't even listen to us. They refuse to believe the big people are really gone so they won't let anyone outside at all, not even to gather food. They're so scared of being hurt outside the cave that they're willing to let everyone inside starve to death!

Sophie was right about that. She's the only person who has brought in any sort of sustenance over the last few days, other than the supplies they had with them and those are all but used up, even with the Elders rationing everything. Someone's going to have to take charge. I don't think it'll be difficult, the people are frustrated and they can't bear the thought of more people getting ill."

"You need a mayor," Amy chipped in.

"A mayor? What's a mayor?" Jack asked.

"A mayor is an elected officer, someone voted in by the public to help with the running of a town or a city. They're mostly figureheads in this country nowadays, but once upon a time they carried out a vital function. They'd have a team of advisors of course, but they would have the final say when it came down to important decisions."

"And how would one become a mayor?" Jack asked.

"Well, one would have to suggest the idea of a mayoral government to the populace at large and then put one's name down as a candidate," Amy said. "You would have to open the floor to other nominations in case anyone else wanted to run for the position, and then take a vote to discover the victor. It'd be worth suggesting a term of office to go with the role, I'd normally recommend a year but a lifespan might be a bit much. Perhaps a month?"

"A month, that's a long time for such a lot of responsibility."

"I think you would struggle to achieve much in less than a month," I chipped in. "I can't see it working with a shorter duration."

"You're probably right," said Jack, "I'll see if I can get some support for the idea this afternoon. I'm sure I can get Sophie in on it." Was I imagining the faint flush that painted his cheeks when he mentioned her name? "There are a lot of discontented people in those caves; I think they'd be happy to back someone ready to take a decisive lead to get things up and running again."

"And you think you're the right person for the post?" I

asked Jack.

"I don't know. There are a lot of faces I don't know in the community now, but something has to be done and if I can help then I want to. We've had a great adventure Tom, now it's time to knuckle down and achieve something."

"You're right. You're absolutely right. You go and start your campaign, I'll be back later." I turned and ran from the scene to the amazement of Jack and Amy. Jack was spot on with his thoughts. A man needed a mission in life. I was happy to help the little people find new homes if I could, but more than that I needed a new purpose of my own. I couldn't continue to while away all the rest of the days of my life.

"Mum, Dad," I said as I opened the door to the family bakery, "I want a job."

"What do you mean you want a job?" my father asked. "Manning the shop?"

"No, I don't want to come here to make some money and then go home, I want you to teach me the trade, Dad. I want to learn everything you know and one day I want to take over Crumbs and run it myself."

The silence was broken by an almighty clatter as my mother dropped a stack of newly washed baking trays and ran to wrap her arms around me. "That's fantastic," she said, "you'll make a fantastic baker, you always did have a knack for it. We won't be able to pay you too much to start with, but we'll manage, we'll manage."

My father took my hand and shook it with his familiar firm grasp. I heard him mutter something about wasted money on an education I'd never need, but the smile on his face was genuine and proud. "We'll start now shall we?" he asked and led me into the kitchen I'd so often helped in as a child. "The breads are all baked for today but I've an order for a cake. We'll start there." With that he was pulling ingredients from shelves and thrusting them into my waiting hands. By the end of the day I was exhausted and my hair was whitened by the flour I managed to dust the entire room with, but I was happy and I felt more fulfilled than I had for a long time, perhaps ever. My father even granted me an offhand compliment about the buttercream icing I put together from his recipe, "You're a natural, son," he said and my heart soared with pride, dulling the ache from the stitched wound in my arm that I was trying my best to ignore. It surprised me how much I remembered of the skills I picked up as a child, and I started to think this might not be a crazy idea after all. I ought to have let Amy know where I ran off to but I knew she would understand. When I hadn't turned up at the cove after another hour she returned to my parent's home and, finding my mother struggling over the books for the business, put her own talents to use creating a spreadsheet that would make the task much easier at the end of each month.

"That's right," Amy was saying as I walked through the front door, "you put the takings for the day in this box here."

"Like that?"

"Just like that, yep, then press enter and you see? The figure at the bottom has updated and that's your profit for the week. It's automatically taken off the expenses you put in earlier."

"That's incredible." My mother was awed by the wizardry of computers and the expertise of her house guest.

"Amy, I'm sorry I vanished," I said as I rushed through the door.

"It's okay, Mary explained where you'd gone," she said with a smile for my mother who quickly bustled out of the room.

"Any update from Jack?" I asked in a low voice.

Amy shook her head no, "He left to put some feelers out to some of the younger little people about a mayoral system to cover the duration of the emergency, but we won't find out how that went until tomorrow. You'll be busier now I know, but we're going to have to do something to help find them a new home. You heard what Jack said, they can't stay where they are."

"I've been thinking about that but I'm drawing a blank on places they could go. We could explore up and down the coast and never find as secluded a spot as the one they were in, but rebuilding that place would be a huge effort. I'm not sure it's even possible."

"What about private land? Could we find them somewhere the general public couldn't get to?" Amy suggested.

"Maybe, but that'd mean getting more people involved, and finding someone to invest and buy the land. I don't know, that seems like a more difficult idea to me."

"Well we have to do something. I feel so responsible for how they're living now. I should never have gone along with Jerry."

"He'd only have brought someone else if you hadn't, and if it wasn't for you he might have Jack and Sophie now. But I know what you mean, I feel responsible too. I thought this would be the end of it. Bring Jack back, protect him and his friends from Jerry and then leave them to it, pop round for a Sunday roast now and then. But I agree, we can't leave them the way they are now. I wish I could think of some way to help."

"Me too."

We sat around the dining room table racking our brains for a solution that wouldn't come.

The following afternoon we discovered Jack hadn't had much luck either. The little people weren't ones to hold grudges and once Jack explained the full tale they were happy enough to put it behind them, like Sophie. They might forgive easily but like the elephant, they never forget. They were perfectly happy to accept Jack back into the fold, but to listen to him and elect him their leader? That was another level altogether. Jack felt that many of the younger people, some only recently come of age, would be willing to throw their support behind the well travelled and world-wise Jack, but the Elders held a lot of sway and they weren't budging.

"They won't believe their old homes are gone, they think I'm making it up to try and get the little people to take part in some grand exodus or something," Jack said to me and Amy in exasperation. Sophie was with him today and she looked just as frustrated.

"The Elders are so worried about what'll happen if we're seen that they're happy to let us waste away in those cursed caves. They're scared of their own shadows, that's what it is," Sophie ranted.

"I don't know how we can persuade the general populace to accept your idea Jack, but as to the first part surely we can let the Elders see their old homes for themselves. It'd take them a day or more to get there, but we could take them in a few minutes." It was Amy who made the suggestion and Jack and Sophie were keen to try it. They weren't able to persuade all the Elders to come along, but three of the seven leaders consented to being carried to their former homes, under cover of darkness. So it was that late at night on the nineteenth of September Amy and I found ourselves meeting three Elders in an oddly formal ceremony. They insisted on making our acquaintance before being carried, and solemnly shook our fingertips with both of their hands. Including Jack and Sophie, we were to be burdened with five little people, too many to carry in hands which would be needed for crossing the rocky coves in the gloom of night. We took inspiration from Amy's quick thinking when she hid Jack and Amy in her shoulder bag, and padded the bottom of it with scraps of fabric to make it as comfortable as possible. Amy gently passed the little people down into the dark confines of the bag, carefully placing them beside one another. I held the torch as we walked and she concentrated on jolting the bag as little as possible as we clambered toward the site of their home. Despite her care five dishevelled looking little people stood in a group once we had arrived and freed them to look around.

"No," an Elder woman said and fell to her knees at the horror of the scene before her. I pitied her. Her life's work as an Elder was to protect this place and now there was nothing left.

The reaction reminded me of newscasts of natural disasters where residents would escape with their lives, but return later to find their houses flattened by tornado or consumed by wildfire. In those situations you could shake your fist at the sky and mutter at the incredible force of nature we humans think ourselves so impervious to. In this instance I could blame no one but myself. I flicked the first domino that started the chain which knocked these houses down. As I watched Jack show a pair of Elders around the devastation I couldn't entirely regret my actions, the best friendship I had ever known came from them, yet it was with sadness and gnawed again by guilt that I surveyed the scene. It looked worse in the moonlight, particularly as the retreating ocean had dragged away much of the rubble leaving the site looking bare and utterly ravaged.

Amy knelt low beside the stricken Elder and spoke to her with soothing words and Jack vanished from sight with the other two Elders, no doubt continuing to explore the ruins.

I felt a sudden clarity of thought in my moment of solitude, as I watched the moonlight dance on the distant ocean and felt the stillness of the night as something almost tangible.

I had the answer. I knew how I could help the little people.

But it wouldn't be easy.

CHAPTER TWENTY-NINE

"Okay, here's my proposal." My parents exchanged amused glances at my serious tone; it was out of character for me. To get to this point I had worked nonstop for several days, relearning my new trade in the mornings and spending the afternoons with Amy, putting together the details of our plan. Jack was hard at work too; the newly elected mayor of the little people was working out the finer points of our great endeavour from his side. Jack won the hand-count election by a landslide after the Elders saw the devastation of their homes and gave him their backing. Despite Jack's age and the limitation of his mobility which the little people weren't altogether accepting of, they knew decisive action was required. I don't think it harmed his campaign having a couple of big people on hand to help, the more astute members of the community realised this could be a factor in their improving fortunes. We had already made their lives more comfortable by providing a ready supply of food and transferring some of the furniture and goods previously locked away in the cavern close to their old homes. The little people love tradition and values handed down through the generations, but when a change is truly necessary they affect it with a speed that left me stunned. When you only have three hundred and sixty-five days to call your own each moment is precious, and it helps to make speedy resolutions.

My mother and father held back the laughter that danced behind their eyes as I passed them the handouts Amy and I had prepared so diligently.

"The first document you'll see in your pack relates to the bakery. Amy and I have put our heads together and we think some extra marketing and exploring of other avenues for sales, such as online retail, could really increase the profit margin of Crumbs. I know you've lost a lot of business to other bakeries and to supermarkets, but Dad, what is it people do keep coming back for?"

"I suppose that'd be the cakes," my father replied thoughtfully.

"The cakes! Your cakes are so popular around here that we think we could expand sales further afield around Cornwall, and even to a wider audience than that by posting them out as people order on your website. We could offer an easy customisation service where a paying customer fills in one form with what they want written on the cake, along with any thoughts on shape, colour and so on. No one likes making phone calls anymore, so we make it as easy as possible to do it online. You'll get a lot more orders. And we could post other things too, genuine Cornish pasties, boxes of cupcakes, even your special recipe fudge Mum."

"But Tom," my mother chipped in, "we don't even have a website."

"That and it seems like a lot of extra work, I don't know if we have the expertise or the time for all of this," my father began but I cut him off.

"It will be a lot of work, but remember I'm on board now so I'll be managing this side of things. We need to make things more profitable, I've seen the books. I know you'll struggle to pay me a full-time salary if we don't, you'll struggle to even stay afloat for long. And hey, I need some money if I'm going to get my own place.

"That leads me nicely to document number two. On the top of the page there you will see a photograph of the other cottage you own. If I'm correct in my assessment of the situation you put it on the market not long after I left but haven't been able to sell it, most likely because it's not in the best condition, am I right?" My parents nodded dumbly. "I propose that you let the property out to me. In exchange for slightly less rent I'll be willing to do the decorating and renovation that's needed, with Dad's help for some of the bigger structural jobs of course. It's habitable as it is so I could move in straight away and work on it in any free time I have. I was thinking I could move in this weekend."

"Tom, that's only a day away. You can't be serious!"

"I am serious, Mum. Document number two shows the projected increase in worth that a few simple jobs around the house could do. Amy and I have calculated the value against the estimated time it would take to complete the updates, and subtracted it pro-rata from the average monthly rent that a property like this one can hope to make in today's market."

I always thought the expression regarding a jaw hitting the floor was a figure of speech, but I saw some truth in it on the day I explained my proposals to my parents. Their mouths fell open at the sight of their son so organised and so carefully planning for his future. In truth, the majority of the carefully rehearsed words I wowed them with were Amy's. She was much better at this sort of thing than me.

"The plan for the future would involve me buying the property from you, once it's all done up and I have a bit of money under my belt from bringing in extra income to Crumbs. That would be the best solution for everyone; I would be on the property market and you would have a nice nest egg to retire on whenever you fancied it."

We talked back and forth over the details as the ticking of the kitchen clock counted the evening away, but eventually my parents were satisfied I had considered every argument and outcome. Amy was a silent witness to the talks, but she beamed with gratitude when my mother insisted she continue to stay with them rather than live in a building site. I expect my canny parents were also keen to reduce the unspoken temptation as well; no son of my mother's would be caught living with a woman outside of wedlock, even if the relationship was purely platonic.

As to that, I wasn't entirely sure how platonic our relationship was.

Amy and I had grown closer throughout this experience and during our collaborative work on Phase One of the plan, Parental Buy-In, but the romance I secretly yearned for hadn't blossomed. There was the occasional brush of skin as I picked up a document and caught her hand or a gentle touch when I moved past her crossing a room. Once I thought she intentionally leant her knee against mine, causing my heart to thud so loudly I was sure she'd be able to hear it. I found myself falling asleep thinking of her smile more and more each night, and more and more each morning I counted down the moments until I could see her again. There was a smile she reserved for me in the mornings, a wide grin that brightened her face even more than her usual happy countenance.

I took it to mean there was a chance my feelings were reciprocated but the thought of broaching that conversation terrified me. What if I was wrong? There was more to it than my racing heart as well. Each time I searched for an opportunity to discuss such topics I felt a hesitation like a physical barrier placed between us. She had thrown herself into action on behalf of the little people, but deep down inside I wondered if I could genuinely trust her. Her initial reaction to the little people, it had reminded me so forcefully of Jerry that I couldn't help but fear she would vanish one day, along with Jack and the other little people.

I wasn't the only one doing battle with affairs of the heart. As I returned from the bakery one afternoon I spotted Amy deep in conversation with little Sophie Lake. They hadn't seen me, approaching as I was from behind, and so I heard some of their chatter as I drew quietly closer.

"He thinks he's too old for me, that's the problem. He says he's beyond all that and that he chose his path when he went off to travel the world. I don't care about his age, I wish he'd see that," Sophie said, pacing up and down in frustration. Emotions ran so highly in her that it seemed she had to expel the excess energy through motion. I can't remember ever seeing her sit still.

"It's nonsense anyway. It's obvious he likes you. Besides you're what? Three months younger than him? That's nothing," Amy replied.

Nothing to us perhaps, but three months to a little person? That was a significant age difference. Now that I thought about it, it was unusual that Sophie wasn't already married with children. The little people tended to pair up at a relatively young age.

"Why don't I get Tom to have a word with him? Maybe they can help each other to see sense," Amy said with a sigh that sounded wistful to my inexperienced ear.

I decided to feign ignorance regarding the knowledge gained from my eavesdropping and made a show of huffing and puffing as I approached so they would hear me coming.

"Hi Tom," Sophie said in her tiny voice, "Jack's not here yet. He said to tell you he'd probably be late. He was meeting with the Elders to talk through some problems, like the rain that came through the crack last night and soaked everyone's dry clothes. He said not to worry though because he's still making time for Phase Two."

"How is Phase Two going?" I asked.

"It's helping a lot having Amy take a couple of people at a time over to see the old town. You can be told a hundred times that it doesn't exist anymore, but seeing it really opens up the eyes. I think once everyone, or the majority at least, have seen it they'll all be ready to move on. No one's thinking we can stay where we are at any rate and no one knows of any other place to go, so the more Jack suggests the idea the more people are going for it. The young'uns are downright excited to see a new place and settle in there, something that has the older folks frowning. I think they worry your influence will have them all running off to explore and leave their people behind, no matter how much Jack tells them that's not the case."

"He'll have a while longer to persuade them, Phase Three will take time and that can be run together with Phase Two," I said.

"I know Tom, we all know the plan," Sophie replied with arms folded across her chest, as though she were addressing a child. I suppose in some respects that's what I was to her; she'd be almost double the equivalent of my own age. "When will Phase Three start?"

"Tomorrow hopefully," Amy answered for me, "that's when Tom will have access to the new site and then we can start looking around at what needs doing."

"I've got that list for you Tom," Jack said, he arrived while we were talking, making his way slowly across the rocks. Jack was a man full of energy still, but I noticed he was more cautious than he used to be manoeuvring around on his crutches. A fall at his age would be more hazardous than a similar mishap in the days of his youth. Jack's disability continued to cause concern amongst the little people. It astounded me that a people so forgiving and good natured could be so intolerant of those incapacitated by anything other than old age. It explained why John Meadows had struggled to find the words to tell his son he still loved him, when everyone in his world classed Jack as broken beyond repair. "Here are the names of all the people I think would be good to scout the new site. They've all an eye for construction, having worked to make our current cave a bit more homely, so I think they're the best men for the job. They're sympathetic to our aims with the new site as well." Jack handed me a miniscule piece of paper bearing names I would only be able to read through a magnifying glass.

"Thanks. Sophie says Phase Two is going well?"

"Well enough. Persuading the People," Jack grinned as he spoke, "you definitely gave me the hardest phase to manage."

"Oh I don't know about that, there will be plenty more difficulties to come yet. We've not even started on the plan for moving everyone to the new site," Amy chipped in.

"Such a positive bunch you are," Sophie muttered, taking the sting from her criticism with a smile.

We whiled away an hour, the four of us together, and enjoyed a break from our responsibilities before Sophie and Jack returned to the temporary residence of the little people.

"I know you heard us speaking," Amy said. Nothing slipped by her. "You should talk to Jack for Sophie, they would make such a good couple and Sophie really doesn't care how old Jack is. She doesn't want anyone else even if they might be closer to her own age."

"I agree," I said, pausing Amy in mid-speech, "but he'll be hard to convince. He knew what it was like to have parents who would get to their end before his coming of age. I don't think he wants to inflict that possibility on any kids they might have."

"Their end?"

"When they die, the little people call it their end. Jack's end will be on the twenty-fourth of December so they would have to have children right away for him to see them come of age." Amy stared at me, wearing an expression of horror.

"How can you say that?"

"Say what?" I was confused.

"That Jack will die on Christmas Eve. How can you

just come out with that? Doesn't it bother you?"

"Of course it bothers me! But it's a fact of life, of their lives. That's the end of his lifespan and there's nothing I can do to change that. We all know it. He's fine with it, why shouldn't I be?"

Amy struggled to grasp a concept that had taken me nine months to master. We talked of other things for a time but her usual smile was distant. Perhaps she was coming to the realisation I had considered since hatching our five-phase plan; if we were to complete it before Jack's lifespan came to an end we were working to a tight timescale.

There is a world of difference between holding a piece of information in your mind and genuinely accepting what that information means. Amy was aware the little people live for just one year from her first meeting with them, but it was only now that she was starting to understand what that implied. Her budding friendship with Sophie would come to a close sooner than most human relationships would take to build, and we had less than four months to spur the little people to action and have them settled if Jack were to see his legacy come to life. It is a hard task, acknowledging that life isn't eternal, and that we each have a limited time to live it.

Those were big thoughts for a leisurely Saturday afternoon.

- PART FOUR -

REBUILDING

CHAPTER THIRTY

This seems as good a time as any to let you in on the details of our little plan. In all honesty, I never considered my parents' rental property as somewhere I wanted to live, primarily because I didn't expect to return to the area after my university days. Now it seemed the perfect solution. It was a quaint little cottage, all white with small windows and a tiled roof and climbing rose covering one side of the building and plastering it with colour in the summer months. It stood nestled onto the edge of a cliff and boasted beautiful views of the ever-changing ocean far below. My parents purchased it when I was young and house prices were more reasonable. It was a shrewd investment on their part. The rental income provided a boost to the money brought in by my Dad's famous sponge cakes. The house featured three small bedrooms, a living room and a kitchen-diner with beautiful old fittings that, with a bit of love and paintwork, could soon look pristine again.

The biggest boon of this little cottage in terms of our plan however, was its location.

It was set on the outskirts of the village in which my parents lived, on its own plot of land. The garden wasn't enormous, but should you walk out of the kitchen and onto the patio, past the small fishpond and an area laid to lawn, beyond the tool shed and the plum tree, you would come to a small gap in the hedge through which a secret garden could be found. It wasn't a practical space, sloping quite steeply as it did toward the cliff edge. I imagined that was why it had been sectioned off, but to my mind it was the best part of the land. Not much would grow there, exposed as it was to the fierce winds of winter travelling across the ocean and bearing a hint of snow and ice from the north. It was also composed primarily of bare rock, but it had a lovely view of the seaside and, most importantly, was secluded enough that no passersby would be able to sneak a peek at the wonders to be contained within. It was this more than anything, which made me think of the property not simply as a home for myself, but as a home for the little people.

I explained my thoughts to Amy with excitement and while she agreed that it couldn't be a more perfect plot, she soon spotted many holes in my feeble plan.

"Come on Tom," she said with exasperation, "you can't expect things to happen by magic, haven't you ever heard of setting goals? We need to break this idea down into manageable and attainable chunks that we can divide between us. That way we stand a chance of making it happen."

I agreed emphatically, primarily because I loved to see the passion on her face as she gathered paper and pens toward her with the force of a whirlwind, and started to sketch a multi-coloured diagram highlighting the many considerations we would need to address. I was more focussed on her delicate fingers pointing out the red-marked challenges adorning pieces of paper than on the writing itself, but I covered my distraction well. Eventually we whittled the notes down to a concise five-phase plan:

Phase One – Parental Buy-In.

Phase Two – Persuading the People.

Phase Three – Setting up the Site.

Phase Four – Making the Move.

Phase Five – Creating Home.

For each phase Amy created a wad of paper stuffed into a plastic wallet, detailing ideas, potential pitfalls and the required involvement of the little people. To this day I don't think I have ever met a more organised person. For my part I couldn't wait to introduce Jack to a new home and to assure him that the little people would be safe for countless generations to come. For Amy, the formulation of the plan itself kept her going, though I know she also harboured a sense of satisfaction at the thought of settling this miniature race into a happy home.

Phase One passed without a snag, with my (Amy's) carefully calculated presentation persuading my parents I was more than responsible enough to take on the management of a property.

It boded well that our plan started so successfully. We had set ourselves a hard task, but a structured plan and months to complete it in smoothed away the lines of worry from our foreheads.

Many of the little people were still reluctant to move to a new site, several miles away from their old homes. It would be a move that would take them away from the close proximity to the ocean, and they concerned themselves with details I had not even thought to consider, such as how to provide food and materials for crafting their wares without the ever versatile seaweed on their doorstep. The coming of age ceremony was another headache; how it could continue so far from a beach was a topic thrown about in discussions of the Elders and the wider populace. By this point they at least acknowledged that moving was a requirement for their continued existence, but many voiced their desire to find somewhere closer, somewhere more familiar. Jack met such resistance on this front that we spent an afternoon walking up and down along the coast, Amy and Sophie in one direction and Jack and I in another to cover more ground and try to spot potential resettling sites. We found nothing. Every likely location suffered from too much footfall from passing locals or tourists, or an environment unsuited to the little people if they wished to live out their short lives free from the fear of being drowned by a particularly high tide or discovered by an adventurous child.

Amy and I left that problem to Jack and Sophie. Jack would work on the Elders while Sophie dropped hints in her conversations with the people about the beauty and wonder of their new promised land. The pair saw gradual success but I held doubts in my heart as to whether all of the little people would want to leave when their new houses were ready.

I was forced to put those misgivings to one side, because we had enough to worry about in the pile of unanswered questions surrounding the remaining three phases of the plan. We would need enough space to house the current population of two hundred and thirty-six little people, divided as they were into sixty-two families. Somehow we needed to construct or excavate a minimum of sixty-two dwelling places in the back garden of my new house, all without attracting any undue attention. We hoped to house a few building crews of little people on the new site as the work progressed, but we were reluctant to disturb the community at large until the new village was at least partially constructed. As yet we hadn't even started to address the dilemma of how best to move a group of two hundred and thirty-six little people several miles from their current location.

One problem at a time I reasoned.

Crumbs was closed on Sundays, giving me a full day free from other responsibilities to transport all of my possessions, accumulated within twenty-two years. The cottage was furnished in a very floral fashion, not exactly to my taste, but at least it provided me somewhere to sit and sleep amidst the boxes containing my world. My parents offered to help of course, but I insisted this was something I needed to do myself. They nodded sagely. In reality Jack was in my pocket and I was desperate to show him the secret section of garden that would be his home.

So eager was I to introduce it to him that I inconsiderately left Amy to carry the bulk of my things into the new house as I ran to the garden. At first I paced around the site with Jack on my outstretched hand, and then I placed him down to pace it for himself. I followed behind, stooping to hear him mutter about the houses he could erect here and the meeting place that would fit perfectly there. He poked his nose into the cracks between rocks and seemed satisfied that what plant life was growing on this cliff edge would be a good start to sustain the little people. I watched as he used a small piece of stone to sketch an area for a large pond we could populate with plants and small fish. I marvelled to watch my friend create a village with his imagination, and rushed inside to find paper and pen to record his ideas. By the time the exhausted Amy dropped to the floor to sit beside me we had sketched a plan for a beautiful town filled with plentiful housing, planted walkways and common areas where the little people could meet. Jack even insisted we explore the farthest reaches of the site, where the cliff sloped dangerously and I could barely pick a way down without breaking my neck. His idea to bring bucket loads of shells to sprinkle around the area would make this a challenging coming of age climb.

Any residual anger burning in Amy's eyes at being left to unpack someone else's house diminished as she regarded our plans.

"Oh Jack, it's marvellous," she exclaimed, and began to add her own suggestions for improvements to the layout of the village.

"I hate to be the one to cast a pall on all of this," I said as the evening shadows lengthened, "but how are we going to build all of these houses? This will take months, if not years to finish and we only have a couple of months until, until Christmas time." I couldn't bring myself to say it aloud. Until Jack's end. Until Jack's death. It sounded too final, and altogether too close.

"We'll think about that tomorrow," Amy said, ever the voice of reason. "For now it's time for me to head back to your parent's house and for you to get settled in. Do you need a ride home Jack?"

"No, thanks Amy, I'll stay here tonight I think."

She left us to it. We sat in the burgeoning twilight and watched the stars wink into life, candles set afire by some unseen match on a tapestry of black. I struggled to find the words to broach the conversation Amy had requested I start. In all our travels discussions about the opposite sex and relationships had been vague and general, nothing like this.

Before I could decide how to phrase my opening gambit, Jack said, "I'm going to ask Sophie to be my companion, Tom."

"Your companion?"

"My wife, you'd say," Jack replied.

"Wow, okay, are you sure?"

"I'm sure."

"And she feels the same way? She wants to be your companion?"

Jack shrugged, "I think so."

"Well, great," I said, feeling proud of myself for managing what had promised to be an awkward conversation so successfully.

"I'll suggest Friday."

"You'll ask her on Friday you mean?"

"No, I'll ask her tomorrow, I'll suggest Friday for the companionship ceremony."

"Whoa, whoa, wait a minute. Isn't that moving a bit quickly?" It was easy to forget that five days was the rough equivalent of a year to the little people.

Jack looked at me in confusion.

"I guess not," I said and stared at the stars, trying hard to turn my thoughts to Jack and Sophie's upcoming nuptials, rather than the way I wished I could find the courage to ask Amy a similar question. Jack made it seem so simple. Perhaps knowing your time on earth is limited is the key to open the door to acts of courage trapped behind locks of fear.

CHAPTER THIRTY-ONE

It was a beautiful ceremony.

My parents kindly offered me some time off to settle into the new house which left me free to enjoy the full day. The secret section of garden was a mess of a building site already, but Jack insisted he and Sophie become companions there, in the place that would be the future home of the little people. He genuinely believed in those words, but he also took it as a wonderful opportunity to show off the site and convince the stragglers how perfect a location it would be to live in. Amy and I were left with the logistical nightmare of transporting more than a hundred little people from their current cave to the new house. Amy was busy with Sophie making the garden look as pretty as could be, so it fell to me to be the pack mule, transporting a dozen little people at a time in an ingenious contraption Amy thought up. It was made from an egg carton. With some customisation a little person could sit quite comfortably where an egg used to rest. They couldn't stand up while the box was closed, but the journey wasn't long and it allowed me to transport the little people in bulk and in relative safety, even if it did take ten trips.

I left the last group to escape their transport vehicle

with willing hands pulling them free from the cardboard, and went to track down Jack. He was in the house, pacing in a nervous manner he hadn't exhibited in all the days of his life.

"Whatever's the matter Jack?" I asked.

"Oh Tom, am I making a huge mistake here? She's so young. She'll have months without me, and what if there are children, how could I bear knowing I'd have to leave them so soon? Companionship should be for young people with their lives ahead of them, not doddering old fools like me.

"And what of my going away and leaving these people, my people, for so long? I abandoned them to their fate; I brought all of this on them. It's supposed to be anything for the people, not anything for yourself. I don't deserve this."

I let him talk. A tiny selfish part of me screamed that now was the moment to sabotage this day. What with Jack's mayoral duties and now his responsibility to a new wife, I worried he would have no time for me. Jack had less than one hundred days remaining to call his own and I was jealous of his time. If my dealings with Jerry had taught me anything however, it's that friendship occasionally means doing what is not in your own best interest for the good of your friend.

"Do you love her?" I asked after quieting my own internal debate.

"More than anything."

"And does she love you?"

"Yes. I know she loves me too." Some of the cares seemed to drop from Jack's shoulders as he spoke, but he remained downcast, staring at the kitchen tile he stood in the centre of.

"Then what's there to worry about?"

"I'm broken." I barely heard the words that Jack squeezed out in a whisper. The hot prick of tears stung my eyes as I watched the grey head of my very best friend battle with a word which had tarnished his life since his dad first mentioned it in the days of his youth. We never talked about Jack's crippled leg during our journey, aside from the practical measures of designing new crutches or ensuring his comfort. It didn't mean anything to me, I hardly noticed his handicap, but now I suspected it was the reason Jack had turned from the cove of his childhood without looking back. Returning here to Cornwall and to his people had ignited the never-extinguished coal that screamed of his defective, mutilated, broken leg. Words leave longer-lasting wounds than any physical malady.

"You are *not* broken Jack. You're the bravest man I've ever known, to overcome everything you have. I know you aren't broken, and Sophie knows it too. She loves the person you are, and your injury is a part of who you are."

Jack expelled a deep breath. The lines of concern marring his forehead were smoothed away as a smile broke out on his lips, and I was reminded of the sun rising and chasing away the shadows of a dark and dreary night.

"Don't wait too long Tom," Jack said as familiar humour coloured his tone once again.

"Don't wait too long for what?"

"To talk to Amy of course."

"Oh, well, there's no rush there, I have more time than you, and I'm not really sure if she's, you know, the one."

"Jack shook his tiny head and smiled. "You never know what's coming tomorrow Tom. Talk to her. Enjoy her company for as long as possible. Even if I could spend a hundred lifespans with my dear, dear Sophie it wouldn't stop me wanting to become her companion today."

Jack was always right these days. It was infuriating. I wonder if it was the wisdom gained by age.

Jack didn't look three months Sophie's senior as the two stood together beneath a cardboard arch draped with the petals of purple delphinium flowers Amy sourced from the village florist. The joy that suffused his face took years from him, and he could have been a youngster again, grinning with pleasure at his first love.

Amy was the artist behind the arch. She stayed up late into the night cutting out all sorts of shapes of cardboard to decorate and make the building site a more festive scene. Purple ribbons and petals decked the entire garden. It was picture perfect; the pair of little people were framed by flowers as they looked out to the distant ocean. An Elder presided over the ceremony as, one after another, Jack and Sophie promised to love, care for and cherish one another until the day of their lifespan end. I felt a lump in my throat seeing Jack so happy. He had loved our travels, we both had, but this was a different sort of glee. This was the unspeakable and indescribable joy that only comes from meeting the person with whom you are destined to journey together for the rest of your days. It was a joy bolstered by the purpose he had come to realise in his life, becoming the chief architect of his people's redemption. His face beamed with peace and with exhilaration mirrored completely in the countenance of his new bride, Sophie. I saw Amy wipe a tear from her cheek as she, like me, lay on her front beside the assembled little people to fully hear all that progressed during the ceremony. As I looked at Amy watching the giving and receiving of intricately weaved belts symbolising the commitment of one little person to another, I felt my doubts about her fade away. Within this world there will always be the temptation to get rich quick at the expense of another, but there are moments of beauty that transcend the seduction of wealth. In that moment I was convinced that Amy, like me, would do nothing to jeopardise this community.

The little people brought instruments with them for the festivities, the same type used in their funerals. They played merry tunes into the night and danced by the firelight of small bonfires carefully erected around what would become the main square of the village. Once or twice I saw Jack leave his blushing bride to show some part or other of this new home to little people who were yet to be convinced about the relocation. Sophie was too radiant with happiness to care. She would grab any passerby to swing them into the dance, once even taking hold of my little finger and giggling with glee as I tried to spin around, bent over at an awkward angle to allow my hand to reach the floor and trying hard to make sure I didn't step on anyone. Amy was on the floor crying with laughter at the performance. I discovered that I didn't mind making myself the fool, if it brought a smile to her face. I was elated for my friend when he brought his blushing bride over to me at one point in the evening to introduce me to the new Sophie Meadows.

As the long night drew on we realised it would be impractical to take the little people back to their cave until the morning. Amy suggested pitching the tent Jack and I used on our travels. It was still stuck in the boot of the car, along with a pile of other things I wasn't quite sure where to store in the new house. Putting up a tent wasn't an easy task, given the uneven and rocky nature of the secret garden, but we managed it and soon the little people were merrily settling themselves in, curling up in pieces of fabric Amy tore from an old bed sheet.

"This is it Tom, this is what we've been looking for."

"What is?" It had been a long day.

"Don't you see?" Amy sounded impatient with my slow-wittedness, "We want to bring all the people over together, yes? But it'll take too long to build all of the houses to do that anytime soon."

I nodded mutely.

"They're all living together in that cave system at the moment aren't they, without much privacy, so why not move them here into the tent? It'd be more comfortable than where they are now, and more watertight. We can make sure the ropes are well secured so it'll be okay in rough weather, and we can use shoe boxes or cereal boxes or whatever we can find to make divided areas for families. That way we can get them all here and that'll give us more hands to help with the building too. They can get settled into the area and move out of the tent gradually as the houses are built. It's perfect!"

"You're right. You're absolutely right," I said and picked her up, twirled her around and placed a kiss on her cheek. She looked utterly startled as I released her. Startled, but not displeased.

It was perfect, and I couldn't believe I hadn't thought of it.

Phase Four, Making the Move, could begin as soon as we had the final okay from the little people and securely set up the tent. With our egg carton transfer system that would be an easier job than initially anticipated too.

Everything was going according to plan.

CHAPTER THIRTY-TWO

My father once told me if something seems too good to be true it probably is.

On the day after the wedding Jack and Sophie reported that the vast majority of little people were now happy to make the move, and were excited at the prospect of finally getting out of the damp and cramped cave. Though Amy and I continued to work making the building site as level as possible and creating more egg carton transport solutions, I was in a surprisingly relaxed mood about bringing everyone over. Jack and Sophie were radiant in their newly wedded bliss and I was keen to afford them a bit of privacy before bringing their entire community to live in one space, albeit a space like a vast concert hall to the little people. Though we gave the couple as much privacy as they desired, it was also a wonderful opportunity to really get to know Sophie and to spend time with them together. The four of us had many memorable moments in the house, growing closer over board games and food. I well remember tears of mirth when the feisty Sophie ran around the Monopoly board, kicking over Jack's hotel after finding out how much she'd be forced to fork out for landing on his Mayfair square. She was a wonderful character, and so well suited to Jack. It was no wonder to me that she was unattached until he came along, because they were two puzzle pieces that joined so neatly they couldn't possibly have found contentment elsewhere. I'd met a few more little people during this time, and none were as bold and brave and daring as little Sophie (besides Jack). She was cut from a different cloth to the little people at large, and so it was that the rigid and unchanging little people found themselves governed by two free spirits. It made sense; Sophie was utterly devoted to Jack and to the little people at large. Nothing was too much effort if she could assist a member of her kind, and though everyone knew to avoid her temper, they were quick to contact her when they needed someone they could count on.

Sophie's character endeared her to me, but it was Jack's utter devotion that firmly convinced me of her worth. I never thought of Jack as an unfulfilled person, but in those few days he seemed more complete and whole than in all the time of our travels. I suppose there are moments when we don't realise something is missing from our day to day journey until it jumps out at us, and suddenly we can't live without it.

Happy as we were ignoring the world for a while, we eventually set a moving date for a Wednesday, a couple of weeks after the wedding ceremony.

"That's fine," Jack said, "that means they'll all be in for when Sophie gives birth. I'd rather she was here for that than in the cave."

"I'm sorry, what? Sophie? Giving birth? Are you? Is she?" I opened and closed my mouth like a goldfish and gawped at Jack. He grinned back mischievously. The usual advice to enjoy being married for a year or two doesn't really come into play when you only have one year to live but even so, they'd moved quickly. If I didn't know better I'd say Jack was quite proud of his achievement.

Moving day arrived with grey clouds on the horizon. The

year up to this point had been particularly clement, with temperatures warmer and days drier than the startled British residents had known for years. It suited Jack and I well on our travels, though the yellowed lawns and wilted flower beds of houses told a tale that not all life approved of the extended dry season. The rain held back to give us a glorious day for the wedding and an enjoyable fortnight following it, but it could wait no longer. By the time I returned from work in the afternoon the rain was lashing against the side of the cottage with incredible force. The wind whistled through cracks in the old window panes, sounding like a creature uttering its final dying cries. The white tipped waves of the ocean showed that conditions were rough well out to sea.

Amy and I wrapped up in raincoats and made our way to the entrance of the cave system in which the little people huddled.

"We'd best put it off a day or two I think, Jack," I suggested. Jack and Sophie stood beneath an overhang of rock to avoid the heavy drops of rain. He nodded in accord and we waited, and waited, and waited, but the rain showed no sign of giving up on its relentless soaking of the country.

We weren't completely idle on those rainy days. Amy and I battled the elements to carry building materials to the site, and with Jack and his select team of builders and creative minds who stayed on after the wedding we started to mark out plots for houses. The group of little people spent many an hour huddled over pieces of paper in my kitchen, and when I snuck a glance at their work I saw they were putting together plans for how best to build small houses for their people. They opted for a combination of wood and stone to put together what might end up looking like a model village. I was amazed at the designs. A knowledge of building must have been passed down from one little person to the next over the years, from those who had originally worked on the cove they had called home for so long. We left them to it and continued with the grunt work of transporting goods and digging out the allocated spot for the rock pool. The endless rain was a danger to the little people, and though we tried our best to rig a collection of umbrellas and tarpaulin to cover the area of work, most of the building was halted on those soggy days.

The rain continued to fall one Saturday morning. It was a rare Saturday for me, one completely free from work at Crumbs, one that I was looking forward to using to make more headway on the pond. Before the first swing of my father's borrowed pickaxe I heard Amy screaming my name and ran as fast as I could over the wet stones back to the house.

"It's time Tom, the baby's coming," Amy exclaimed.

"Oh. Wow. What do I do?" I asked her, a deer caught in the headlights.

She laughed and clapped me on the back. "Look after Jack. Childbirth is something for the women here I think, not the husbands."

With that Jack and I were relegated to the sitting room to wait. He paced the carpet back and forth and back and forth with his tiny crutches until I'm sure I could see a worn path marking his steps.

"Calm down," I tried to put as much encouragement into my voice as I could. "She'll be fine." Jack only started at me in silence, wrung his hands, and continued his relentless march. I chuckled to myself and wished I had some suitable liquor to offer the father-to-be. I'm not sure how a little person's system would deal with alcohol, but now would have been a perfect moment to find out.

Seconds became minutes and Saturday morning dragged slowly by.

"Does it normally take this long?" Jack questioned.

"You're asking me? How would I know?" I laughed back and was rewarded with the flicker of a smile.

Eventually, after what seemed like weeks rather than a

little under an hour, Amy came to the door to call Jack into the kitchen.

"You have a son," she beamed.

Amy and I stood over the tiny family, an exhausted Sophie cradling a bundle of crying material and Jack gently stroking her hair murmuring sweet nothings we couldn't hear.

Eventually he looked up at me and with the widest smile I've ever seen decorate the face of any person, little or otherwise, introduced me to Joe Meadows, his son.

We didn't achieve much during the rest of the day, and Jack and Sophie decided to stay the night at the house instead of returning to the cold damp cave with their precious baby boy.

And so it transpired that they were with us when the phone call came the very next day.

In all of my unpacking I had happened on an old mobile phone and decided it might be useful to leave it in the cave while the people were split between the two sites, in case of an emergency. My own number was saved as a favourite and assigned to a speed dial key to make it as easy as possible for a little person to call me. Battery charge hadn't worried me, as I expected the move to happen soon and those old phones kept their power for a long time. The trickier part of the job was getting the phone into the cave system. Its narrow entrance was one of the reasons the little people chose to use it, as it would be very hard for anyone to see within. I managed to cram the phone through, poking it with a stick to fit it through the long crevice through which the little people entered their main cavern. The little people looped a piece of weaved seaweed around it, and ten of them tugged together in some kind of deranged tug-of-war game to get it into the cavern and somewhere water wouldn't drip on it.

I'd all but forgotten I had given it to them when my phone rang.

"Tom, phone," Amy called.

"Answer it would you?" I was making us a late lunch to eat as we pored over the shopping list of items the building team insisted they needed. I could hear the musical tones of Amy's voice as I buttered bread but couldn't distinguish her words, so I wasn't prepared when she ran into the kitchen in a state of panic.

"We need to leave, now," she said and pulled me by the arm away from my lunch. I sent one longing look at the fresh bread, my own handiwork, and cheese as I thrust on a waterproof coat. "We'll take the car. It'll be a bit closer for them, and safer in the rain too. Grab the egg cartons by the door, and that umbrella," she shouted instructions to me and I followed them blindly, tailing her into the living room where Jack and Sophie sat.

"What on earth is going on?" I asked.

"It's the cave Tom, it's flooding." Jack jumped to his feet in an instant. "We need to get them all out now, we can find somewhere to put them once they're safe but we have to act right now."

Jack beckoned to me and I reached down to pick him up and put in my pocket, but Sophie stepped into the path of my fingers, the sleeping Joe wrapped up in her arms.

"What are you doing?" Jack said in a raised voice. "We're in a hurry here."

"I'm coming too," Sophie replied.

"It's too dangerous," Jack implored. "You and Joe stay here, I'll be back soon."

"I said I'm coming too. They're my people as well." She planted her feet and I recognised a dangerous expression creeping onto her face.

"She can ride with me," Amy interjected, staring at her watch. "They'll both be fine with me."

Amy scooped Sophie and Joe into a roomy pocket and I grabbed Jack. I was soaked to the skin from the brief journey from front door to driveway.

We parked as close as possible to the cove and dashed

over the slippery stones faster than was safe. As we drew closer I could pick out small screams carried on the stiff breeze, cries for help mingled with the desperate shrieks of names and echoed through the cave system as we crouched beside the entrance. Little people were crowded there, trapped between the steadily rising water within the cave and the torrential rain and wind that swirled outside with gusts easily strong enough to carry them away. I remembered Jack telling me that at the bottom of this little system of caves and crevices was a rock pool the little people had been able to use for some sustenance, though it was a perilous climb down to it. The pool had never overflowed, but days of solid rain and an uncommonly high tide must have caused it to rise through the cave system, threatening to carry away any persons left behind. With each wave crashing dramatically on the shore the water level would rise. There were twenty-one little people in the building team at my new house.

That left us with two hundred and fifteen people to rescue.

Over the pounding of the surf and the endless patter of the rain I could hear an ominous sloshing sound coming from within the cave and knew lives were at risk with every second I dawdled. Hysteria was taking hold as those closest to the outside were shoved forward by the crowds pushing at their back. If they stayed where they were they would be drowned. If they moved out of the safety of their shelter they would be torn to pieces by the weather.

We were their only hope.

Time. I need more time, I thought to myself as I racked my brain for a plan. We had four egg box cartons, which meant enough space to transport forty-eight little people at a time. That would mean a total of five trips, if my panicked brain was calculating its sums correctly. Would there be enough time for the last group? Perhaps we could move them out of harm's way and then shuttle them to the car from there? I scanned back the way we had come for a likely spot but couldn't see anything beyond the rebounding raindrops. Finally I resolved that whatever happened we had to move and we had to move now.

"Amy," I shouted over the storm, "get the umbrella, see if you can wedge it here by the exit so they can have some cover as they leave the cave."

She leapt to obey my instruction. The fierce wind turned the umbrella inside out the moment it was open, but together we wrestled it into place with its handle wedged between two rocks. I doubted we'd ever free it again. It wasn't perfect but it offered some extra shelter for the little people, to save them being swept away by the first big gust of wind. I opened the first egg carton, the cardboard already soggy, and placed it as close to the entrance as possible.

I dropped Jack out of my pocket beside it. "Jack, get me twelve people now." He nodded understanding and counted the first twelve who ran as fast as their little legs could carry them to the shelter of the box. I shut the lid to offer them further protection, and put the next box in place. "Twelve more, now!" Another twelve little people darted from the cave to the box, one tripping and falling on the way. I scooped the little girl up and deposited her in the space left vacant by one of the many eggs rolling around in my fridge. I noticed blood on my hand and hoped she wasn't too badly wounded.

"Amy, take these two cartons. See if you can find a sheltered place on the way to the car to leave them. If you can't then run them to the car and leave them in the boot." She was off at a sprint before I finished my sentence, having left Sophie and Joe with Jack beneath the overhang of the cave entrance. I turned back to Jack and Sophie, urging them to count out the next twelve people. Though I could feel an almost physical wave of panic rising from the shouts and screams within the cave system behind, it amazed me that the little people responded to the instructions of their leaders without question. Only twelve at a time ran from the mouth of the cave and there was no jostling for place or trampling over one another to reach safety. Word must have been passed down the chain of the impending rescue, as my final egg carton was full of children who had been pushed to the front of the queue. Their young terrified screams would haunt my dreams for many a night.

Where was Amy? My two cartons were full but I wanted to do this in a relay, leaving one of us here loading while the other ran two full cartons to safety. Where was she? Each second felt like an hour as I waited until I saw her running back toward me, the empty egg cartons tucked under her flapping raincoat; she'd not even stopped to do it up.

"Go, go!" she shouted to me. "There's a ridge, not far back, you'll see it. There's room for most of them under there."

I nodded my understanding and sprinted as fast as I could in the direction of the car. My foot caught a seaweed smeared rock and I tripped, holding the cartons as level as I could as I fell to the ground without my hands for support. The jarring fall aggravated the old wound in my arm but I ignored the pain and jumped back to my feet to continue the journey. I was in such a hurry I almost missed Amy's ridge. I only saw it when I happened to glance to my right to see two dozen little people jumping up and down to get my attention. It would have been funny in any other circumstance. Skidding to a halt I opened my two cartons and watched as many willing hands pulled the little people clear and into the shelter.

It took an inordinately long time for my cartons to empty, but soon I was back on the run. I followed Amy's example and tucked the soggy cardboard containers under my coat in an attempt to maintain their structural integrity for as many journeys as possible. Amy was ready and waiting with her cartons filled and started running for the ridge before I had reached the cave entrance in this perverse relay race.

Jack and Sophie continued to fend off panic and kept the people in order as my third load was completed. Though I worried for the young Joe I was glad Sophie was present, no one dared to countermand her instructions, even when seawater started to lap around the ankles of the little people and the screams from inside the cave system grew in intensity.

Amy was still kneeling beside the cave when I arrived after depositing the passengers of my fourth trip. One and a half of her boxes were full. That meant there were only a few little people left to come, but there was no sign of anyone else waiting for a ride.

"What's going on?" I shouted over the barrage of wind.

"My babies, let me get my babies," a heavily pregnant little woman was crying over and over again, restrained only by her fellow little people.

"I'll go," I could just here Jack's words over the rain and wind as I knelt closer.

Sophie placed a hand on Jack's arm and smiled a sad little smile. They both knew Jack wouldn't be much help with his leg the way it was amidst the pressure of the rising tide.

"I'll go," Sophie said and thrust Joe towards his father.

"No Sophie, please, don't," Jack pleaded and I couldn't tell if it was raindrops or tears that rolled down his cheeks.

"I have to. Anything for the people, remember?" Sophie pulled Jack into a fierce embrace and I looked away, embarrassed by the intensity of it. "I love you," she called as she disappeared into the dark cave, the water up to her calves even before she moved downhill into the rest of the system.

Time stood still as we watched the water rising from within, starting to lap the rock outside. Still there was no sign of Sophie, or the two missing children. Jack held tightly to the squirming Joe and stared intently into the water's murky depths.

Suddenly a great splash rent the surface as first one child and then another surfaced as if pushed from below. Their mother, freed from the grasp of her peers, ran to them and wrapped them in her arms. Amy scooped the tangled mess of limbs into the remaining spots in the egg carton.

Sophie emerged behind the children. She lay on the floor, exhausted and coughing water from her lungs when another enormous wave crashed over us. The spray carried on the wind and stung our hands and faces as we huddled together against it. Amy used her body to protect her charges. I was knelt beside the entrance to the cave and Jack kicked at my hand to get my attention. He thrust the baby Joe into my cupped hand. I didn't dare to move. If you've ever felt nervous holding a new born baby just imagine the terror of holding the child of a little person, knowing how easy it would be to crush him unintentionally between two fingers. All I could do was remain kneeling and cover the child with my other hand like a clam shell to shield him from the rain.

All I could do was watch as Jack threw his crutch to one side and lunged to reach Sophie's hand. Their outstretched fingertips brushed before she was sucked toward the cave under the backwash of the wave.

"Sophie! SOPHIE!" Jack cried, lunging after her only to be beaten back by the next wave's approach.

The little people were homeless once more, and Sophie was gone.

CHAPTER THIRTY-THREE

I ever so carefully rolled the baby Joe into the outstretched arms of one of the little women in the egg carton and sent Amy off to take the last load to safety. I don't like to think how long it must have taken her to load every person back into the soggy cartons to journey to the car, and then from the car to the tent in the back garden. I felt bad leaving her to it, but I knew she understood. She could take her time now that the threat to the lives of the little people was over.

Jack and I remained.

We searched until the greyness of the day turned to inky darkness and we could search no more. Jack shouted himself hoarse for his bride and we thoroughly explored all around the cave system, but there was no sign of her.

"We'll try again tomorrow," Jack said finally.

I nodded, too exhausted and numb to speak the truth we both knew.

We were soaked to the skin and freezing cold when we finally returned, my fingers were pruned as though I had spent the day in a bathtub and I noticed Jack couldn't stop shivering. Whether that was from the cold or in reaction to the day's events I couldn't tell you. Amy had worked wonders in our absence, setting the little people up within the watertight tent and establishing a triage area to one side of it. In the scuffle of getting free from the cave there had been numerous injuries. Most were scuffs and scrapes that she, and a team of little people helpers, had been able to treat with clean water and tiny strips of bandages Amy had scavenged from my house. There were a few more serious injuries, several broken bones and one old man who Amy suspected of having internal bleeding. "His end is only two days away," Amy said in a hushed tone, "I'm not sure he'll make it."

The cold water that soaked the little people to their skins was another danger. All of their spare clothes were left behind in the waterlogged cave, not to mention all of their other possessions. I noticed several little people wandering around in blankets made of squares of tinfoil. Amy shrugged when I asked her about it, "I figured they use foil blankets for humans if they're worried about hyperthermia," she explained. She had found any old towels, blankets, sheets and even clothes that she could get her hands on to make comfortable areas for the little people, and to give them something dry to wrap up in. A collection of older women in one corner of the tent fashioned scraps of material into poncho style dresses by cutting holes out of the middle of each piece with small, sharp stones. These were secured around the middle with a belt of fabric to provide rudimentary coverings. By the next day all of the rescued little people were attired in the same way. In the midst of sadness I had to fight a strange temptation to laugh when I saw a group of little people, just shy of coming of age, walking around in ponchos made from my old pyjama bottoms.

Jack surveyed the scene in a daze, clutching Joe to his chest as though he couldn't bear to put him down. The news of Sophie's plight spread rapidly, and Jack was greeted with sympathy by his peers. Sophie was well liked. She was the only one to try and source food for the starving little people in their initial exile, and it was she who managed to persuade many of those still undecided about the move to the new site with her clever words, friendly smiles and, perhaps, the fear of her wrath. It seemed so wrong that the last time the little people had congregated in this tent they were celebrating the joyful union of Jack and Sophie, a little more than two weeks ago.

All I could do was shake my head when Amy asked for news of Sophie. Putting words to something gives it a sense of finality, and I wasn't ready to accept what I feared to be fact. Jack still had hope. I tried to find some within myself but all I could identify was grief and exhaustion and that last memory of Sophie's tiny face as the unstoppable ocean pulled her away from us with currents stronger than any little person could master.

I sneezed myself awake in the morning. My time exposed to the biting wind and rain had left me with a stuffy nose and a sore throat but I didn't let that stop me returning to the cave with Jack, even if it was a good excuse for failing to attend to my duties at the bakery. We left Joe safe and sound with a little woman who had given birth a few days before. She was happy to care for the extra baby. It wasn't a difficult task with all the help to hand more than happy to assist in the looking after of Sophie's offspring.

The calm morning mocked us. Birds called serenely and the sun crested the residual grey clouds as we reached the cave. A tattered umbrella beaten out of shape by strong winds was the only evidence of yesterday's struggle, that and a few scraps of miniature clothing and other items washed out from the entrance. The tide was out now. It lapped the shore gently, like a tame lapdog and not the vicious and rabid brute of the previous day. Jack slipped inside the damp crevice to explore the cavern system in the hope Sophie might have found shelter in a nook or cranny within.

I traipsed around the outside of the cave system. I call them caves, though really the caverns were more like small pockets of space beneath overlapping stones that happened to leave room underneath big enough for the little people. Their refuge was an interweaving network of such small hollows, and it had provided enough space for the whole community to survive for the last few weeks. I found the pool that was the cause of yesterday's overflow and sat beside it, looking for any evidence that Sophie had somehow been expelled here with the force of the retreating wave. There were some additional possessions of the little people scattered around but I couldn't see a person, no matter how hard I looked.

What I did see caused a sorrow so agonising I felt it like a physical jolt in my stomach that gradually spread to my other extremities until even my fingers were tingling with sadness.

There, lying atop a few scraps of clothes and the carefully handcrafted toy of a child was Sophie's belt, the companionship belt Jack had given her one week before. It was a distinctive green and red colour and I recognised it instantly. She was wearing it when she emerged from the cave with the two young children, I was sure. It must have been torn from her by the force of the water, a force that would surely have smashed her petite frame into the unforgiving rocks.

I scooped up the pile of little people paraphernalia, including the belt, and returned to the cave entrance to wait for Jack. It might have been the longest wait of my life, with nothing to do but mull over the news that would break his heart into pieces.

Eventually Jack appeared, looking older and more tired than ever before. He saw the beautifully weaved belt held between my fingertips before I could say a word and dropped heavily onto his good knee. A sob racked his tiny body. Jack took the belt from my fingers and clasped it between his hands, folding himself over it as a rush of grief extinguished the last flickering flame of hope.

I couldn't tell you how long we remained there, Jack on his knees and me praying silently to a God I didn't know for a miracle. My cheeks were damp with my own tears.

"I should never have let her go," Jack croaked. "Why didn't I go instead?" He beat the ground beneath him with his fists.

I wanted to reassure him, to tell him Sophie was right and there was no good he could have done in the cave. I wanted to let him know it wasn't his fault, but I knew he wouldn't hear those words today. There wasn't a lot of space on the rocky outcropping beside the entrance to the caverns, but I found a way to squeeze myself beside Jack without intruding on his grief. In solidarity I placed a single finger on his back, the closest to a hug I could offer.

Eventually, in unison, we stood to our feet and I scooped Jack into my hand, and then into my pocket. He gripped the belt until his tiny knuckles turned white. The walk home felt like a funeral procession, so slow were my footsteps. I couldn't bring myself to hurry to deliver our dreadful news.

No matter how hard we try to slow the pace of time, it's impossible to put off the inevitable. Jack was engulfed by comforting arms as I deposited him gently in the tent in the midst of the little people.

Sophie had met her end.

Amy and I shared in the grief we saw before us, but confusion battled my sadness. I had seen little people die before and it was nothing like this. End days were happy occasions where life was celebrated. The little people grieved, of course, but this was entirely different. The people were so subdued that even the air seemed still and no one spoke a word louder than a whisper to break the sombre silence.

Our grief wanted time to stand still. It seemed wrong for mundane tasks to take precedence over our sorrow, but the sands of time keep falling and a subdued routine formed over the following few days. One of the younger Elders unobtrusively took over Jack's responsibilities, pushing the building teams and the many willing volunteers to work on the first row of houses. Amy and I helped the construction work to progress quickly. We could lift beams and pieces of rock to form roofs quicker than any crane. The young Elder also organised a team to return to the caves with the intent of tracking down any usable items. Secretly I believe they were also looking for the body of Sophie Meadows. At a later date I discovered that in all of the rich history of generations and generations of little people passed down by the Elders, there was no mention of a situation like this, where a person prematurely met their end without a body to bury. There was no precedent for recognising Sophie's end, and so it was that the people were industrious and lively during the day, but returned to the shadow of a pall cast over the tent at night. Jack took to sleeping on my bedside cabinet again with his rapidly growing son, to spare the other little people the sight of his anguish.

I was accustomed to the little people; I had even learnt to accept that one year of life was enough for them. The one thing I could never get to grips with, something that makes my head spin even now, is the thought of knowing the very day your life will draw to its inevitable conclusion. There is no surprise in death for a little person, no sudden deterioration from illness in a person far too young with far too much still to offer, no unforeseen visit from the police about a car accident snatching away a person you love. Little people had died from a variety of hazards before, from cave-ins and falls and even in the dangerous coming of age ceremony, but in those instances there was always a body, and usually time to say a swift farewell. I wondered if bereavement would be easier for humans to deal with if we knew exactly when it was coming.

The Elders finally reached a conclusion a full week later. The little people would bury Sophie's belt. A patch of earth to one side of the designated housing area of the little people was established as a burial ground, and a small hole was excavated. The little people gathered outside of the tent to speak their stories of the departed, though their words sounded hollow and strained without the little person about whom they were talking there to listen and laugh along. High clouds painted a brilliant whiteness across the sky as person after person told tales of Sophie's bravery and heart and fierce spirit. Even in her youth she was determined, traipsing further than tradition demanded or her Guide advised at her coming of age ceremony in order to find the most perfectly formed shell she could discover. An end ceremony typically lasted an hour or two, giving the little people chance to get on with their appointed tasks for the day, but Sophie's was a full day affair. Everyone had a story to tell. Jack sat stolidly by as the words of the little people rolled over him. He never expected to deal with this I thought with a pang, his end should have come months before hers.

My reverie was broken as Jack stood to speak, leaning heavily upon one crutch, "The first time I met Sophie, she punched me in the face. It was the happiest day of my life." A hint of his old smile twitched his lips as his words brought a chuckle from the assembled crowd, not many knew the circumstances of Jack and Sophie's meeting. "She was the brightest ray of light in my world. I never expected to fall in love when I returned, and try as I might I can't wish that I hadn't. A fortnight as her companion was enough to change my whole life for the better. A day would have been enough. I will miss her laugh and her beautiful face and the fire of her heart to my last breath, but I am so thankful that I knew her, even for a little while. I'm so thankful." Jack's voice trailed out. I think he ran out of words to do justice to his bride. My gaze wandered as I tried to imagine what he must be feeling, and I found myself looking at Amy. She sent a small, sad smile my way, and I pictured what it would be like never to see her again. The pain of the thought was a dagger to my heart and my lungs struggled to find enough air to stay inflated. I felt my palms grow sweaty. In a couple of weeks she would be leaving for her job all those miles away in Birmingham. Would I see her again? With a new life to distract her I would be far from her mind. I was so lost in thought I didn't notice the procession had started. Jack led his friends and family and beckoned frantically for me to fall into step with them. I jumped to my feet so fast an elderly couple had to sidestep to avoid being trampled. I couldn't hear their words, being so far above them at my full height, but from the shaking of the old man's fist I'm sure they weren't complimentary.

Jack held so tightly to his Sophie's belt as he walked that I wondered if he would be able to surrender it. I wondered if he would want to, or if some part of him would wish to keep hold of this memento of the happiest day of his life.

I carried on walking.

It wasn't a great distance, from one side of the secret garden to the other, but it took a long time at the pace of the little people. It gave me plenty of time to think, and I realised Jack wasn't one to keep mementoes. He had nothing to remind him of his estranged father or beloved mother. The explorers who turned out the cave for anything useful brought back clothes and practical items, but nothing that might hold extra significance. With only three hundred and sixty-five days of life to remember, the little people don't need anything to prompt the memory of specific faces or events. They would never face that horrible sensation of desperately clinging on to a memory, only to feel its clarity diminish with each passing year until it is unclear what is the true memory and what we are painting with our own imagination. It was a nice thought to have. Jack might have lost Sophie, but he needn't worry that his recollections of her would be dulled by the passage of time.

The mood was solemn as Jack gently relinquished his grip of the belt to the cold embrace of the earth. I had yet to see the graveside portion of a person's end before this day; it was a simple affair. Jack held his wriggling son on one hip and dropped a handful of loose earth into the hole, as did those closest to Sophie, her remaining family members and dearest friends. The hole was all but full by the time Jack took his place at the head of the queue once again. With his bare hands he scraped the remaining soil into place and patted it down. Joe stood beside his father on unsteady feet, and then crouched down to imitate his actions smoothing the earth. He was growing so quickly.

In ones and twos the little people drifted away, one of Sophie's sisters collected Joe from his father's arms, and I heard a lively piped tune floating towards us on the breeze. I guided Amy away with an arm around her shoulders. As I glanced behind I saw Jack kneeling alone beside the flattened ground holding the only remaining trace of the love of his life.

CHAPTER THIRTY-FOUR

On the morning after Sophie's funeral Jack was nowhere to be seen. He spent the night in the tent with his people rather than on my bedside cabinet, but when I asked after his whereabouts I was answered with sleepy shrugs.

There was no sign of him at the burial ground. In the passing of one night it was already difficult to identify the spot where Sophie's belt was buried. The little people don't bother with gravestones, Jack told me that one day as we drove past a cemetery. He was bemused by the concept. Little people don't return to the site of internment after the day of the end, and something like a gravestone would seem a silly idea when the person buried would pass out of living memory within one year or less. Small stones were commonly placed at the four corners of the burial site to ensure the same plot of land wasn't insensitively excavated soon after a funeral, but that was it.

A small group of little people clustered around a diagram depicting construction details for the new houses. It was a challenge this building work; the rocky nature of the garden meant digging foundations would be nigh impossible, and yet no one was particularly keen on the idea of a sudden gust of wind blowing their home away.

Given that the stone itself was good and stable, the little people adopted a plan to build their dwellings on top of stone blocks. These could be positioned and shaped according to the sloping landscape, creating a more stable bed for the properties than I had first imagined possible. I didn't entirely trust the design. The stormy winds that occurred on the day of Sophie's death could easily strike this exposed location and the last thing we needed was more tragedy. With that in mind I managed to get hold of some steel wire in the hope it could be run over the houses and bolted to the solid stone ground. I wasn't exactly sure how it would work, but tethering the foundationless properties was a sensible decision, no matter how much faith the builders had in their plans. I wondered if my wire was the topic of discussion. One little person was pointing at a roll of it which stood significantly taller than himself.

I walking over to add my suggestions to the mix and noticed the man in the centre of the builders, holding up the plans and gesticulating wildly at the wire, was none other than Jack. For the last week he spent his time staring into the distance, lost in thoughts that I didn't dare to disturb, barely stirring from his reverie even as Joe started to crawl and then to walk. Seeing him take action in the building of his dream felt like a weight falling from my shoulders. He was going to be okay.

Jack's resolve sharpened to the point of a blade. He was happy to leave the tedium of organisation to the young Elder who took on the role during Jack's period of mourning. It freed him to focus on spending every ounce of his energy to get the little people out of the tent and into their own properties. Amy and I made the tent as comfortable as possible, even managing to retrieve some pieces of furniture that had lain hidden since the little people left the site of their original homes. We partitioned off different areas for individual family residences and sacrificed many items of clothing and bedding to make it comfortable. Still, it wasn't ideal and as we reached the middle of October I worried at how cold that temporary dwelling would be for the little people. Holes in the tent's fabric could help with ventilation but would let in the rain, and without them the little people were left choking in the smoke of the fires they tried to light. Eventually I had the idea to run an extension cable outside to plug in an old oil-fired radiator. It took some of the chill off the nights, but it had the adverse effect of making a part of the tent uninhabitable for the little people who found it too warm close to the heat it provided.

A hint of Jack's old self returned as the days passed by. Time is a healer, though I'm sure it was Joe who stitched the tattered fragments of Jack's heart back together. He learnt to smile again at the antics of his son who had inherited Sophie's temper and Jack's adventurous spirit from a young age. More than once I stepped in to rescue Joe as he toddled his way into the midst of the building work or toward the edge of the cliff. The more reserved little people sighed and shook their heads but with an understanding smile, given the lad's heritage. I know Joe wished he knew his mother as he grew, but he suffered no great lack from a parenting perspective. He had a village full of mothers and fathers and aunties and uncles and grandparents willing to take him under their wing and look out for him as Jack worked hard to establish the new community.

If Jack's smile was less ready than in his youth and his eyes took on a faraway look from time to time, no one questioned it. If anything I was amazed at how quickly Jack did recover from such a devastating loss when I still felt it so keenly, but I had to remind myself the equivalent of two years had passed now since the day Sophie was lost to us. Jack's new found diligence was a way to mask his pain, I'm sure, but at the same time he knew he needed to get on with his life. I was convinced the little smile that lifted his lips at odd moments was at the thought of what the sharp-tongued Sophie would say about his moping around and doing nothing.

The first house was completed on a Tuesday, three days after Sophie's funeral. I went to work in the morning, and when I returned in the afternoon there it was, standing proudly, finished with a slab of slate lashed carefully to the stone below with steel wire. The other four houses on the row were all but complete as well, only their roofs needed fixing. Amy must have walked up and down the coastline for hours looking for suitable pieces of slate and then carried them back up to the house. I marvelled at her resilience. She had struck up a friendship with one of the building team, a Gerald Flowers. He would ride on Amy's shoulder, gripping onto the fabric of her shirt, and the two would go out together looking for adequate materials which she carried back in her shoulder bag. I felt bad that my responsibilities at the bakery kept me from more active involvement, but Amy had a passion for the work and didn't seem to mind the labour. "It'll be different soon," she said when I asked if she needed a break, "I'll be stuck behind a desk. I might as well enjoy the fresh air and exercise while I can. Besides, Sophie was desperate to see her people housed. It's the least I can do." Amy's beautiful blue eyes darkened and she turned away to hide a tear. Sophie's death shook her more than she cared to admit. Neither of us had lost a close friend before. I wanted to comfort her but I couldn't find the words. Instead I rushed off to help move some stones around the site.

I am not an architect or a builder, and so I didn't understand the finer details of the construction of the houses. I helped to move stones, position roofs, cut up bits of solid driftwood into planks, drill holes for the supporting wire, all at the instruction of the little people. The houses were built of a wooden frame, overlaid with small stones held together with a type of mortar the little people knew how to mix, and then topped with a slate roof. Internal walls were created in much the same way as those I helped John Meadows to make so many months ago. They were dry stone walls created from the many tiny pebbles Amy and I lugged up from the shoreline.

I was concerned the houses would stand out like a sore thumb on the stony land, but Jack's original site layout was crafty beyond my skill to appreciate at the time. Houses were clumped together into unassuming groups and all windows and doors faced away from the main house, toward the ocean. At a cursory glance it would be easy to dismiss the homes as unusual piles of stone unworthy of a second look. Only a closer inspection revealed the structures to be homes.

Amy wrapped the first completed house in a giant ribbon, and as all the little people gathered around she helped Jack support the weight of a pair of scissors easily as big as him (they were the smallest she could find). The ribbon fell to the ground to an almighty cheer from the assembled onlookers. Many rushed forward to squeeze through the press at the door to see what the interior of their new homes would be like. Jack insisted over and over again that he wanted this house to go to someone else but they would have none of it, and proclaimed this first finished structure to be his own. I watched him run his hand over the doorframe as he entered. He looked satisfied, though I knew more than anything he wanted to share this moment with Sophie. He wiped his tiny eye with a hand, straightened shoulders increasingly bent with age and strode into his house with Joe on his tail.

When Jack stepped back out into the chill breeze of the day it was to a sea of beaming faces who took up a chant, started by the youngsters, "Jack and Sophie's house," they cried. The name stuck, and for as long as I knew them, the little people referred to that first building as Jack and Sophie's. As the years passed by it was shortened to Jackie's, and though no one really knew why it bore the name they never changed it. Tears rolled down Jack's face as he stood in his doorway, his hand on Joe's shoulder. The name was a reminder of all he had lost, but he would have it no other way. This vision was as much Sophie's as his, and without her it would never have been realised.

New houses sprung up like spring bulbs every few days from then on. The entire community was spurred to action. Even the smallest children could be seen carrying stones to and fro or supplying refreshments to the builders. Amy and I provided all the food the little people needed during this building time to allow their great work to continue unabated. With more than sixty houses to build altogether we knew it would take some months for the village to be complete, but at least the tent became less crowded with each finished home.

There was the matter of long-term sustainability to think of. I was happy to feed the little people, but we talked at length of the importance of their not becoming completely reliant on us for everything.

"What if something happened to you Tom?" Amy asked as we walked over the same conversational ground. "We need to make sure they can get food and make clothes and whatever they need."

"That's what the pool will be for," I said for the umpteenth time.

Amy bit her lip as was her wont when thinking hard, "I'm not sure the pool will work, not as a saltwater pond anyway. Without the ocean to replenish it the salt content will drop each time it rains. It's going to need to be a fresh water pond and that will mean different species and life forms to what they're used to."

With Amy's wise words echoing in our minds we took a trip to the nearest garden centre late one afternoon, and spent more than an hour studying the different types of plant life we could put in a freshwater pond. Amy brought along an ancient looking little woman with wispy white hair and a walking stick. Amy carried her with incredible deference, and it was a challenge to keep her hidden as we asked her opinion on the various types of plant life. She was most reluctant to hide in a pocket or bag, considering it an affront to her dignity. Instead she insisted she remain in a hand, arguing that no big person would notice her anyway. She was right. At one point she sat plainly on Amy's palm when a harried store attendant rushed by. He noticed nothing untoward.

By the end of the trip Amy had filled pages of a notebook with information regarding the reeds and plants which would be the most useful for crafts and for food. We would return to purchase them once the pond was up and running, but in the meantime we acquired pond lining, a pump to keep the water running fresh and some other necessities. This was one job the little people couldn't help with, other than offering the advice they were always very keen to dispense. I chipped away at the specified location until my palms were blistered from gripping the pickaxe and my back ached. It's not easy, creating space for a pond in a bed of solid rock. Amy cleared away the rubble as I dislodged it, and a line of little people judged which pieces might be fit for the ongoing building work and which should be discarded. I was proud of my efforts. Or at least I would be, once a long bath had soothed sore muscles I didn't know I possessed. There was a bit more clearing to do the next day and then we would be ready to start lining and filling the pool, and as the next day was a Sunday that meant uninterrupted work time.

I had completely forgotten it was also the day Amy was due to leave.

CHAPTER THIRTY-FIVE

My aching body refused to leave the comfortable nest of duvet and pillows when my alarm clock blared so I rolled over, went back to sleep and didn't surface until close to noon. I gingerly pulled some clothes on and ventured into the weak autumn sunlight.

I was surprised to see the entire assembly of little people gathered together, with Amy in their midst. As I stumbled over I noticed they were presenting her with a wreath, made from some seaweed we'd scoured from rock pools on the coastline for their various crafts while the new pond was under construction. It was tiny, not quite big enough to slip onto her little finger, and she held it as delicately as the most fragile china. The little people always kept a distance from me, or perhaps I from them, but Amy was much loved amongst the community. She spent many hours listening to their stories and helping with the construction in more visible ways than me. We were both involved in the rescue from the cave, but for many of the little people Amy was their hero. She was the one to deliver them to this new land of promised safety and bounty.

"What's going on?" I murmured sleepily. Amy turned

to me with a sad little smile and suddenly I remembered what day it was.

"Oh Amy, I'm so sorry, I forgot. Let me get organised and then I'll take you to the station."

"It's okay Tom," she said and clasped one of my hands in her own for just a second, "I've ordered a taxi. It'll be here any moment now."

I stood mutely by as Amy knelt down to offer farewells to a few special friends, and finally to Jack.

"You'll have to come back you know, to see him grown," Jack nodded toward his son, leading the other young children in a game of tag through the legs of the disgruntled adults.

"I will, I promise. I just wish, I wish she was here too, I wish I could say goodbye." A tear fell from Amy's nose and fell perilously close to Jack's head, it would have soaked him.

"I know, and she knows," Jack patted Amy's index finger with a hand and the two were silent with their memories until the beep of a car horn startled them. "You take care of yourself," Jack said, and nodded towards me. Amy rose to her feet.

"I guess that's your car," I mumbled.

"I guess so."

We stared at each other awkwardly and then I stuck my hand out formally for a shake. She took it with a sound I couldn't distinguish, it might have been a sob or a laugh or both of those things rolled into one.

"You'll make sure they get enough food? They'll still need it for a while until the plants are in and matured."

"I'll make sure," I said.

"And you'll help to secure that last house we built? We ran out of time yesterday to get the cable over it and I don't want it forgotten."

"I'll remember."

"And you'll email me pictures? Lots of them?"

"I promise."

Amy nodded but continued to stand at my side, as if giving me the opportunity to say something else. The constriction in my heart begged me to grab on to her, to tell her not to leave, to confess my undying devotion but I couldn't rationalise my feelings into cohesive words and so I remained silent.

"Well. Goodbye Tom," she said at last.

"Goodbye," I replied and followed her through the house to the waiting taxi. The driver threw her bags into the boot and she climbed into the backseat. My mouth opened and closed with words I couldn't utter. As the taxi pulled away I waved, and felt stricken with a sensation that the taxi was stealing the colour from my world, leaving me in greyscale misery with a hole in my heart.

I stumbled back into the garden and started throwing pieces of rubble out of the nearly completed pond. I almost flattened Jack with one particularly large piece, he had to scramble on his crutches to avoid it and he furrowed his grey eyebrows at me.

"What are you doing here Tom?" Jack asked after accepting my apologies for nearly turning him into a pancake. "Go after her."

"I can't go after her. She's gone now. It's for the best."

Jack picked up a tiny piece of rock, threw at my foot with all his strength and let out a roar that caused a few little people to scamper quickly away.

"You go after her right now!" Jack shouted. "What I wouldn't give for another minute with my Sophie, another second, I won't let you throw this away."

"I... I have to go after her, you're right. Jack you're right." I picked him up in my hand and swung him around in a great circle. "But the time, I'll never make it in time."

"Go Tom, you'll make it."

I deposited Jack in a heap and sprinted to the trusty Volkswagen, roaring to the train station at a speed I'm not proud to admit.

In the week after Sophie's death I tried to encourage

Jack to talk about how he was feeling. He was mostly unresponsive, but he did tell me that he thought he experienced the worst pain life had to offer when a seagull tore into his flesh with its talons. He was wrong, he informed me. Sorrow was a pain deeper than any physical wound. I thought of his words as I raced to the train station. It would be so easy for him to be angry at the world, but even now he was thinking of me and trying to ensure I could experience the happiness he had known, however briefly. My eyes grew blurry with tears again. "Get a hold of yourself," I growled to the empty car.

At the station I rammed the car into the first available space, didn't bother with a ticket and ran as fast as my legs would carry me to the station. There are no barriers at these small Cornish stops so I ran straight onto the platform to see the train vanish around the corner, whisking Amy away from me.

"No!" I shouted.

"Alright lad?" A passing conductor asked.

"Where does that train go? Where does it stop?"

"That one? Well it's up to Camborne and Redruth, then Truro, St Austell and on to Liskeard and Plymouth and beyond to the north. Wait lad," he called to my retreating back, "you'll never catch it, better to get the next one."

I barely heard his words. I was in the car in a flash and plugging Redruth train station into the sat nav as fast as my fingers could manage.

So began my first and only race with a train.

Amy's carriage was long gone by the time I pulled into Camborne, raced out of the car and reached the platform, and at Redruth too.

"Come on Tom, think about this," I said to myself as I sat in the car park. "You'll never catch her hopping station to station."

I plugged Plymouth train station into the GPS and set off, hoping against hope to avoid any police cars or speed cameras on the way. It gave me an hour and a half to think about what I could possibly say to Amy, and I was no closer to a conclusion as I ruthlessly beat an old woman to the only available parking space in the small short term parking area.

This time I couldn't reach the platforms without a train ticket, so I fumbled at the automatic machine to buy the cheapest fare on offer, checked the board and raced to the platform indicating Amy's train was due to leave at any moment.

And there it was, sitting at the station, the doors still open.

"Amy," I bellowed, "Amy!"

And there she was, sitting beside the window, staring at me in amazement.

"Tom?" she mouthed. She ran from her seat onto the platform and I pulled her into my arms and into the sweetest kiss I've ever known. The world was a blur of motion and sound around us, but all I could see was Amy, her face, her smile, her soft lips. I pressed her against me and kissed her again and inhaled the smell of coconut from her hair.

"Uh, sorry miss, are you getting back on this train?" A uniformed man tapped Amy on the shoulder.

"Yes. No. I don't know." She turned to me, "I have to go Tom."

"I know," I replied. "I love you."

"I love you too," Amy said and nuzzled against my chest. I wrapped my arms around her again and held her tight.

"I'm so sorry I waited so long. Come back and see me at Christmas?" I implored.

She nodded and pulled away, glancing at the platform attendant who pointedly cleared his throat.

"I'll call you," Amy said and climbed back on to the train. She returned to her seat and I watched her until the train started to move, and then I jogged to keep up for as long as I possibly could until she vanished again and the train became a spot in the distance, and then nothing.

I have never known loneliness like the moment that train sped Amy away from me, and yet my whole body was suffused with warmth and happiness at having finally said something to her, at finally taking action. Still, it would be a long drive home, with plenty of time to muse on how the little people had rubbed off on me. I met Amy just three months ago, and now I was driving seventy miles home after a seventy mile journey to spend two minutes with her. I didn't regret it for an instant.

I was left with a strange conundrum as the miles clocked by. I longed for time to pass quickly to enfold Amy into my arms again, and yet the swifter the passage of time, the closer the next goodbye.

CHAPTER THIRTY-SIX

Life returned to some semblance of normality over the next month, though I would hesitate to call it a happy ending. Jack continued to apply himself to the building projects with a level of energy I can only hope to possess if I reach the equivalent of his age in human terms. He never did resume the mantle of mayor. His young successor was unanimously voted in for a month long term, following his effective administration in resettling the little people and catering for their needs. Jack was happy enough dedicating his time to getting as many people settled as possible, and to spend precious moments with his rapidly growing son.

I tried hard to put the upcoming December date that would herald Jack's end out of my mind, but there were moments when I silently pleaded with time to stop. Willing time to slow is like trying to stop the tide. As children we made barricades of sand and wondered if they could stop the relentless flow of the incoming water, but despite our best defences the ocean would always trickle over the bulwarks and leave us sandy and soaked and laughing at our futile attempts.

I worked hard at my trade and brought the little people freshly baked bread each day. My father and I spent the odd hour working to do up my own home (though I always kept him out of the garden) and I gradually replaced the dated furnishings with those more to my taste until the place felt my own.

I won't bore you with details of those unremarkable days; they don't make such a good story as the rest of this tale. Suffice to say we were as happy as we could be, and the village grew larger as contented little people left the shared tent to take ownership of their own homes. Jack couldn't be dissuaded from helping with the work, but his pace started to slacken as we entered December and felt the bite of the first winter frosts.

On the fourth of December when I turned twenty-three I was touched to find Jack waiting by the kitchen door when I returned from work. It was a long walk for him these days, and he stood leaning heavily on his crutches and breathing hard, holding a small package in one hand.

"Amy told me a long while ago you big people give gifts on these, now what did she call them? Birthdays?" He handed over the tiny package wrapped carefully in a leaf. I used a fingernail to prise open the present and there within lay Jack's coming of age necklace, the piece of shell cleaned and polished to a beautiful white gleam.

"Jack, I can't take this," I said, completely humbled.

"Why ever not?" he asked. "It's not like anyone would doubt I'm of age now is it." He broke into a gruff laugh that tugged at the corners of my mouth. "A little something to remember me by, that's all," he said and patted my finger, shaking his head. "Sometimes it's so strange to look at you Tom. You look exactly the same as that first day I met you and here I am drawing close to my end."

I smiled but inside I was broken. Less than a year ago I thought this was all so much fun, watching someone grow older in the space of a few months, but now I would do anything to stop it. I didn't want to lose the best friend I'd ever had. My relationship with Jack had changed so many times over the months, from younger brother, to older brother, to father and even grandfather figure, but through it all we had remained the very best of friends.

"I've something for you as well," I said to Jack, "wait there." I darted up the narrow cottage steps to fetch a memento which had suddenly sprung to mind.

"I kept this. I thought you might like to see it one day but I completely forgot about it until now," I explained and revealed the seagull feather torn from the beast that maimed Jack's leg all those months ago. Jack was silent for several minutes, running his hand over the soft barbs.

"It's amazing, what you can overcome when you set your mind to it," he said finally with a small smile. I carried him and the feather back to his house to save him the long hike. He told me he planned to hang it on the wall, as a lesson to Joe that nothing can stop you achieving your dreams.

Amy returned on the twenty-second of December. She drove the long way down in her new car, a more modern Volkswagen Golf than the hunk of rust still decorating my driveway. I swung her around in my arms and hugged her so tightly she wriggled in complaint. We spoke every day on the phone after her departure, but I missed the smell and the sight and the feel of her. She insisted she would stay with my parents again, having grown close to them in her previous trip, and knowing my mother would have it no other way. I was happy enough to have her to myself during the days. Myself and the two hundred and forty-two little people she was eager to be reunited with.

I showed Amy the village, now boasting more than thirty completed houses, an established and thriving pond and a cliff edge laden with more shells than coming of age ceremonies would need in my lifetime.

"It's incredible Tom, you've done so much."

"I only wish it was finished. I wish I'd been able to get

it all done for Jack to see before, well before, you know."

"I know. But Tom you must know Jack won't be disappointed. He has seen the finished village. If he hadn't seen it all those months ago there would be nothing here now. This is his vision come to life."

She was right of course. The building teams continued to use Jack's original site layout and construction designs, even if he was too old now to partake in the construction.

We spent much of the next two days with Jack and the now teenage equivalent Joe. I sensed there would be some great trips to be had once Joe was old enough to explore the world, though perhaps not such long forays as the adventure Jack and I undertook together.

As I pulled the blanket tight around me on the night of the twenty-third of December I willed myself to stay awake. It was a stupid idea, but somehow in the gloom of the evening I felt that keeping away the sleep threatening to overwhelm me would somehow halt the coming of the following day.

It was a day I dreaded since I first grew close to the young Jack Meadows. I had no idea how to say goodbye to someone who had impacted my life in such a way. Were it not for Jack I would probably still be in my parents' house, wondering how to make a go of life and moping for days at a time. I wouldn't have the new found respect for life and appreciation for time that an acquaintance with the little people can't help but bring. I would never have met Amy.

Knowing Jack had altered my life beyond recognition, and tomorrow I would see him for the last time.

As sleep finally overtook me, the thought circling my mind was that no human effort can stop the wheels of time rolling steadily onwards. No matter how much we may wish it otherwise, tomorrow will come.

Christmas Eve dawned with a brilliant blue sky. The cold winter sunshine cast diamonds onto the surface of the ocean.

The celebration of Jack's end started early, because every little person wanted to be a part of it. Jack was the hero of his people. He brought them to a new home, saved them from the great flood by his friendship with me and Amy and prepared a new life for them here. Phase Five of our original plan, Creating Home, wasn't exactly finished as there were still several families living in the tent, but what Jack had achieved was a marvel and his community wanted to express their appreciation. Despite the chill of the day the assembly gathered outside as one little person after another told stories of Jack. We heard from a friend of his youth, of days spent playing and exploring and how he refused to let his injury stop him from living his life. We heard more recent tales of Jack's help with house setup, and the responsibilities he undertook as mayor. Every word spoken pointed to the rich life this little person had lived. It was a sad day for me, but I couldn't help thinking Jack had achieved more in one year than many of us would in a lifetime. In our journey he saw wonders beyond the comprehension of most of the little people, and yet in returning he poured himself out to create a space for them to live in security and happiness. He lived life full to the brim, and now he would die empty, having drained himself to make the lives of those around him better. If there is a greater way to live I have never seen it.

Jack sat with a serene smile on his face and held the hand of his son as he listened to all the little people had to say.

"I'd like to speak," I said when all had said their piece. There was some grumbling amongst the older residents at this break from tradition, but the mayor, newly elected to his third term, nodded approval.

"I asked Jack once if he ever wished he'd done things differently in his life. He looked at me and laughed and said, 'Why would I wish that? It's a waste of time to wish away the choices you've made. You've done things the way you have and now you have to make the best of the situation you're in.' Those words will stay with me for the rest of my life, and I vow I won't waste my life wallowing in regrets. I will take what chances come my way and enjoy the things I have.

"There are so many stories I could tell you of Jack but it would take more time than we have to recount them. Instead all I'll say is Jack, you've changed me for the better, and I think that's what friendship is all about. I'm going to miss you, we're all going to miss you so much, but know that as long as I draw breath you won't be forgotten."

I planned a longer, more grandiose speech, but when it came to it there were no more words to do justice to this day. Jack's face, carved with lines of wisdom and age, broke into the widest smile I ever saw and he beckoned me closer to speak in a voice made croaky by his advanced days, "Take care of my son Tom, as you've taken care of me."

I nodded and Jack sat back, the smile still playing on his lips as he whispered his final words and closed his eyes for the last time, "I'm coming Sophie."

I struggled to see through the mist of my tears as we marched in procession with the little people to the burial plot where a small hole loomed before us. Jack was carried on a sheet by some of the younger little people who would normally place him into his final resting place. Instead they gently lowered the sheet to the floor beside the hole and looked expectantly up at me. Shakily I lifted the still form of Jack into my hand. He was lighter in death than he ever felt in life. I lowered him into the hole, and took up some dirt between my fingertips to sprinkle over his supine form. Joe followed suit, then Amy, and then all of the long line of little people until the hole was a hole no longer but a grand mound of earth. Joe knelt to smooth the dirt with his bare hands and the burial was complete.

Amy slipped her arm through mine as we walked

toward the village of the little people, to the accompaniment of a merry tune played by a solitary pipe.

CHAPTER THIRTY-SEVEN

The village was completed of course, halfway through the next year. We built extra houses too, for the little people to expand into as their population grew. The pond teemed with life and youngsters learned their front crawl against the gentle flow of water from the pump that kept it clean. Together with a team of little people we planted wildflower seeds to line the paths between houses, until the village teemed with colour and the bumble bees much beloved by the little people, despite the intimidation of creatures as large as their heads floating past on a warm summer's breeze.

With the housing work completed, I started on a gate designed to look as though it were a part of the hedge. It completely closed the secret garden away from the outside world, unless we needed access in an emergency. I did leave peepholes for us to keep an eye on the community, but after Jack's death we decided it would be best to limit our contact to allow the lives of the little people to return to normality. I erected a bell close to the gate so the little people could call us in an emergency. Its peal reached to the house and would send us running to assist our small friends. The bell rang often in the first few months, for fear of seagulls or lack of food in the days of their settling, but as the generation we knew rested in eternal sleep the bell grew still and silent. It is some years now since I heard its song echo through the garden.

We weren't completely cut off from this marvellous race however; the Meadows clan would often sneak under the hedge to meet with us. I've had the honour of knowing Joe, Jake, Jacqui, Jan, Jeffery, Jade, Jemima, Jody, Johnny and more Jacks than you can count. There has never been another adventure like the trip Jack and I shared, but Amy and I often took the odd intrepid soul out for a weekend to see the world beyond their borders.

Amy returned to Cornwall after completing one year at her firm and we were married soon after. She achieved her dream, today she runs a small firm helping local business owners to concentrate on what they do best, while she manages their finances in her wonderfully organised way. My own parents retired some years ago and I manage the bakery, now a successful online enterprise as well as a staple in the local community. My son, James, is keen to learn the trade so I pass on the knowledge my father passed on to me when he returns home from school. We aren't rich, not as I once thought I would be with my prestigious university degree framed on my wall, but I have learnt money is by no means the key to happiness.

Our own children love to interact with the Meadows folk, and I often see them peering through the cut-outs in the hedge to keep an eye on the little people at large. I felt nothing but pride the day they presented Amy and I with handmade badges, cut out of cereal boxes and decorated crudely with the words 'Guardians of the People.'

"Not the little people?" I asked my daughter, Alex.

"No Dad, that's what *you* call them, they call themselves the people," she insisted with a roll of her eyes.

Life has taken a different turn to the path I once anticipated, and all because of Jack.

Sometimes in the dead of night, even today, I wake up

and expect to see Jack asleep on my bedside cabinet and I miss him anew. But then I remember that his influence lives on in the community of the little people and in my own family.

I shared a year in the life of Jack Meadows, and I will never be the same for it.

ACKNOWLEDGEMENTS

Thank you, first and foremost, to you my reader! Without readers there'd be no purpose for stories and then I'd be out of a job, so thank you for making it through to this point. For a double, extra special thank you with sprinkles on top, please consider writing a review of this book on the website you purchased it from. Reviews help other readers to find new books to read, so please spare a few moments to add your thoughts.

Jack Meadows would never have been born, lived and died were it not for the unwavering support of my husband, Dave, who dealt with my neurosis on a daily basis and supported me in the writing process, even when it took several times longer than poor Jack had to live to get it all finished.

My heartfelt appreciation also goes out to my family: my parents, Andrew and Brenda, my sister Angela and my uncle Pete, all of whom convinced me there might be a point in continuing after the first few pages.

Thank you to Jessica Shepherd for creating such beautiful artwork for my cover, and for being the amazing encourager you are. And to my church home group friends; your gentle promptings and prayers kept me going when it would have been so easy to give up.

Friendships are a great enrichment to my life, and there

are too many people who have spurred me on through the months and years to mention them all by name. You know who you are, those who stood by me and nagged me into continuing with weekly progress checks and encouraging words. Thank you, thank you and thank you again.

ABOUT THE AUTHOR

UK author R.L. Waterman lives on the border of the New Forest in Hampshire, which she loves to explore with her dog, Steve. She also likes to disappear into a good book, play the occasional videogame and travel as often as she has the chance. Her first novel, A Year in the Life of Jack Meadows, was published in 2017.

Discover more at www.rlwaterman.com and on Twitter @RL_Waterman.

Printed in Great Britain
by Amazon